News Flash: Most of the Best Science Fiction is DarkSF
(e.g., Blade Runner, Dark City, Invasion of the Body Snatchers, Frankenstein, Metropolis, & many more…)

DarkSF is the Dark Chocolate of Science Fiction

DarkSF Novels by John Argo
- This Shoal of Space
- Streamliners
- Day Flies
- Meta4City
- Robinson Crusoe 1,000,000 A.D.
- Doom Spore San Diego

Empire of Time Novels by John Argo (Future History)
- Star Mate: Cosmopolis, City of the Universe
- Mars the Divine
- Pioneers
- Time Train
- Tellerine (Moon Berry Wine)
- Lantern Road
- Runners: Escape Prison World or Die

Also by John Argo:
- YANAPOP (wild urban fantasy)
- Neon Blue (suspense)
- The Sibyl's Urn (historical fantasy)

Meta 4 City

A DarkSF Novel

**By
John Argo**

DarkSF is the Dark Chocolate of Science Fiction

Clocktower Books

San Diego

Meta 4 City by John Argo

Copyright 2007, 2017 by John Argo. All Rights Reserved.

You may not reproduce any part of this book for any purpose without the publisher's written permission.

This novel was previously released under the title Monopol City

Cover Design:CTB/JTC

Photos: iStockphoto, Fotolia

This novel is a work of fiction. Names, characters, places, and incidents are products of the author's imagination. Any resemblance to actual events or locales or persons, living or dead, is entirely coincidental.

Clocktower Books

P.O. Box 600973

Grantville Station

San Diego, CA 92160-0973

editorial@clocktowerbooks.com

http://www.clocktowerbooks.com/

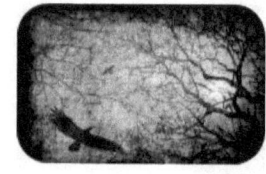

Meta 4 City

A DarkSF Novel

By
John Argo

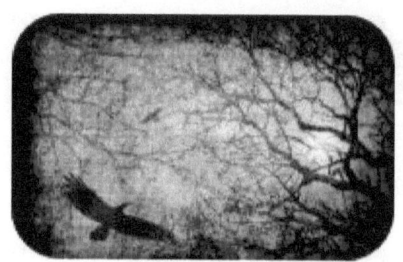

Contents

Part 1 - Crimes Unspecified

Prisoner of State

Chapter 1

Two orderlies wheeled a deeply sedated female prisoner down long, shadowy corridors within the bowels of West Gotha Military Hospital No. 325.

The young woman was blonde, with thick wavy hair framing a thin face that was as much shadowy as it possessed a bruised attractiveness.

The two air force corpsmen's shoes squeaked on the clean, waxed floors. The gurney's wheels rolled with a faint smacking of grease like chewing gum in its wheel hubs. Each corpsman wore off-white scrubs of a faintly gray discoloration, spattered with tiny droplets of blood and body fluids that might be new from today, or baked in from years of endless laundering in the hospital's gray, steaming basement laundries. Under his tunic, each hospital technician wore a wide, black leather belt from which dangled a small 35 mm automatic in a triangular licorice snap holster. Trained and alert as they were, ready for hand to hand combat or a gun battle if necessary (not unusual in the divided world of West Gotha and East Gotha), the two men could not be aware of a fourth figure who shadowed them.

Following through an endless series of gloomy archways, through long tunnels black as night, was a man in dark camouflage: the spy, Alton Hedrock, Tedda's lover. Neither of the two orderlies could possibly know that.

If Tedda knew, it was only dimly so. They had knocked her out with mephisterol, veritol, and other powerful drugs designed not to kill her or make her unconscious. They filled her blood stream, permeated her meat and brain, and saturated her neural kelp. They had been injected by cold and cruel experts to make her thoughts and memories an open book for the Inquisitor who was about to probe into her crimes and conspiracies.

Tedda was dimly aware of being a disembodied soul inside the contained ocean of who she was, inside her skin, a floating sentience in a dark evening sea. She was the sea.

By a parallel metaphor—permitted only within the house of mirrors of mephisterol, where logic and illogic were mirror images--she was the hospital. The tunnels and halls through which she rolled or floated were not brick or concrete, but sinews and bones, arteries and pulsing neural networks within her own body. She was remotely aware of the endless war and nightmare enveloping all life in the two Gothas.

The two corpsmen were part of her dream state as much as they were part of their own waking reality. With pounding regularity, as the gurney rolled past passed rain-streaked windows hemmed in by tight steel-mesh, a bluish-gray light from outside would illuminate the prisoner's battered figure with a kind of chrome, underwater light.

With similar manic predictability, enemy streakers droned in from high up, some from orbit, and exploded on the city's force shields, seeking a weak spot. The prisoner's wan and slack features would flicker with lightning reflected upon her bones and eye hollows.

West Gotha was in a perpetual state of war with her twin sister state, East Gotha. The two nations, in fact, shared a divided capital. A high wall, topped by barbed wire, ran down the center of the City of Gotha, capital of the nation and the world. Stationary mines, starving dogs, and all-seeing videobots on tank treads patrolled the no man's land. The dead zone was a 100 meter wide strip, on either side of the brooding, rain-damp wall. Frightened and armed guards, with orders to shoot and kill intruders on sight (or be shot by a military police firing squad) patrolled on foot, on motorcycles with sidecars, and in armored cars. This was the world in which Tedda hovered between a drug-induced coma and fitful consciousness. Chained to the gurney, wheeled by combat-trained orderlies, she was dimly aware of distant explosions in the night.

Each detonation outside, following constant enemy provocations, was nearly soundless, felt only as a dim and distant shudder; that meant the incoming rocket had not chanced upon a momentary server-down somewhere on the invisible dome. The occasional hit that got through could devastate an entire factory or neighborhood, and the East Gotha side had been getting a similar drubbing day and night for as long as anyone could remember. Meanwhile, the force fields did not prevent rain and wind from slipping through—there were other filters to sift out chemical, biological, and radioactive weaponry. The world was so beaten down with all the poisons of war, however, that both sides had by necessity retreated to the use of still potent but cleaner weapons.

The patient was a prisoner. She had committed a crime of passion. Time and again, she saw motion-blurred images of herself astride her victim: two naked persons, one astride the other and holding that person's hair while raising a huge kitchen carving knife. It was a scene so horrid that she always blanked it out in her mind when the knife reached the top of its arc of travel and started descending for the final lunging stab deep into pulsating red flesh awash with fresh blood.

The patient wore a flimsy gown with microscopic flower patterns whose attempt to convey warmth and femininity failed amid the sour smell and rips in the worn cotton fabric. She had a grayish sheet draped over her thin, sprawled legs. The soles of her feet looked orange-dirty, and her ankles looked knobby in proportion with the starved thinness of her calves. The gurney's back was cranked up, permitting her to sit, with her wrists manacled to the dull iron rails on either side. The woman's head was slightly raised, her mouth slightly open, her eyes staring straight ahead as if in alarm. A whitish, dried trail of drool fanned out from each corner of her mouth, running into the dimple of her chin. Under her left eye was a purple, puffy bruise with green and yellow underscores.

They stopped before a door marked simply in brown, painted-over numerals, 909. While both men awkwardly turned the long gurney with its huge, chipped-white wheels, one of them knocked on the door.

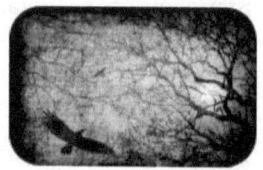

"Come in," said a man's oddly caressing, cruel voice.

"Room 909," one of the men told the woman, if she could hear. "This is where we go in. The Inquisitor is waiting for you."

When the men were gone, the woman sat, still chained, on her gurney, in an uncomfortably large and barren office.

The woman had trouble turning her head, because her neck hurt from the treatment she'd been given.

She laid her head back on the cloth headrest and looked about with large eyes.

Her body ached, but she was more in pain from the tightness in her muscles—the fear and anticipation of the terrible things yet to come.

"Relax," the Inquisitor said. He was a well-groomed man with a pale, soft face and cleanly shorn brown hair. He wore a tight black uniform on his lean frame, with a wide lapel flap open. "Do you smoke?"

The woman did not answer. She did not smoke, nor did she have the extra energy to tell him so.

Like many things, it no longer mattered.

He left her in her sitting position, walking around her in wide, thoughtful circles while smoking an elegant machine-rolled cigarette, long light-green job with gold edges.

Smoke billowed around him as he looked down at the floor, formulating thoughts.

The air took on a tinge of blue from the floating smoke, and the woman lay back, ignoring the nightmare thoughts of her recent interrogation—the mild, Step One variety.

The smoke reminded her of her father, long dead, and she cursed inwardly, silently, this intrusion upon her cherished memories.

"Let's just talk a bit," the Inquisitor said as if seducing her. "Look outside at the rain dribbling down the windows. Think about how this is your home, your nation, and how you want it to remain so. Would you like some water?"

He paused, looking at her expectantly as if she were his client and he wanted to please her. But there was an icy, pragmatic glimmer in his eyes, as if he were looking at a piece of meat he were about to barbecue.

She realized that, yes, she was parched, and strained to croak out a reply.

A glass of water appeared before her face, and she leaned forward to drink.

The Inquisitor was surprisingly accommodating, not teasing her for it as the night questioners had. There was little sensation as the liquid dribbled into her swollen mouth and soaked down into the purple, engorged intestine that was her throat. She could not lift her chained hands, so he patiently held the glass while she drained it one grunting, effortful swallow at a time until she choked and spurted water all over her lap.

He set the glass aside. "I find it encouraging that you display such a calm, cooperative manner. I can make things easier or harder for you, depending on your understanding of the dire situation in which you find yourself. In fact, I find myself in a dire situation trying to find a certain Captain Alton Hedrock who has betrayed this country and will cause grave harm unless we locate him. He is your husband. Do you remember him?"

She nodded with a last ounce of defiance. She acknowledged the love of her life, the man to whom she had sworn herself, with a sharp snap forward that made the gurney creak and her chains clatter.

"Still loyal, are we?"

She felt drained, and sat leaning forward with her chin on her chest and her head feeling heavy.

"Get over it," he said. "Hedrock is as good as dead. So, my dear, are you unless you cooperate." He stiffened, sitting up, seeming to become larger and more elongated as he looked threateningly at her. "Where is he?" he barked.

As the sharpness of his voice echoed around the room, like a whip crack, she suddenly slumped. Her body seemed to surrender to the inevitability of what she was about to do. Her shoulders seemed to grow smaller, and her head fell back against the grimy headrest, while her eyes gazed emptily at the ceiling.

"Where is he?" he repeated, slapping his palm softly on the desk. He leaned forward as if he wanted to suck the truth out of her marrow. His eyes looked dark and burning.

She slumped some more, letting her chin fall to her chest. Her manacled hands were clutched together. Keeping her face downcast, she raised her eyes toward him so that their whites showed while her pupils rolled upward in hate and shame. Her lips moved.

"Speak louder!" he shouted.

She told him where her husband was when she had last seen him.

The Inquisitor sat back, clapping his hands together in delight.

Even as she spoke in a sobbing, quivering voice, Tedda raised her palms to her eyes. She realized she was betraying her most cherished love. She was destroying everything she held dear, even all the things she could not consciously remember because of the drugs. She began to cry brokenly, and her sounds fell like broken glass around her. The Inquisitor, who saw that he was succeeding in his torture of her, simultaneously began to grin at his success.

Hedrock—if they could capture him, they would torture him until all the secrets of East Gotha came squirming and worming out of his innermost gut and the remotest inner coils of his brain. Licking his lips, he asked her in a voice that could not contain its hunger and impatience:

"Where do you think Alton Hedrock is at this moment?"

"I don't know," Tedda said amid sobs.

From his silence, she knew it would not go well for her. She did not really even know who Alton Hedrock was, but she knew she would die for him—if she knew anything, which she no longer did.

"Tedda," came the Inquisitor's menacing voice, like a razor blade inching through black, invisible space. "This is your last and only chance. Tell me what I need to know, or you will be thrown into the pit of hell, never to return."

Chapter 2

Tedda, chained inside the van with three other women prisoners, felt a chilly draft and smelled fresh air from somewhere in the darkness—probably where the seals on the doors were worn out. It was all part of the numb realization that she kept waking to in her thoughts: nothing was going to change. She'd gotten life plus fifty for a murder she could not remember having committed.

Then again, she had visions of sitting astride another woman while holding the woman's head by the hair, and raising a huge kitchen knife for a series of fatal stabs. All because of a seductive man with a small mustache.

She writhed slightly, knowing it was hopeless and she'd never get out. She felt some deep need, some urgency, some overpowering sense that she must do something important, save someone, serve the nation whatever that was, but she had no idea what it meant. The feeling came at the oddest moments, and always passed.

Thunder boxed and growled around in the night sky, and lightning flashed dimly visible in the thick swollen gray rain clouds. The roads in the wilderness were black and slick, shining before a dirty white prison van that slowly made its way through the dense forest. Rain drops cascaded down, left and right as the wind kept changing direction.

The inside of the van smelled of dust and oil and something rotten, like a carton of milk or a half-eaten hamburger left under the torn leatherette seats days earlier. The women sat with their hands fastened together in mid-air, as if praying with fingers folded, and chained to the ceiling. They looked at each other silently, afraid. Two were hardened, with the dead look in their eyes and a slight sneer. Tedda was slender, with raggedly clipped thin brown hair lying on the pale skin of a long boyish neck. Her features were plain, androgynous, with freckles and sullenly darting blue eyes. The fourth woman, Estana, was shorter, more solid, with thick curling black hair and lush South Pacific features, eyes black and blazing as wet coal.

The van started making rocking motions and bouncing so that the women's chains, by which they were fastened to steel braces above, swung back and forth in steady arcs rattling. Tedda could smell the steel, and the oil of the canvas in which it was packed when not in use. "Hey," one of the hardened women said in protest, ever ready to blame someone for everything that happened to her—so Tedda thought, averting her gaze lest the other woman make eye contact and make Tedda her instant enemy for life. One couldn't afford that at life plus fifty. Might become life minus fifty.

The van stopped. Leaning forward together, the women peered through a small window in the wall behind the cab. They could see a lantern swinging steadily back and forth as the wipers labored full force to push sheets of water aside. A figure in a yellow slicker drew near. The driver opened his window, and Tedda heard: "Road's about to wash out. If you go across, you may not be able to get back out any time soon."

The driver, a young black man, replied: "I've got my orders. I deliver these honeys over to Edgemoor and then I do my best to get back across."

"Don't do it," said the man standing by the window. The glow of the lantern filled the cockpit, illumining the drivers with a somber orange light.

"Look man, I've got no choice. The longer you hold me up with this chitchat, the more likely I'll be spending the night at the prison."

"All right," the man said. The lantern withdrew. "Good luck. It's a long way across this canyon when it's full of ripping flood water."

The driver muttered something, put the van in gear, and shot forward. For a few seconds, the van seemed to slide this way or that on an asphalt road surface greased with melted clay. Then the van gained traction and rumbled across a steel bridge whose surface was lined with loose planks. Soaked wood made slamming and ringing sounds as the heavy vehicle rolled over it.

"Something is wrong," Tedda heard one of the hard women say. Estana looked terrified, her dark eyes glittering as she looked frantically about. The other hard woman regarded Estana with contempt, her sneer rising a fraction as she looked at Tedda in a silent challenge to do better than Estana.

At that moment the driver yelled something. The van twisted around in a quick, sickening motion. The other driver's arm was visible waving about as if he were trying to steady himself. The driver got the door open and tried to jump, but it was too late. The bridge gave out in a loud crack of snapping timber and tossed railroad ties. All four women screamed as the van rolled backward. Tedda felt acid terror stun her body with its electric charge. It was terrifying to be enclosed in a box like this, illumined only by the dull, dirty-yellow dome light; and chained, while the van slid backwards into a raging river. Women screamed. The back doors crumpled as logs ground against each other. Instantly water rose up, icy water, and Tedda felt it taking her, rising past her sensitive thighs and crotch, up her waist, to her breasts—the warmth in her prison jump suit gone, replaced by numbing cold. Still the water rose. Tedda had a glimpse of Estana staring at her with those big dark eyes full of terror. The other two, the hard ones, were already gone, only their dead hands sticking up from the foaming water with their chains, and their hair floating like seaweed. Estana was next: Tedda caught a last glimpse of Estana's dulling gaze underwater as she sank down in a trail of bubbles. Already Tedda's scream was turned into froth as the water rose above her mouth. Tedda pulled herself up toward the ceiling as best she could. Her whitened knuckles gripped the icy steel chain links, which were slippery with wetness. Oh God, it bought her maybe a foot, maybe a minute of life, before the water took that away too.

The van landed in the river with a splash of white, and twirled in circles like a cocktail stirrer in the mad flood of debris and foaming chocolate water, seen dimly under repeated lightning strikes. As it twirled, the van suddenly turned over, striking a huge boulder in the wash. The van rolled over, slowing for a few seconds, and the roof tore open with a loud, hideous grinding noise. The van turned fully over, bobbed away, and joined tons of other floating debris on its way to some larger lake of deadly flooding.

Tedda thought: this is it.

Then she noticed that a weld seam in the steel plate holding her chain to the rack had split. Her chain was stuck! If only she could get it free.

She took a deep breath as the van ground over the rock. Then the van spun off the rock and turned again, filling totally with water. Sounds turned to angry mumbles like in a tossing dryer as she fought underwater to get free. She pulled herself toward the ceiling and planted her booted feet against it. Nearly blind in the darkness—the yellowish dome light was flickering and going out—she pulled her chains this way and that.

The van lurched with increasing speed and the motion made her stomach sick. Her air was going sour and her ears felt like exploding. Her lungs were on fire. Her stomach muscles fluttered with the desire to breathe, and she fought the instincts of her body.

There: the chain came free. She had a glimpse of the three women hanging together like dead rabbits a hunter was taking home. She kicked free, and the current rushing through the broken van sucked her out the back door. She caught a last glimpse of the dead drivers: the one's brown head with short hair, the other's foot sticking up. Gone. And she was next. She took a terrified gasp of air, coming up, saw the van fly away from her, saw the foaming waters rushing up to strangle her, saw the powerful currents twirling like braids on a giant green glass rope, and—

Felt a shock as her chain caught on something.

She hung numbly while refrigerator water poured around her. She was caught on a huge log, on its roots, sticking out where it had fallen. She was a thing like a speed boat, rising to the surface, bobbing as the laminar flow sliced around her tearing her clothes. She felt one boot go, then the other. It was as if someone sentient pulled her heavy wet socks off. First one then the other. They flew away on the current. Any second now, a heavy log would fly by and impale her. She gave a yell, and pulled herself up. The motion flipped her around on her belly and pulled her in the lee of the huge tree. She saw that it was shaking like a palsied hand, for all its size and tonnage. Eventually it would give, and would crush her as it took her down under and out to the lake or sea or whatever lay downstream.

She summoned her last ounce of energy, pulled herself up on the trunk, and lay gasping for a few minutes. The hard wood under her sang and trembled, and she thought she felt it move an inch, she felt it give a little. That made her pull herself up, as if sitting on a horse, in a saddle. It made her shimmy down toward the shore a foot at a time. Her wrists were still manacled together, and about four feet of slender steel chain links dangled from the manacles, ending in a broken link. She rolled over, tossed herself free, just as the huge log made a protracted groaning noise and slid several feet with the current, preparatory to being unwedged from the bank.

Tedda rolled free, crawled up a bank of packed wet sand in a drenching downpour. She was numb with cold, but alive. That alone gave her energy to keep on. She half crawled, half staggered up the bank until she found herself at the edge of what looked like a huge parking lot. Wind whipped across the flat black surface, and tree branches bounced around like twigs in the storm. She heard a cracking noise behind her, and looked. There went the five or six ton log she'd ridden minutes ago—torn from its anchorage, rocking majestically like a heavy boat as it floated away in the fast tide.

Tedda held her hands to her eyes to shield them from cold stinging needles of rain in the wind. She staggered toward a mass of distant lights atop a fortress-like structure. As the wind howled around her, pushed against her, she abruptly lost her energy and crumpled in a heap, welcoming the numbness, the darkness, like someone falling asleep. It felt almost cozy, the kiss of death.

Part 2 - Neo-Deco Terror

— Gotha —
City Divided

Chapter 3

Major Walther Tonsonby had a pit of foreboding in his stomach as he speeded through rainy, nighttime city streets in a staff car. The unexpected summons to see Leader Moss had come in the middle of the night, ordering Tonsonby to appear before the fatherland's leader by dawn. Tonsonby had an inkling it was about the doomsday rocket, and it couldn't be good.

As he stepped from the car, while an aide held the rear door open, Tonsonby put on his gold-trimmed, peaked General Staff officer's cap. He wore a gray uniform with gleaming black boots and blue-edged riding trousers. Aides hovered about him, silently opening doors, holding umbrellas, and shielding him with their bodies. Tonsonby was oblivious to all of it, concerned only for his precarious staff position.

Tonsonby ran from the car up the steps to the cathedral vastness of the West Gotha State Chancellery. He was a big man, but fast, and two aides hurried to catch up with him.

It was so early in the morning that night still gripped the city with its rain, its sirens, and its search lights while enemy bombers probed and growled in the clouds far above. Tonsonby glanced up, with raindrops on his troubled expression, and guessed that the enemy in East Gotha were unaware of the horrific weapon being readied across town to destroy them.

Tonsonby entered the building, dripping rain water, and stopped to let his aides catch up. His chauffeur (a fat man in charcoal Uniformed Civil Service uniform) took his dripping coat, while his secretary (a slim woman with mousy hair and steely eyes) handed him his briefcase. Nodding curtly, Major Tonsonby left the two at the service entrances and hurried into the main hall. He tucked his peaked cap under one arm, and carried the briefcase by its handle.

Tonsonby had been summoned by none other than Leader Moss—top man in the rulership of wartime West Gotha. It was only Tonsonby's fourth or fifth visit to the headquarters of fifty million patriotic West Gothans. Tonsonby, like all West Gothans, had pilgrimaged through these halls as a school child and considered it a sort of national cathedral.

The summons had come tinged with ominous hints, Tonsonby thought as he clattered across the vast marble floor where the paths of hundreds of central government functionaries crossed his own.

The main hall was a basilica, with ornately scrolled ceilings edged in gold. Buttresses and heavy square pillars framed high, narrow stained glass windows. The windows glowed in the endlessly rainy ambient gray light from outside. Night and day, kaleidoscope fragments of weak, cool color spattered across the porphyry-tomato floor expanse. The windows revealed patriotic themes, built from disciplined quadrilles of red, blue, yellow, and green glass. Silvered scrolls etched into the glass bore black words in Gothic alphabet. The scenes were sentimental: Victory waving aloft a sword, standing knee-deep in naked corpses on a battlefield, looking back with urgent eyes to send more troops against the enemy; Motherhood, pinching a full, stiff breast to nurture wounded men with agonized expressions, who crawl to her on their knees as one of them continues to hold aloft the West Gotha battle flag; Fatherhood, in the form of a huge grim figure handing a sword to one son and a rifle to the other, while they bow their heads and the enemy sends in yet another violent light-show barrage; and so on, sixteen windows in all in this cathedral of state and duty; each scene much like the others with a huge central figure holding some object while being served by multitudes of tiny men suffering for their nation.

Going up the central staircase, itself a marvel of grandeur, Tonsonby barely noticed the crowning image: Nation, consisting of a huge father image whose face is characteristically of the Moss clan: round, with fierce little black eyes that inspire men and women to sacrifice themselves for the Nation and the Leader; against a huge tapestry of war and sacrifice, filled with little scenarios populated by gigantic, muscular men and women. The muscled giants of West Gotha lift hammers over anvils, raise torches to light beacons, bear children, send children to war, received the glorious dead back from battle, and on and on.

Tonsonby's path took him briefly outside on a passageway that wrapped like a slender concrete thread around the skin of the administrative headquarters. Like shadows in a hurry, couriers and secretaries and military officers hurried back and forth this windy deck, with only a glass wall to keep one from falling off. As preoccupied as he was, Tonsonby couldn't help but gaze across the magnificent vista.

Anti-aircraft lights, sweeping their cones back and forth under mottled rain clouds, illuminated the night sky above West Gotha. Sirens wailed in a slowly rising and falling chorus.

On the city's outer defensive perimeters, particularly facing the enemy city of East Gotha, force curtains rippled in the air like artificial green auroras. Sometimes, East Gotha bombers made it through to the innermost defenses, and ak-ak would begin pounding the skies until one or two burning bombers would slowly keel over and disappear to crash in the far countryside.

The city looked lovely from a distance: mountains of hazy light from thousands of windows piled into skyscrapers, one behind the other, in a soft, huge pyramid of buildings rising toward the center. Here, where Tonsonby walked, the central administration building rose like a magnificent basilica of stained glass windows and creamy Deco towers.

Closer up, the city had that wartime shabbiness characteristic of the grinding nightmare of wars seeming to go on forever. A sign atop a high-rise might be missing a letter. A wall might be peeling and long overdue for a paint job. A street might be potholed. Despite a million such inconveniences, the patriotic and dutiful people of West Gotha put on a brave face and soldiered on. The survival of the fatherland depended on their support of the Leader, and Tonsonby was heading to that Leader's office at this very moment with fear lining his stomach.

Tonsonby was unaware of a small but important drama that had played out only hours ago, yesterday evening, elsewhere in the city, between a baroness and a spy. The union of those two was about to start having a frightening impact on Tonsonby's career and in fact on his very life.

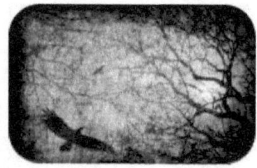

The citizens of West Gotha valued whatever time they could steal from the grind of work and fighting, to pursue love or pleasure. Behind the thick blackout curtains of a luxurious industrial executive suite, such a drama played itself out tonight. The hereditary executive of one of West Gotha's top wartime industries, a beautiful young baroness, had been working alone at her huge desk. As the evening wore on, she often stopped to chew her stylus and look up at the clock. She was expecting someone, and he was late. Or was he coming at all? She put her stylus down, closed her laptop, and rose. Sensually fingering her delicate wrist in its lace ruffle, she strode across the marble floor to the wet bar. There, she poured two crystal glasses of premium sec champagne from a bottle leaning in an ice bucket draped with linen hand towels. She loosened the kerchief around her neck, and fluffed her blouse open a button or two. Holding one of the glasses, she sauntered over to the entertainment bar and twisted a few knobs. The room filled with the seductive rhythms of recorded big band music. The atmosphere dimmed a bit she switched off the working lights.

The ambience in the room, already seductive with her light perfume, turned amber, at the edges verging on rouge.

The tall double doors opened at the other end of the hall, and a man stood in the high rectangle of light. She clutched her bare neck, fearing for a moment that the servants had intruded at a compromising moment. "Alton!" she said, recognizing Captain Hedrock's handsome features despite the shadows. He had to be the most charming, reckless man she'd ever known, but she would throw her sizeable share of West Gotha's wealth at his feet if must be. He closed the doors, locked them, and strode confidently toward her, taking off his jacket and tie. He wore the uniform of an officer in the West Gotha Guards, but she knew he worked for East Gotha. Her hope was to turn him—to help her overturn both wartime governments and restore peace to a newly unified city that ruled the world. As he approached, he grinned in his seductive, irresponsible manner and opened his arms to take her. They flew together, kissing hard in an embrace that could not be enough. They refilled the champagne glasses and toasted each other. Outside, in a grim and different reality, bombs fell on the city's force shields and exploded with deafening echoes. Inside the muffled executive suite, there was only sinuous Latin dance music and the sound of their laughter and heels as he spun her around on the marble floor. Only gradually did she notice the lipstick on his shirt, and smell the other woman about him—and thus another kind of war was about to begin.

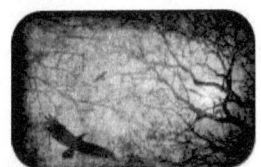

As Tonsonby came to the end of the dizzying walkway above West Gotha City, the first tendrils of daylight streaked the horizon from black to gray. Glad to get back into shelter, he entered the far half of the administration building.

He entered a wood-paneled lobby where uniformed figures with hard mouths and suspiciously swiveling glances stood smoking and exchanging conspiracies. Up Tonsonby went, two steps at a time on a wood staircase with blood-red carpet runners. He dodged between streamlined staff officers, and one-armed or one-legged infantry officers retired to administrative duties.

Hugging his tan leather briefcase under one arm, and holding his cap in his teeth while he pulled his black gloves off, Tonsonby came to the third floor. As he hurried along the mezzanines overlooking the grand hall. The passages up here seemed claustrophobic and overpopulated. They smelled of paper and ink, of wet coats and soggy leather boots, of harsh coffee and thick cigarette smoke that cast a pall resembling that of the battlefield. Tonsonby had both arms and legs intact, a fact of which he was exquisitely aware in this retirement farm of blinded, limping, amputated combat veterans.

Tonsonby, however, was not a paper pusher. He was an important cog in the Strategic Information Group (SIG), a central intelligence service attached directly to the Leader's offices. He was also a distant Moss cousin, which explained much to anyone who cared or dared to ask.

As he hurried into the increasingly plush, quiet, and sparsely populated mahogany row area, male and female desk clerks rose and snapped to attention like a series of dominoes rising rather than falling, and each held a telephone receiver to one ear to announce his arrival. For that reason, the double padded doors of Chancellor Moss' office suite seemed to swing open without need of a knock.

"Come in!" said the round-faced man in brown suit. He had a harp of thin black hairs combed meticulously over a round skull gleaming like aged cheese in yellow wax. "Just in time." He offered a cigar from a silver *etui*.

As custom required, Tonsonby politely refused. This was Leader Moss, a grandson of the Original Leader.

Leader Moss did not look happy as he stuck the huge brown rod in his thin mouth. Immediately an aide snapped forth with a lighter.

"Did you bring the device?" Leader Moss said as he puffed on the cigar, and dry acrid smoke filled the air.

Dawn was breaking, and its harsh light etched itself on the already harsh figures of Leader Moss.

The office was wide, with oriental carpeting and rich antique furniture. The windows were framed in dark wood, and part of an edge-down orange-slice effect running across six irregularly shaped double panes of heavy glass.

From here, Leader Moss had a panoramic view.

The city, with its domes and rectangles under gunmetal-gray roofs, glowered under charcoal clouds that looked smokier than Leader Moss's cigar smoke.

"Bring in the detector dock," Leader Moss ordered.

On command, within minutes, three corpsmen in drab fatigues wheeled the refrigerator-sized electronic unit across the thickly piled carpets.

Moss asked Tonsonby: "Is the latest upgrade fully functional?"

"Yes, Leader." Tonsonby addressed his cousin in the prescribed manner.

Laying the briefcase open on the glass-topped desk by the window, Tonsonby donned clean white gloves. He extracted a flat, rectangular container of creamy factory porcelain from the briefcase.

Opening this, he carefully removed from its padding a wide green circuit board etched with myriad gleaming silver patterns.

Gingerly, he lifted this into the cold gray light so that its silver lines glowed like molten, flowing chrome.

Tonsonby wondered if the day would become any brighter than this as morning wore on.

The dozen or so orderlies in the room, hovering in the shadows until bidden to light a cigar or fetch a brandy, let out a barely audible gasp.

Tonsonby stepped up to the tall, rectangular electronics closet and offered the circuit board to a wide mouth-slot.

He heard whirring inside the unit, and felt the circuit board pulled away from his fingers and into the maw of the machine.

It would travel on rails through a sort of digestive system until it came to rest in the unit's functioning core brain area.

The newly added component would raise the unit's artificial intelligence by several exponential factors.

"Readings are normal," said a technician nearby after a moment of silence.

"Good," Moss said. "Now we wait. Brandy?"

It was too early in the morning, but Tonsonby nodded. Nervously licking his lips, and feeling his hands suddenly cold and trembling, he stepped beside Leader Moss. Brandies arrived (smooth, sweet, tangy, nutty—not the cheap, harsh fluid of average little citizens).

Out in the distance, a rocket nose cone stood out like a needle above a forest of supporting gear.

Gantries hemmed it in on either side, and many lights glared with a harsh bluish-white intensity almost like arc welders.

Tonsonby saw the first major sign of activity before launch: a vast white cloud of steam grew over the launch area, so that only the nose cone and a few bluish-harsh lights were visible anymore.

"Launch time is minus 35 minutes and the clock is running," a female technician's crisp voice announced in the office where Tonsonby and Leader Moss stood looking out over the city.

"Patch into the tower chatter for us," Leader Moss commanded with quiet authority.

A minute later, there was a constant chain of quiet, efficient conversation as the launch engineers talked among each other and the final countdown sequences began.

Tonsonby stole a glance sidelong at his cousin.

The older Moss had a veiled, unreadable look as he smoked quietly and regarded the city with slightly red, smoke-rasped eyes.

Far off in the distance, past a faintly shimmering force field, Tonsonby could see mountains in East Gotha, in enemy territory.

Far away, when the clouds shifted, one could see the defensive domes and turrets of the massive fortress that was the equal and the deadly enemy of Tonsonby's motherland.

The nose cone atop the rocket contained sixteen MIRVed antimatter warheads. Each Multiple Independent Reentry Vehicle could dig a crater a mile deep.

One such warhead would impact the central headquarters of East Gotha within the hour.

Leader looked so proud of himself.

Hopefully, this great weapon of the Fatherland would end the generations-long war of the sister states once and for all, with total defeat for the Eastern upstarts, and a great victory for the glorious West.

Chapter 4

The two spies sat in a van. Parked on a promontory, overlooking West Gotha, was Captain Alton Hedrock of the East Gotha National Information Processing Agency (NIPO). Hedrock was the quintessential tall, dark, and handsome lady killer with a small mustached pressed hard on the rim of his upper lip. With him sat the West Gotha professor of computer information systems he had seduced into becoming a fellow spy—his boss in the West Gotha Special Projects Branch (SPB), Dr. Moira. They sat silently sipping lukewarm coffee that filled the van's dingy cab with a wood-like aroma of artificial cream, too much sugar, and too-thin brew of chicory with a sprinkle of real coffee. Rain pattered on the roof and echoed in the van's half-empty interior. Moira had one cold, trembling hand on his thigh. He considered pushing her hand away, but calculated that she needed reassurance more than she needed warmth.

"How could I let you lead me to betray my fatherland?"

He was absorbed in the distant view of the West Gotha launch port, and almost did not hear his lover speak.

"You're a cool one," Moira said.

He gently patted her icy hand, which gripped his knee, and smiled at her. He was fond of her, well enough, though his duty always came first and she was expendable like any other attractive woman he seduced in the line of work. He raised a pair of small, strong binoculars and scanned the city for reference points only he recognized. Moira had helped calculate the triangulation of three seemingly innocuous microwave patterns that would intersect at a dumb, blind transponder hidden in a tower among the many towers near the launch gantry.

Chapter 5

Let's talk a little about the purpose of today's launch," Leader Moss murmured softly, so only Major Tonsonby could hear. Moss put an arm around Tonsonby's shoulder, and guided him out of earshot. They stood by the cold, frosty window glass overlooking tawdry streets with dim neon cheer below. Cars and ant-like citizens pushed through the drizzle and vapor on the dark streets. The very street lights were still lit, though it was midmorning. "Good day for a launch," Moss said with a tight little grin. He clapped Tonsonby on the shoulder a last time, then sat on the window sill in a pensive mode as if he had much to say. An orderly tiptoed near to refill their brandies. After the quick dip here, there, of the bottle, Moss waved him away. Moss said to Tonsonby: "I'm afraid I have disturbing news for you."

"I was afraid you might, Leader."

Moss shrugged disarmingly, though his eyes had a dangerous light that contradicted his words. "Nothing to fear. I have it all under control."

"What, Leader?" Tonsonby's gut wrenched. He thought sickeningly of his wife, his two little children, his safe and comfortable existence...how easily it could all fall away into an abyss. The thought of losing it all suddenly loomed terrifyingly—perhaps even spending the rest of his life in a dungeon somewhere, with his family told he'd died in a plane crash while on duty or some such nonsense.

Moss took a quiet breath, utterly in charge of himself and the world around them, and said: "I'm afraid we have learned that your subordinate Dr. Moira is working for the other side."

"No." Tonsonby felt horrified as his world started to melt around him like candle wax.

"I told you not to worry," Moss said. He gave Tonsonby another cold, domineering, but somehow vaguely reassuring clap on the shoulder. "Drink your brandy. You look as if you need it."

Tonsonby obeyed, shooting the burning sweet liquid down his throat. He almost choked, fearing it was a trick and they'd put something in there to corrode his insides and make him collapse of a faux heart attack. He regarded Moss with utter terror, like a drowning man looking up at someone coldly amused by his plight. But the feeling passed. The brandy was good and warm. Moss wasn't amused by his terror but apparently pleased to have outwitted the other side. Every such victory gave off a rewarding glow, since such triumphs were few and far between in this endless, nerve-wracking war to the death between two alienated super-states that dominated the entire Earth between them.

"The launch isn't going to happen," Moss said quietly.

"It isn't?"

Moss nodded. "Think about it. They have a new technology for stopping our launches dead. If we were to actually send up nukes today, they'd blow them up over our heads. No, my dear fellow, we're after a different brace of game today. We'll reserve the antimatter bombs for another day. Today it's all a show of pyrotechnics, while my agents swoop in and clean up the nest of spies you've been brooding like a hen in your shop over there."

Tonsonby stumbled back and clicked to attention. "Leader, I beg your forgiveness."

"Stop making a scene," Moss growled through gritted teeth. "Play it straight, you dunderhead. We don't want these boys to understand that something is afoot."

"Of course, Leader." Tonsonby was still sweating, and trembling, but he pulled himself together as best he could.

"Ten seconds to launch," said a controller's voice far away at the rocketdrome, echoing in Moss's office public address system.

Chapter 6

Ten seconds to launch," said a controller's voice far away at the rocketdrome, echoing faintly over the eavesdropping radio in Hedrock's van.

"Oh my God," Moira said, "what have I done to my fatherland?"

"Relax and enjoy the show," Hedrock said, giving her his seductive, boyish smile. "You are helping me save the world. There must be one Gotha under a new leadership, not East or West, not Moss nor Grunt."

Visibly disgusted with herself, Moira shoved him away. Her unexpected violent motion made him spill hot coffee over his lap, and he jumped up cursing.

No time to humor her now. Too bad if she was unhappy with herself.

He ran a fingertip over the miniature control display bar overhead behind the windshield glass. All the indicators looked green, with the occasional flicker into warning amber but quickly back to green. No red lights at all. The wide array of tiny signals looked good clear across from one side to the other.

Today's abort would put a huge dent in West Gotha's strategic capabilities, Hedrock thought. His handler here, and his coordinators on the other side, had promised him a bloc of time to himself. He did have a special matter to pursue—a woman. She was special, and he actually hoped that he could salvage their damaged relationship.

She too was a professor—a mathematician. Hedrock liked his women attractive and brilliant. Moira came close, but Amy was the ticket. If most women were little more than a brief lyric, Moira was a minuet, but the wealthy, powerful, and intriguing Baroness was a symphony. The fact that she possessed knowledge that could reshape history on this planet was almost not a consideration right now. Hedrock had a different plan for her, a strategy unlike any he had ever considered. He was about to betray both East and West Gotha for her sake. First, though, he must find her and cautiously try to repair the damage he'd caused to their relationship—for Amy, whom he had married in a secret ceremony, his wife under secret laws of neither East nor West, had discovered his liaison with Moira. Amy had become suspicious, spied on them, and caught them in bed together in a mediocre downtown West Gotha hotel—complete with missing T in the pink neon Hotel sign outside the window. He'd almost expected Amy to kill them both, given the rage and pain he saw in her eyes as he and Moira lay frozen with pink neon washing on and off across their naked skin—and perhaps that would have been merciful compared to the rage he'd spotted in her only after glance as she fled from the home he'd briefly started sharing with her in the family castle.

"Three, two, one," said the distant voice.

Moira sat frozen, staring at the red rocket glow starting to warm up the billowing vapor clouds around the nose cone.

"Launch is go, lift sequence engage, full burn all engines go," said a *melange* of voices blending together in one urgent mix of cryptic words.

Hedrock crossed his fingers and glanced at the head-up display, which showed the microwave outputs were active and beaming, aimed at the transponder and the rocket's brain core from three different locations within West Gotha.

Moira gasped as the cloud grew redder and flashed into a yellow-white sun before instantly dimming into a cold blue glow that died out within choking gray-black roils of burning rubber and machinery.

"Yes!" Hedrock said. "We did it." He laughed as he turned on the engine, put the van in reverse, and started to back away from the stone wall overlooking the promontory.

At that moment, he saw a half dozen West Gotha police cars come streaking toward him. Their overhead light bars twirled in various colors, and their white metallic shapes hurled through the damp air. *What?* Hedrock stared in disbelief at the undoing of his scheme. In the same instant, he realized that Amy Hedrock wasn't the only one who hated him. He stared at Moira, his lover, and saw the flat, slate rage in her eyes directed at him.

"I couldn't go through with it," she said. "I turned us both in."

Chapter 7

As the fires flared up on the distant launch pad, and pale assistants dashed to the window to point and yell in anguish, Moss pushed Tonsonby into a small side office and closed the door behind him.

They were alone in the small room, which was too brightly lit with too many fluoros, and contained blonde furniture (a table, chairs, bookcase) littered with white paper printouts.

"This is a chess game," Moss said. "You were blind-sided, and I am going to insist you shake up your internal staff."

"Of course, Leader." Tonsonby felt his knees trembling.

People were pounding on the door, demanding Moss' attention, but he called out "Leave us alone!"

He sat Tonsonby down in a chair and loomed over him, face to face so that Tonsonby could smell the other's rancid cigar and brandy breath. "You, Tonsonby, will now have the need to know, and will be further enlightened, so that you can fulfill your next duties in continuing to deceive the East into thinking we are as stupid as their Captain Hedrock evidently thought we are. Are you ready?"

"Yes, Leader."

Moss was shaking with rage, and red in the face. He jammed a thick, dirty index finger into Tonsonby's mouth so that Tonsonby felt his choke reflex mauled and attacked.

Tonsonby started retching helplessly, failing the courage to attack back. He closed his eyes and thought of his family. *Oh God, anything but that, anything but lose them.*

"So you understand what's at stake then!" Moss shouted. His eyes were small and vicious, and spittle flew from his small meat-red lips. He made the finger into a fish-hook and tore a knife-like fingernail through the soft tissue in Tonsonby's mouth as he extracted the finger.

Tonsonby leaned forward retching up brandy and blood. His mouth felt as if it were on fire.

Moss shouted: "I'm going to put it in your record that you failed to supervise your people on several of the most sensitive projects the state has entrusted to you. If you succeed in the next phase, I will consider removing the damaging information from your record. Family or no, cousin or not, this nation cannot succeed with dimwits like you entrusted with important matters. That is why I had my people infiltrate your department when I got word of the traitors working for you."

Tonsonby sobbed, kneeling before Moss and holding the man's knees in his hands. "I am sorry, Leader. I am so sorry. Please forgive me."

The words choked in blood and chyme that kept making him spasm and splatter the carpet, so that Moss slapped him across the face and jumped back.

"I am so sorry, Leader, so sorry..." Tonsonby repeated amid sobs and choking.

Chapter 8

The gravel parking lot of the high park overlooking the city filled with small white police cars. Hedrock backed the van up, put it in gear, and made the van jump forward. As he did so, instinct told him it was going to be a rough ride. He tugged his seatbelts tight.

Everything seemed blurry. On his left, he saw the city, and a flashing white streak as a patrol car cut him off. On his right, he saw Moira struggling to jump from the van. He reached over, grabbed a handful of her hair, and violently yanked her toward him. As he did so, he gunned the van and rammed between two police cars to try and escape. Meanwhile, Moira was struggling, clawing, crying, punching. He held her hair and slammed her head down on the steel floor. She sat stunned and bleeding on all fours. He held the wheel in both hands as he did bumper-cars among the police cars, which were all lighter and smaller than the van. Shots rang out. The windshield shattered. Cops were jumping from cars with drawn guns.

Alton Hedrock reached up under the ceiling, pulled down the assault rifle, crouched half-upright, and sprayed the parking lot. As the assault rifle chattered, he saw legs and shoes in the air. He knew he must not let them overwhelm him like this. What to do?

Throwing the assault rifle aside, he gunned the car again. The engine roared mightily as the clutch let out. Moira was just starting to put one hand up on her seat to get up. He ignored her, holding the wheel with both hands as he crashed through the low stone wall. The van lurched upward like a missile. Bits and blocks of stone and mortar as well as weeds grown in cracks exploded outward. For a second, the van looked like a bread loaf spinning in empty air. No more shots hit it—the cops must be stunned.

Moira screamed briefly and then fell silent as she clutched the seat. She couldn't get a grasp, and her hands slipped. He saw how white her desperate fingers looked. Her eyes, too, looked white and scared. She regarded him with sheer terror written in her gritted teeth, her frozen scream, her beautiful eyes.

All he could do now was hang on.

Somewhere below were streets, neighborhoods, escape routes if his luck held.

The van impacted in a tree crown and slowed. Amy still writhed, trying to gain a grip on the slippery, dirty old leather of the seat. The van slowed, then started moving again.

Branches cracked, snapped, exploded, and yielded. The van started sliding fast again.

Branches slammed into the cab.

Hedrock managed to duck down and cover his head. The last he saw of Moira was her legs as she was pulled from the shattered passenger window, impaled on a branch.

Already, her legs made death twitches, in just that second before the van tore loose and sailed down into the houses below.

Hedrock lay back in the seat, crossed his arms over his chest and face, squeezed his knees together, and thought of the rising sun flag of East Gotha. He had never imagined that would be his last thought as he faced death. He liked it. It seemed patriotic. It validated all that he had achieved. If this was the end, it was a decent way to go.

No time for more thoughts as the van dropped through the air.

The van landed on a slate rooftop, which braked its fall.

Slate crackled and shattered in thin layered plates all around him.

The van's chassis buckled and twisted but the vehicle held together. Roof timbers cracked, groaned, cracked, and then snapped.

The van dropped down into a bedroom, onto an empty bed whose owners had luckily gone to work or whatever. The van came to rest on the bed like a lion draped over its kill.

Bleeding from the mouth and ears, Hedrock unsnapped himself from the harness. He laboriously kicked the bent door open enough to let himself slither down the side and onto a splintered wooden floor that groaned dangerously. Glancing up, he saw cops yelling and shouting about 300 feet overhead. They looked tiny and didn't dare shoot. People in the house were beginning to scream.

Hedrock managed to distance himself from the van and get through a door into a hallway.

As he made the final leap to safety, the floor buckled and the entire room crashed down, van and all, into the next story, which then collapsed and sailed down through the next story, and so on down six or seven floors.

Hedrock heard one or two brief screams, and then silence as he lowered himself down the broken piles of rock floor by floor. He saw a few places soaked with purple blood and macerated body parts.

Main thing, he was still mobile and moving fast now. He'd ache later. He'd find a place to lair down and hide until his bruises healed. Maybe he had broken bones. Right now, with adrenaline pumping through his system, he didn't know or care. He felt nothing, except the exhilaration of chase and escape. He'd managed to survive yet another close call.

Climbing out through a rear kitchen window, he hobbled away through someone's vegetable garden, through a back gate, and down a rear alley, even as only the faintest distant keening of sirens became audible.

He'd live to fight these bastards another day.

More important than that, he must find his wife and promise that now everything would be different.

Part 3 - Femtoverse War Gaming

Bit Cave

Chapter 9

Tedda woke, strangling, falling out of bed. She lay on the floor convulsing as she tried to breathe The cold kiss of her manacles, the clatter of her chains like the rattle of an attacking snake, woke her from the pitch black dream in which she had been submerged. She lay on an icy, coated concrete floor, gasping and wriggling desperately like a fish out of water.

She had a brief, fading vision of a knife, and a terrible episode, a handsome man, but the details were no longer clear. At some level, she knew clearly she was being offered an exchange: peace of mind from her terrible past, in exchange for cooperation with the fatherland.

Unable to breathe, she tried to scream. Her choking, heaving motions brought forth what seemed like acres of green water filled with bits of broken leaf, twigs, bird feathers.

Lights came on. Voices shouted. Boots splashing in water ran toward her. As her lungs emptied, she began to take in racking, sobbing breaths. She lay like a crocodile, hands splayed on the floor, and opened her mouth wide in short bursts, snapping it shut, drawing in sweet oxygen.

She took big gulps of warm air, smelling the rubbery finish on the floor under her palms. She could almost kiss the floor, so grateful was she to be alive, though terrified once again: *where am I?* she wondered.

Chapter 10

Tedda lay in some sort of mummy wrapping on a gurney under a pinkish light. It was like the light in a dentist's office, round and pink with concentric plastic rings in its cover.

Sedated—that much she could feel.

The turgid metal of some opiate swirled in her blood stream like mercury, making her feel dull and amputated but free from pain. Amputated from pain, she lay in her cocoon feeling numb and warm and safe. This was better than being dead, even though this hurt dimly, but it was not as painful as the cold.

Tedda felt her fingertips pressing against her thighs, so her manacles and chains must be gone.

That much was good.

Why am I here? she wondered.

She was wrapped in blankets and around those, tied with straps, to a hospital bed. Two I.V. poles stood nearby. Bags of saline hung suspended, clear and wrinkled, and stabbed into those were various piggy-back I.V. medicines, and it all went *drip, drip, drip* down clear plastic tubules toward the parts of her body invisible to her beyond the horizon of sheets and straps.

This was a place or a condition of endless monotony.

It was a large room with peeling white walls and dull floors.

Under the dull ceilings, a double row of long fluorescent tubes mostly were not working, and the few that worked were all different shades of pink or yellow or gray.

One kept winking on and off.

Their chargers hummed.

She felt a twinge of that awful need to run somewhere, do something, save someone, help someone, a warm someone—but the feeling eluded her.

She could make no sense of it.

Tedda looked toward the only motion visible.

To her left was a row of long, low windows that could be leaned open, but they were all closed.

Above those were big square panes of glass that could not be opened.

Outside were huge green tree crowns full of leaves and rain.

Wind pressed leaves against the windows.

Tedda could hear a faint howling and realized the wind outside must be very strong.

Not a good night to be outside.

She looked with glazed eyes at the endless runneling of rainwater down the window glass.

It was good to be inside here, warm and dry.

What the next second or minute might bring, she had no idea. But for this instant in time, she felt warm, dry, and safe.

Chapter 11

Sunlight flooded into the room.

Tedda sat dully waiting, with her hands folded together in her lap, on a hard wooden chair with a curving back generously sweeping around her and under her forearms to provide resting spots for her elbows.

She sat with her feet crossed at the ankles, and twiddled her thumbs.

The drugs were not out of her system yet, and the clinic had given her other drugs to counteract nausea and dizziness. In that cocktail of gel capsules was also something to take the edge off her terror.

Nearby sat the gurney, cold and dead now, with sheets and blankets tightly folded and placed very precisely in a harmonious and military looking pyramid with the pillow near the top and a white towel and washcloth folded on top of that.

Dust motes twirled in the bar of sunlight that streaked in and exploded silently on the waxed floor.

The large, rectangular room smelled of floor wax and harsh soap.

Somewhere, voices echoed in hallways. Someone whistled. A man laughed.

Two women joked.

A man made a seductive comment.

Two women laughed.

Tedda caught it all in the periphery of her awareness as she sat waiting.

A hand bag sat by her side with a few possessions in it; nothing personal in there, unless she counted the plain pine toothbrush with frayed bristles, which she had been using for however long she'd been here.

At one point she rose. Her legs were stiff and shaky.

She wore a plain blue mid-calf gown, and on soft lace-up boots like the ones she'd lost.

The memory of near drowning terrified her.

She closed her eyes and held her palms to her ears as she saw again the swirling loamy water, the dead women hanging from their shackles liked skinned animals, the van tumbling away downstream.

Quickly she opened her eyes, counter-instinctively, and moved her palms across her mouth to stop herself from screaming.

Tears flowed from her eyes and dribbled over her fingers, dripping onto the hard floor.

Her tears, she saw, were real. They spattered when they struck the brownish, dully gleaming floor that smelled of hard, institutional, cruel wax.

She walked across the floor, her inner ears ringing and pounding.

She had to stop once or twice as the floor seemed to shift like a carpet being swirled, but the feeling passed.

She actually felt better, as she stood with her fingers loosely intertwined over her pelvis, and looked down into a cobblestone courtyard nearly two stories below. It was nearly two stories because the ground tilted slightly away from the main building, and there was a little grassy slope, kidney-shaped, that she could make out below looking through rich leafy tree crowns.

Looking into the distance, she saw a grassy strip receding toward a distant line of trees.

To the left of the grassy strip was a rough road, at times cobblestone, at times gravel, at times muddy with puddles, and to the left of that a long, low wall.

Upon a second glance, she saw that the wall connected a series of small, gray stone buildings whose rounded portals and heavy wooden doors overlooked the rough road.

Tedda glimpsed a man in uniform, with a riding crop in one hand, leading a huge white horse by the halter. The man wore black jodhpurs and riding boots, and had short blond hair.

"Child," a woman's voice said warmly, interrupting Tedda's studies. Tedda turned.

A nurse stood in the doorway, wearing a dark blue wool cape over her white uniform, white socks, white shoes, white wing-cap. "I'm Amit," the woman said in an accent that might be Delhi or Bombay. She was light-skinned, Brahmin, with a red dot on her forehead. "I'll be in charge of your recovery, child. Are you ready to check out?"

"Check out?" Tedda said uncomprehendingly.

"Yes," Amit said, pointing to the ugly gray grip by the chair. "Take your bag, child. We have to go."

"I am going?"

"Yes."

"Home?"

Amit looked at her strangely. "Child, you are going down to the lockup. This is a prison."

"What did I do?"

"I don't know. It's not for us staff to know. I know only that you have been a good patient here, and that is the extent of my concern."

Tedda walked to the chair, picked up her bag, and joined Amit who stood sideways with one hand on the door latch, impatient to pull it shut. "I don't remember anything."

"That is to be expected," Amit said pulling the door shut. A large number 909 was embossed on the door in grayish-blue lettering upon routered particle board. They walked down a dark hallway that gleamed with plaques on either wall. Sunlight glowed in through overhead skylights of wavy glass blocks. The hallway took them down several steps, past office doors (dark doors, with frosted windows, and severe-looking black lettering in an alphabet Tedda didn't understand) and up more stairs, then curved around and opened into a large enclosed space framed by heavy concrete pillars and surfaces at right angles. The ceiling high up was black, impenetrable, lit by small sharp track lights.

As Tedda walked with Amit, she became aware of guards and heavy steel security bars. The guards were a mix of middle-aged and younger men and women, wearing black leather belts and heavy side arms. They wore black velour helmets, as if for polo, but with a gleaming brass sun emblem in front. Tedda caught a glimpse of one close up: Many fine small rays formed a cruciform star, emanating from a rounded disk on which writhed an eagle, screaming. Across the eagle's beak unfurled a banner with writing on it. In one set of talons it clutched a sword, and in the other a scroll.

Tedda noticed a large version of the same symbology under a large clock high up in the concrete vaults. "What does it say?"

"It says Union of States in West Gotha. That is our nation, the fatherland, child."

"I can't remember a thing about it," Tedda said, feeling the presence of a deep and persistent terror inside herself.

Amit clucked as they approached a gate that was surrounded by guards, shadowy figures with high leather boots and black helmets. Several carried radios, others rifles. "Prisoner Tedda 823495837459," Amit read from a card.

Tedda stood in an alcove with her legs slightly apart and her arms outstretched to the sides. Female guards watched as lights traveled around inside a recessed arc, shooting faint beams at her: she glowed alternately green, red, blue.

"Pass," said a stern woman wearing much silver braid on her black uniform.

The gate rumbled open, and Tedda walked through alone, carrying her bag. She turned to look back.

Amit stood in the center, surrounded by guards. "Go on, child. I will monitor your health from over here. Watch yourself. Stay out of trouble."

The gate rumbled shut. Steel chattered on concrete as the wheels dug in, grinding through a groove. The lock found its mate in the wall with a clang, and tumblers inside ratcheted shut.

Tedda felt rain droplets on her face, and a cool cleansing wind. For the first time, she inhaled fresh air and the smells of wet grass, as well as damp concrete and exposed soil. The sun darkened as a cloud moved over it.

Chapter 12

For a second, Tedda thought she was alone—and free. Then the guards came from either side and took her by the elbows, not painfully, but firmly and gracelessly. An NCO walked past, waving one arm and speaking directions, while keeping the other hand in the side pocket of his open pea coat. He had three large red chevrons stitched upside down on the upper sleeves, and various hash marks and other insignia—all frayed, worn so the thread stuck out and the dark base underneath showed. Tedda noticed he had mud spattered over his high boots and up his dark blue trousers. He wore a visorless cap pushed back on his head, and had a lanky, careless way of walking. He was a powerful, seamy-looking man with cool blue eyes, nearing forty, and a bit of a slob. Less military than a farm hand, she thought. As they walked in the direction the NCO pointed, Tedda shook the restraining hands from her elbows. The two young soldiers, teenage boys really, seemed glad to let go. Their eyes told her they didn't relish bullying a woman. Good for them.

"Watka," the NCO introduced himself. "I run this yard. You stay on my good side, I'll make sure you eat good and don't get too hard work. You mess with me, and you'll be one unhappy woman. You got that?"

"I understand. I don't want any trouble," she said.

"Whoa," said one of the boys, "she's got school."

Tedda mulled this over. What did this mean? They took her down the curving little hill, where she got her ankles damp in the drippy grass. It smelled good, fresh, after her confinement inside. Down they went along that gravel road, feet crunching in the stones. The boys had heavy boots that tore in, while the NCO shuffled in slamming steps, and Tedda felt positively feminine in her soft boots. Down the street, she spied the officer with the white horse. He held the reins, while an older orderly dressed like Watka but without stripes brushed the animal down. Must have been out riding, she thought. The officer looked at her and froze. She could sense his laser-like attention from 1000 feet. Did he find her attractive? Was he offended by her? Was he just curious?

"That's Major Grün," Watka said. "You might get to meet him. He runs this place for the Colonel General, his old man, at headquarters."

With a last glance down the road at the magnetic major, who was talking with the orderly now, but still glanced over his shoulder at her,

Tedda followed the others into a headquarters office. There, a pair of unsmiling young female adjutant clerks in crisp khaki blouses and dark green skirts went slowly about their tasks. The room smelled of flowers or perfume, faintly, and cigarette smoke and horse dung. In a corner, a black iron stove hissed lightly; reddish flames danced in the glass eye of its door, and wisps of steam leaked from the dented seams of its heat-discolored tin flue that ran up along the dingy white-washed walls. Tedda also smelled typewriter ribbon ink, and paper by the ream, and machine oil from the teletypes in a corner. Somehow, Tedda sensed there ought to be more blinking lights and fancy electronic equipment, but she wasn't sure why.

Watka told her: "They'll take your information, however much you remember, and process you in."

"How long am I here for?"

Watka put both hands in his pockets and cocked his head back while rubbing his back in the doorway. "How the hell do I know? Or care?" With that he turned and walked out. The two young men looked at each other, shrugged, and followed him.

As a message came in, one of the teletypes started to chatter loudly. The tall charcoal-colored metal boxes with rounded corners shook, while its strike-keys made oily whacking noises on cheap paper. "I'll get it. It's War Department D.O.A.G.," the younger woman said moving toward it with a pen in hand.

"Come here," said the older of the two young women to Tedda. She seemed cold and preoccupied, probably annoyed at having to stop what she was doing to put a form in a typewriter and start documenting Tedda's arrival. "Name?"

"Pardon me?"

The girl's head snapped up and her eyes blazed. "Your handle, you dumb shit."

Chapter 13

Tedda stepped out of the warm office—which, despite its rude girls and mix of pungent smells, seemed cozier than this strange dreary place with its rain and rumpled-looking soldiers. She found a young woman waiting for her on the grass just off the street.

"Hi, I'm Lindy," she said in a strangely soft voice. She seemed to be speculating whether Tedda could be a friend, or if Tedda meant to wound her. The girl—well, woman; she was so slender that it made her look younger--wore a motley assortment of threadbare clothes--an old chasse-green peacoat like Watka's but far older and torn, over a faded, baggy-blue prison jumpsuit; a scratchy scarf the texture of an old brown foot rug; and scuffed shoes two sizes too big. The woman's hair was mousy, page boy hanging ragged down to her loosely flapping woolen epaulets. Her face was pale and bony, with redness where she seemed to continually run a finger along one sinusy nostril. Her mouth was wide and expressive, her eyes pale gray and speculative.

"I'm Tedda." Tedda offered a hand, cautiously, palm down as if hiding her feelings.

Lindy reached out and shook Tedda's. "I'll show you around. We're cell mates. You're not queer, are you?"

Tedda shook her head.

"Good. I don't mess around. I hope you're easy to get along with."

"I hope the same."

"Maybe we'll get along." Lindy stuck her hands in her pockets.

"Maybe."

"I hope so." Lindy's haunted face flickered. "What'd you do?"

Tedda shrugged. "No idea."

"I didn't know for a while either," Lindy said seriously. "They do things to you with pills. Either they put you on or take you off. When they took me off I remembered."

"What?"

"Cutting my sergeant's throat while he was raping me. That's why I'm in here. Who did you kill?"

"I have no idea."

Lindy leaned close, hands in pockets, butt up, while she studied Tedda's face. "Yeah, your eyes are a little hosed. You're still on drugs. Maybe you better pray they don't take you off and you remember whatever it was. I'll tell you this."

"What?" They started to walk down the gravel road along the interminable seeming dirty white wall, while the air smelled of chicken shit and horse droppings. Lindy led the way, but glanced sidelong over her shoulder at Tedda. "Anyone assigned to this place is here for a long time. Forever." She pulled a large metal key from her pocket, on a purple ribbon attached to her belt under the pea coat. "Tell you something else."

"What?" Tedda inhaled the growing fog, the droplets from an as yet invisible rain gathering like cold sweat on her face.

"They don't mess with you much. No dirty stuff, no beatings. You know what that means?"

"What?"

"It means we are important to them for some reason."

"Who?"

"The government that runs this place."

"This prison?"

"Prison, fortress, headquarters, it's all the same. The Government of West Gotha, that's our country. The Fatherland." Lindy flicked a sloppy, mock salute with the wrong hand past her eyebrow. "May God save and keep our Cheddar, the great Billo."

Tedda had her hands in her pockets and shivered in the growing fog. She laughed. "What does all that mean?"

Lindy laughed too. "Damned if I know. I just overhear things. These are mostly just country people, in case you haven't guessed."

Their feet crunched in rhythm on the gravel as they approached a low, wide circular tower with a black slate roof overgrown with moss, tucked between huge weeping willows. Overhead, clouds scudded in low, darkening as raindrops started spattering on Tedda's head and shoulders.

"So," Tedda said with a sudden flash of insight, "that must mean—"

"What?"

"We are city girls?"

"You're serious."

"What do you mean?"

"You must be joking."

"Did I ask something wrong?"

Lindy rolled her eyes up as she advanced on the cottage door holding the key on the purple ribbon before her. "Girl, you've got it bad. You really don't remember much, do you?"

Chapter 14

As they walked along the white wall of cottages on their left, their feet crunching on the gravel and drizzle peppering Tedda's cheeks, Tedda spied a disconcerting figure. Sitting in a narrow opening in the whitewashed wall was a large, hooded figure in a dark cape.

"Don't be afraid," said Lindy, "that is Confessor Grün. You'll be meeting with him from time to time. He talks with all of us."

Tedda barely heard Lindy. Tedda's knees were knocking together, and shivers traveled up and down her back. The deepest cellar of her mind let loose this thought, which only briefly flashed along the bottom of her consciousness before disappearing back into her subconscious: *Will he learn about what I did with the knife?* There he was, this caped figure sitting on some sort of throne with his back against the far wall, deep inside this space with its missing front wall. He seemed like a fixture. He reminded her of an eel peering out from his cave underwater. As he lifted his head, the voluminous hood fell back, exposing a broad, enigmatic face that radiated power, mystery, and something ominous. His eyes were not so much cold, but seemed animated, heated, calculating, and merciless. Their eye contact lasted only a second, but she fled away. She dimly heard his deep voice say after her, "Child..." and Lindy said something like "He is calling you to him," but Tedda blocked it all out. She felt terrified. The vision, and the feeling emanating from it, vanished in a few minutes as they reached a building on their right.

Chapter 15

Our home," Lindy. They regarded the rounded, tower-like entrance of a yellowish stuccoed multistory building overgrown with ivy on all sides. A large structure, it appeared to be melded with some ancient city walls of gray dressed stones overlooking neighborhoods several stories below.

"That is the university," Lindy said, pointing to a mass of glass buildings with aluminum spires and domes on the other side of a small valley. "We'll be working there together. First, let's get you acquainted with your new home." Lindy pushed through a heavy old wooden door with wrought-iron bars and thick glass panels. Tedda followed her through the round tower lobby with its creaking wooden floors and over-papered bulletin boards on either side. "I'll show you the refectory and the other common rooms like the basement laundry shortly."

They marched up a gloomy flight of stairs, past the open doors of rooms in which silent women sat knitting or paring an apple or washing hands endlessly or just staring out of shell-shocked eyes that didn't blink. They had come to the topmost room along the spiral staircase and Lindy had thrown it open. Now they stood before a room with two beds. Lindy stepped aside, and Tedda stepped inside. The wooden floorboards groaned in faint, tiny voices as she stepped about.

"Not much to see," Tedda said, picking uncertainly at this or that.

"Yeah, well it grows on you." Estana slipped the door shut and turned the key. "You learn to lock things up or they walk off. Some of these sluts are here for theft, burglary, you name it. Not all get treated well either, if they aren't important."

"Looks comfortable enough," Tedda said, walking around the room touching this and that. To the right was Lindy's bed, with a ragged and faded quilt over it.

"I salvaged that from a family who moved through here last year," Lindy said nervously. "Their child died, and they left me her quilt." She shrugged.

Tedda shrugged. "Yeah. That's tough." She ached inside. Moving to the window, she looked down through trees on a grassy hillside on which rabbits played.

Lindy looked over her shoulders. "The rabbits are stupid. Watka goes hunting here on the estate. I like it when they have rabbit cooked in red wine and onions. It's not often."

"What do you eat usually?" Tedda asked as she sat and bounced on her dry little mattress with a stack of aseptic sheets, blankets, and pillow; pretty much the same rubric as upstairs in the hospital room.

"Yuck," Lindy said, sitting down beside her. "Potatoes this, potatoes that. Sometimes we have meat, sometimes we don't. Depends on how the war is going. There is always cabbage. Sometimes we have carrots, which are good. We get salt and pepper to put on everything. Fruits, sometimes. A banana or a lemon, very rarely. Apples. There are orchards near here. Oranges so we don't get scurvy, but they are often on the verge of being brown and rotten."

They both bounced on the creaking mattress and springs, and laughed. Lindy bounced to her feet and skittered across the room. She reached under her mattress and pulled out a flat pint bottle of some cloudy yellow liquid. "Potato schnapps." She giggled. "Want a sip?

Tedda shook her head. "Makes me giddy. I want to have a clear mind right now, what's left of it."

"I agree." Lindy stashed it back under the mattress. "We have to meet your co-workers. Come."

"You're kidding," Tedda said.

"Nope." Lindy held out a hand. "You'll like them." A gong sounded, deep and resonant but faint, as if underwater. Lindy made a face as they bounded down the stairs. "I forgot. It's dinner time."

"I am kind of hungry," Tedda said following her. She felt a little unsteady and held her left hand against the cracked plaster wall in the curving stairwell.

"I hope you like the cast of characters," Lindy said. "Let's stop in and pay our respects." They went down past the ground floor to a lower level that smelled of cabbage and onions. The wooden floor had a weird smell, as if its untreated, raw tobacco-brown surface were soaked in vinegar. A row of disconsolate women stood silently in line holding battered aluminum trays. Most wore the standard bleach-blue jumpsuit. A few wore other odds and ends, like a faded sweater two sizes too big or two small, or a steel woolish scarf like Lindy. At least one woman had vacant eyes and a scar around the top of her forehead; Lindy whispered: "They unscrewed her dashboard and took out a few of the lights." One women, a large shmeery blonde with hungry eyes and some kind of red lipstick, wore a knitted purple hat-thing with mysterious lumps over each ear. "Looks like she can screw horns in if she wants," Lindy whispered about the wool knit lumps. Tedda squinted more closely and realized the lumps were intended to represent flowers. Two women got in an elbow-jamming fight near the French doors leading into the drab, industrial feeding area. Two others quietly hung back and held hands. Tedda already hated the place, and could understand Lindy's distaste. "How long exactly have you been here?" she asked her new friend and roommate.

"Too long. A little over seven years."

"And for how long?"

Lindy regarded her oddly. "Well, that's part of the punishment. They don't tell you." Seeing Tedda's shocked look, she nodded. "You don't know what a torture it is. Every day you wake up and think this is the day they let you go. After a few thousand disappointments, you quit hoping."

Tedda felt that awful jolt of urgency again, like something cutting her inside. She held her hands to her temples.

"You okay?"

Tedda felt as if all her blood had flowed away, leaving her skin cold and pale.

"You look terrible," Lindy said in alarm.

"It will pass," Tedda said. There was no way to understand or deal with these sudden bursts of need or urgency or duty or whatever it was.

Chapter 16

Night had fallen when they were outside. "What did you think of our crowd?" Lindy asked.

"I'm glad to get away from them."

"You're smart. If you're like me, don't make friends with any of them. Don't even talk with them or make eye contact. They are all bad news."

The two woman each walked with hands in pockets, solitary yet side by side. Puddles glittered like black glass. The sky had an undercoating of smoky clouds, amid which distant spotlights roved, looking for enemy air activity.

"If you stay out of trouble, they give you a lot of freedom," Lindy said, as they walked along a high, ivy-overgrown brick wall. "Not those brain-dead broads back there, but someone like you or me."

Tedda didn't answer. She felt a bit tired, and confused. She would sort things out in time. The road went slightly but steadily downhill, and the walls on either side got taller. Pretty soon they passed high walls with windows in them, and yellow light poured out as people worked late at their arcane tasks. "Everything for the war machine," Tedda said from some rote memory that bubbled up.

Faint banging motions signaled a battle in progress. Lindy sniffed the air, as if trying to detect drifting gun smoke. "It's over to the east more tonight. Somebody is bombing someone, or maybe it's artillery. Some nights it goes on for hours."

Tedda had a sense that this had always been part of the scheme of things, and didn't answer. She was more fascinated with the lights and buildings growing around them. "This is neat. What is it?"

"The University," Lindy said. "There are a lot of very smart people here, doing front-line war research."

"Is that what you do?"

"Honestly? I'm not sure. I help people think."

"How is that?"

Lindy shrugged. "I dunno. I'm just there. It's a talent I think you have also. I'm just there and they talk to me. Sometimes they talk around me. Then I see something, and I say something, and everyone gets very quiet. They look at me as if they are thinking about what I said. One time, they applauded. They threw a special dinner for me and gave me a medal, saying I had saved many lives."

"Did you?"

"I have no clue. I didn't tell you that Major Grün called me aside yesterday and said we had a bright new quant coming in."

"What's a quant?" She thought of what it might mean, and laughed.

Lindy laughed also. "No, no, they just say that if they want to. Quants are people who can work incredible masses of equations in their heads. Do you know you do that?"

Tedda shook her head. "No. I have trouble figuring out postage and recipes."

"Ah yes. They're like autists, only we have no social difficulties. Well, not much."

"Like with the ladies back at the dorm," Tedda said laughing. They both laughed. Lindy added: "Yeah, the Miss Gotha lineup. What a bunch of grotesques. I lock my room at night."

"Oh yuck. Any of them ever come rattling the door handle at 3 a.m.?"

Lindy looked at her darkly. "They're mostly chained to their beds at night. So unless they carry their bed under their arm, no."

"So what did they do?"

"I've always been afraid to ask." They walked a bit further. The sky was clearing up, becoming luminous. As the roiling clouds blew away, the sky assumed a dark blue tint that was almost black, but with an ink-blue glow on the horizon. A few stars twinkled. There was no moon, but the buildings around them glowed with a new liveliness. They crossed intersections where cars whispered past, and people waited to walk at stoplights. As the sky cleared, a new cannonade opened up somewhere far away. A hundred guns must be blazing away on both sides, but it was too far to hear shells whistling. The exploding rounds kept up a low murmur underneath it all.

"We're on the main campus now," Lindy said.

"This doesn't seem much like prison." Tedda felt amazed. She didn't want to return to their place of confinement.

A patch of vapor drifted with Lindy's breath, and she lifted her scarf so it covered her nose. "There are supposedly electric fences with barbed wire and dogs, and guard posts with machine guns, but they are miles away. We're on a reservation of some kind."

"Then you haven't seen the fences?"

Lindy shook her head. "No. I never had a reason to go that far. As long as I stay one step ahead, and mind what I do, I have the freedom to roam.

That's all I want." She stopped, grabbed Tedda's arm, and spun her gently but firmly around. "Don't you get it?"

Tedda stepped back, startled. "What?"

Her friend's face was cold and intense. Her eyes glittered darkly, and all expression had drained from her face—except perhaps a vulpine craftiness that seemed to elongate her already thin face. "They, the government, the fatherland, they think they are holding us prisoner here. In reality, this is the safest place we could be. Think about it. We are under attack night and day. Here, you can—." Lindy stopped in frustration. "Come over here. I'll show you something." She grabbed Tedda's sleeve and towed her across the street. They approached a yellow stone building with sharp, pleasing lines. "Get close to the window and look inside." Tedda did as she was told, standing on tiptoe amid bushes near the wall, while a broken sprinkler kept clicking near her right foot and made her sock wet. Tedda was too astonished to notice at first. Inside, under fantastic modern chandeliers, sat dozens of elegant and handsome young people in fine clothing. They were eating on linen-decked tables, waited on by men and women in black tailcoats. They ate with what looked like real silverware, off china plates. Tedda caught a whiff of something wonderful coming out of a large, ornate pewter tureen: a soup containing every nutrient available, doctored with rare spices and salted to taste. Special waiters in white jackets walked around carrying white and red wines wrapped in linen towels for anyone who cared to try. "What is this place?"

"It's the Leadership Party dining hall," Lindy said. "These are the scholars of the nation, who keep everyone safe by inventing the next great thing that counteracts the next great thing that East Gotha throws at us."

Tedda winced. "It sounds like a never-ending cycle. Where does all the money come from to keep it going?"

Lindy shook her head. "I wonder sometimes. People work, and pay taxes, and make sacrifices. It's all for the great cause of the fatherland."

Tedda stood on the sidewalk and had to hold her head. Things were spinning.

Lindy paid no attention. "This way. I'll show you to the Bit Cave."

Tedda shook off her ague and hurried after her friend. "Is that where you work also?"

"I drift from place to place, wherever they need me."

"Do you know Nurse Amit?"

"Oh yes, I know her. We get a monthly physical over at the military hospital. Amit is a nurse practitioners. I prefer when she checks me, rather than the male doctors."

Tedda nodded in satisfaction, glad for once one of her dots connected with someone else's. Maybe she could connect more dots. It seemed her universe had been disintegrating, and maybe now she could start reassembling it; if only she knew where to start. Maybe then those urgent feelings would stop tormenting her.

They came to a round, two-story building that resembled a lantern, of sorts, in that it had continuous bands of glass from the grassy lawn to the flat roof. Soft light glowed from the glass. The other surfaces were a kind of pinkish, rough-finished concrete. From the manicured lawn all around, small spotlights pointed up at the walls. Maybe the lights gave it that calming Depression glass sheen.

"We go in here," Lindy said, pushing carelessly through the main door, a double glass door framed in soft green aluminum. "This is the Lobby."

"Wow," Tedda said as they came into a kidney-shaped reception hall with a round counter of speckled maroon marble in the center, and a pair of elevator doors opposite that. The air smelled of magazines in racks, and floor polish, and a lingering gardenia scent—the daytime receptionist's perfume? The elevators were in a recessed niche amid ribbed mahogany paneling and brushed steel door frames. Everything in the hall was hushed, sepulchral, lit indirectly by soft wall sconces in lemon-yellow and frosted glass. The walls all around were richly paneled in fine dark wood. Lindy brushed past the modern elegance and pressed the single elevator button. It was a see-through plastic square backlit with a faint baby-blue glow. Tedda took a last look around as the elevator rumbled in its shaft. The central apse of the cylindrical building, above the reception counter, was open all the way to the glass ceiling one story higher. Through the glass, Tedda could see stars twinkling and a lone, high jet flying overhead with its sub-fuselage lights winking.

"Here we are," Lindy said as the door slid open. They stepped into a ten-by-ten elevator that showed a lot of wear inside. Tedda was surprised at the difference. Its plain steel walls were dented and scratched, with faint graffiti showing—initials, curses, threats, swastikas, obscene words and images, invitations to fight or have sex. The emergency phone had been torn out, so that an armored cord hung out of the wall and ended in two burned, twisted wire-ends. The car smelled odd, like pheromones, like the hair of violent people, like the smell given off by the skin of those consumed with anger and adrenaline.

Lindy pushed the one button—a battered little black hockey puck on a steel plate. The elevator door closed, and the elevator trembled for a minute. Then it stopped trembling and a door in the opposite wall opened. "Here we are," Lindy said. They stepped outside into a maze of dark corridors lit only by small amber lights high up on corners, and red warning lights atop metal batteries for emergency lights. "You'll like them," Lindy said.

Tedda followed Lindy among hallways done in yellow tiles, like subway corridors, but very narrow. The raw concrete ceiling beams visible looked like those in a bomb shelter. The floors too were plain concrete, and smelled faintly of dampness and cement. Tedda felt claustrophobic, until, five minutes later, they entered into a large auditorium-like room whose extent in all directions was masked in darkness. In the center of the room was a work-area of cubicles. Beyond that lay an undefined blackness striated with mysterious vertical gray lines. Occasionally one saw a flickering vertical red or blue line, or maybe a dancing stripe of yellow or green, very brief, faint, and never standing still. "That's the File," Lindy explained. "You'll learn all about it." She called out: "Visitors on board."

Out from their cubicles came a grinning, congenial half dozen or more young men and women, waving and greeting. A few wore blue prison garb. A few wore uniforms of the various services, Air, Land, and Sea. The remainder wore dark suits and looked very much like intel ops. *Now why do I think that?* Tedda asked herself. *How do I know such a thing?*

Chapter 17

The senior lead in the Bit Cave was Wally, a jovial software engineer whose easy-going smile softened his hard, probing eyes.

Lindy confided to Tedda: "He and I were an item on and off. It's been off for some time now, but we're still friends."

"Has there been anyone else?" Tedda asked casually.

Lindy gave her a strange glance that told her there wouldn't be anyone other than Wally.

In the subsequent days, as Tedda and Lindy walked back and forth from the Bit Cave to the Fortress where they lived, Wally and his staff made them feel at home.

"I see why you like to get away from the Fortress and come here," Tedda said on one of the first nights as they walked back. It was a damp, windy night with twigs and leaves blowing about. The air smelled of wet rubber and stale coal smoke.

"It keeps me from going insane," Lindy admitted. "Locked up forever, with no end in sight, they really keep your mind engaged."

Tedda asked cautiously: "Lindy, do you ever, you know, get to see a man now and then?"

"Oh sure," Lindy said guardedly. "You learn to get yours when you can, when you feel like it, when it's safe."

"How do you know it's safe?"

"Experience," Lindy said with a sidelong glance. "Until you have it, avoid it, for your own good."

Tedda welcomed the pattern that ensued, in which she felt safe, and there was almost a normalcy in the regularity of it. By day, she would sleep into the late morning hours. Lindy was usually up a little earlier, and would come in with two metal cups of coffee to wake her. The cups were plain soldier's tins, brought from a field kitchen run by two huge NCOs with walrus mustaches, knee boots, dirty green trousers, and stained long-john tops. As grungy as the two men looked, their food was always superb. Lindy, who had always already eaten, would bring for Tedda a plain, heavy ceramic plate the color of egg shells, on which sat a nice warm hunk of brownish farm bread. On the bread, a melted pat of sweet butter, and on that one fried egg with the yolk still partially runny and the white edges browned and folded over to fit on the bread. With that came two or three thick slices of crisp bacon, and a few slices of juicy tomato. As Lindy explained, the farm on the northern end of the fortress was self-sufficient and worked by veterans forced from the conflict by wounds. Tedda would eat this wonderful breakfast sitting by a small table in their bedroom, overlooking green trees and the grassy field below. Sometimes, men in long overcoats rode by on horses, with sabers and lances, but slung over their backs also automatic assault rifles. Sometimes the officer on the huge white horse rode with them. The rain would sleet down and the men looked as tolerant and enduring as the horses who trudged in powerful lunges. It was the way the whole fatherland trudged in endless war, like the endless sleet, like the endless bacon that appeared no matter how hard the enemy attacked the city's shields during the night.

During the afternoons, Tedda and Lindy would walk in the fresh air and explore the upper fortress. Tedda gradually learned the lay of it, though it was as complex as the snowflake designs of Vauban. There weren't massed assaults anymore these days, as far as Watka knew when she asked him about it and he spat to his side while pondering an answer. The walls, when she looked down 30 meters to the green forest and swamps below, had lost their naked threat. The even gray stones were now etched with the round sores of lichens, and their crevices thickly padded with moss. Insects luxuriated over the yellows and whites of the lichens. Swarms of insects could be heard droning over the foamy and sewage-tainted moat water amid grotesque water lilies. At one place, a broken cast-iron pipe protruded a forearm's length beyond mid-wall, and a steady gray waterfall splattered down on a mossy parabola further down the wall's slope.

Beyond the swamps and parks lay a distant city skyline. Most of it was successfully shielded by the modern devices invented by those who ate on linen and silver in the university dining halls. A few of the buildings had taken hits. Amid the hundred or more skyscrapers looming amid a humid marine layer of mist and fog, a few looked ragged and blasted along the top, with girders sticking out this way and that way like toothpicks rusting in raw air flow and whitened with bird dung.

On the other side of the fortress, the jewel of the university lay, with its mishmash of neo-Gothic bulwarks and towers amid primly puritanical modern cubes and other sections with splashy, colorful Mediterranean fantasies tending to curves rather than straight lines. Far beyond that, more skyscrapers, more city, more occasional blasted high-rises.

Sometimes the shields guarding the city shimmered in rainbow colors in the distant sky. Eventually, Amy realized that never once had she seen the naked sun itself. Why would that be? Watka explained, spitting to one side, that an ocean lay nearby, and the city was usually engulfed in its marine layer, which formed as moist, warmer sea air blended with the cooler night air from the desert inland, causing condensation. Lindy explained further that as air cools, it can hold less moisture, and so sheds it in the form of precipitation. The city air was almost constantly in the throes of condensation. Like the endless interplay between West Gotha and East Gotha, the air in the city knew neither peace nor rest.

Atop the northern fortress, some eight acres contained not only the military hospital and a huge administrative and digital facility, but sizeable farms, stables, and even an artillery range that blazed away on Saturday mornings.

In the evening, Tedda and Lindy would avoid the beauty queens of the dormitory, and take their meal in an inoffensive little coffee shop slash grocery market in a section of the campus with narrow cobblestone streets and many little shops. This was the Old Town, with its tiny leaded windows and stone buildings. Some of the windows were improbably narrow, others decorative with ogive points at the top. Gargoyles spouted rainwater on street corners, and toward evening, iron-banded lanterns cast their orange light beside major doorways.

In the Bit Cave, Wally walked Tedda through their project. Lindy worked primarily on chemistry-related services in the Compounds section in a nearby room. Wally placed Tedda in an empty cubicle whose previous occupant, he told her, had died from complications of a battle wound. Tedda didn't ask further; it was considered impolite.

Wally was a large, overweight man who often strode about holding a bottle of soda in one hand and a candy bar in the other. The inactivity of his job, and its stresses, would probably kill him at an early age. At the moment, he was a vigorous, funny fellow of 30 with a wife and two children in an apartment down in the southern city. He seemed successful, happy, and well-adjusted. He did, also, have that hard look in his gray eyes.

The Bit Cave people worked in their island of cubicles all packed together, oddly, for the huge open expanse of the former hangar. Tedda asked Wally about that during her introductory tour.

He laughed. "Yeah, the answer is simple. See that pillar there, and there, and there? Those are heat radiators. It gets cold in here. The hangar is almost large enough to have its own weather. At one time, part of the roof on that end"(he pointed southward)"collapsed during an aerial attack on the city below, and we had clouds drifting through here. Sometimes it even drizzled on us, making the papers on our desks curl. We all had colds, and mold started growing on the cubicle walls. The fatherland patched the roof and fixed that, but it's still damn drafty at times. The best they could do, under wartime conditions, was scare up these four heat pillars and keep our cubicles tightly bunched."

He led her to a roped off area, beyond which the darkness shimmered with stray lights, and crackled with excess energy discharging into the air. "Did they explain what we are working on?"

"Nobody has explained anything to me at all," Tedda told him.

"Figures. Okay, this is a top secret data warehousing project that has run into some unforeseen problems of the highest order. We'll get to that in time. For now, though, I want you to know that once you step beyond these ropes"(he loosened them, thick red ropes on stainless steel poles, like at the movies)"you are entering a high-energy zone with special hazards." He picked up a half-eaten banana lying on a table, and tossed it through the air. It exploded in smoke and dripping rainbow-light before vanishing an instant later. "It's very important, therefore, to enter the warehousing zone through the portal, which is here. It's also known as a step-down collar."

He led her down the middle of a long pathway about ten feet across, delineated only by long strips of baby-blue masking tape, four inches wide. The masking tape path led from the carpeted area of the cubicles toward where, in a normal high school auditorium, the stage would be—and perhaps was, until this place was preempted for government research. Now there was no stage visible. Nothing was visible at all, just that opaque smoky fog that masked the far wall.

"Before we go in there," Wally said, "just be aware you'll feel a little queasy passing through. That's your molecules compressing as the energy levels at the subatomic level are stepped downward several quanta."

The question she asked rose up like a bubble from some deep murky place in her memory: "So this takes us through a barrier?"

"If you will," Wally said kneading fat brownish fingers together while he gazed thoughtfully at some blackboard in his mind. "On the other hand, it's also a threshold. Okay, let me try and explain from the start before we go any further. This entire project grew out of an academic paper at the university, regarding information storage, and then object storage. That, in turn, grew out of a project looking for ways to compress data, which originally grew out of a very abstract mathematical paper on number theory. I'm skipping a lot of steps here, so I can get to the gist of it. The author of the paper was researching, for the War Department, laboratory experiments that lie between the realms of physics, chemistry, computer science, and so forth. At the end of this trail lay some very esoteric and fundamental studies on moving energy around, so that the natural quantum shells of atoms moved more closely together. This in turn affected the space around the objects, drastically shrinking the distances among molecules. Let me offer a terribly bad analogy. Suppose you could wave a magic wand and decrease the gravitational energies between our sun and the stars by some integer amount. Suppose, for example, the distance between the sun and the Earth shrank from 93 million miles to 9.3 million miles, a tenfold factor. Ignore where the excess centrifugal and centripetal energies go—let's assume they migrate elsewhere in the overall universe this posits. The net result is that everything gets smaller. The elements don't necessarily change. Understand what this means. The 'normal world,' as we tend to call it, is mostly empty space. This empty space is occupied or defined by extremely tiny particles, from protons and electrons and neutrons down to the quark level. More importantly, it is defined by the relatively vast distances among these objects. By analogy to the universe, the distances between the nucleus and the electrons might be light years. The key factor here, the critical element, is what determines the energies that keep these particles in check from slamming into each other and causing annihilation. What we have managed to do is leach energy from the overall system or universe—it's that simple. By taking energy out of the system, we collapse all the quantum levels into smaller values." He added: "If energy spills into this construct, it doesn't necessarily mean the whole thing blows up again—instead, we think it makes more of the smaller stuff, so the world expands. As you pointed out someplace, this could be very dangerous."

"I did?" Tedda could see the picture he painted, though she had no idea why. Forget the sun and planets analogy about the atom. Picture the nucleus as a fruit basket, and the apples inside being the protons, and the oranges in the basket as the neutrons. Orbiting the basket at vast distances are tiny bananas, or electrons. There are as many apples as electrons. There may be one or more oranges in the basket, which determines the isotope value. The whole thing is an atom, and zillions of atoms form a substance. Maybe the substance is a bar of gold, chemical symbol Au. So Wally was saying that they'd found a way to decrease the energy levels that kept the bananas so far apart from the fruit basket, meaning that the bananas became much closer to the fruit basket, which meant that if this happened in all of the atoms, then the gold bar would shrink to a tiny fraction of its size. If you knew how to control this process, you could determine the size of the final gold bar. It might start out as a foot long bar of gold, and wind up as something so small you couldn't see it anymore, but still contain the same number of atoms. Maybe you could store a thousand gold bars in a volume equivalent to that of a candy bar.

"How do you deal with issues like mass?" Tedda asked.

Wally's face changed as he engaged his mental gears with hers. "That's the next thing. You know about dark matter? Visible matter constitutes less than half of the universe. The ocean bottom of the universe, so to speak, is dark matter." He took a small pointer the size of a pen from his shirt pocket, and aimed a fine red laser beam at an area on the outer transition shield. Immediately, a holographic mesh of virtual controls became visible—a huge and complex interface delineated in fine, glowing amber lines, black work surfaces, and glowing icons: white text, blue notes and underlines, green geometric shapes, red warnings. "Watch this," Wally said. Moving the pointer about, he caused a display to open.

Tedda watched large black dots the size of dinner plates bouncing around against a grayish-white background. "What are they?"

"They are monopole sub quarks, discovered recently."

"Those look like hockey pucks."

"We call them monopole Go-dots, like the black stones in the Japanese game of Go. They do sort of look like black felt dots, don't they? Those are actual images taken through a piggybacked stepdown particle maser looking through a graviton haze in a laboratory near here."

"And what do these monopoles do?"

"Well, we don't know much about them yet, but they exist and they form another layer of reality in the sub-lepton range, which we call Bottom, but that's just a misnomer in itself. There appears to be no smallest particle. There are just layers below layers, each with their own self-contained sets of rules. At one time, people thought atoms were the indivisible. Then a layer of subatomic chemistry opened up, and people thought the lowest you could go were protons, electrons, and neutrons. Soon after that, a whole zoo of particles was discovered by smashing larger particles. Muons, leptons, pions, even tachyons—still part of the so-called material world. Then a new bounding box of self-contained relationships opened up, the six flavors of quarks, and people thought they were done. Well, just as there is no end of the universe where you fall off, anymore than there is no end of the world where ships fall into the sky, so there is no smallest and no largest. We think that the infinite universe is a limitless foam with embedded events that typically spread energy in all directions, pushing particles, whose unity constitutes what our five senses perceive as matter. Not long ago, someone"(he paused, eyeing her with a barely perceivable tightening of the irises)"discovered a way to represent yet another layer. We haven't gotten far enough to give it a name, so we call it Bottom, as in ocean bottom—down in the infinite cold and darkness of a deep sea. That's the metaphor. At this point, all we know is that it is composed of at least two things that we won't even call particles. They seem to have their own sorts of interactions, so effectively it's a two-dimensional plane that seems to be scalable according to the amount of energy—that's the dynamic down there, as we refer to 'energy' in the visible range. In other words, it's so weird that it makes quarks look as normal as the common gumdrop. The two monopoles we know are Black and Gray, and we think there might be a White and a Yellow (actually just shades of gray), and mind you those are metaphors from our own visible energy spectrum." Wally paused and wiped his sweaty brow with a heavy wrist. "I don't know much more about the theory—the fatherland has top people working night and day at this university on the problem, because we know East Gotha has the same information and is exploiting it to destroy us."

"We just need to get there first," Tedda echoed some faintly remembered campaign slogan from her childhood, when schools were let out, and kids marched in uniform down long gray streets. She blinked, shook her head, wiped her eyes, at a vague but persistent memory of stirring martial snare drums rattling so that her heart felt inspired, and rows of children marching under falling confetti while holding long banners over their knees praising the Billo Maximus and denouncing the running dogs and stinking Limburgers of East Gotha. She could hear a man making speeches, and his voice powerfully echoing amid the stone canyons of some city, and confetti falling in chill wind amid the smells of sausage cooking and beer foaming from kegs.

"You okay?" Wally asked worriedly.

"Yes," she said. "Every once in a while an undergone zips through my brain, causing this blippitousness."

He grinned. "Nice sense of humor. We'll be happy to have you working with us."

"Doing what?"

"Thinking," he said; "emanating. Whatever it is that you do best, the fatherland has decided you will be of great help here."

Chapter 18

Tedda and Wally walked along the pathway defined by the blue tape. The tape ended as they entered a tunnel that looked like the hole in a huge donut. The tunnel was circular, and its opening about 20 feet in diameter. The tunnel walls were composed of swarms of tiny particles, like millions of fireflies whizzing about inside dark water. Tedda became dizzy and reached up with a shaky hand to touch Wally's large, sweaty shoulder.

"Technically, this tunnel is called a step-down collar. You'll be okay," he said, putting a beefy hand around her waist and taking her hand in his other, free hand. "I'll hold you steady. It's common the first couple of times," he said. He guided her carefully as the tunnel turned, twisted, even twirled. The tunnel also grew dark as night, appearing almost starlit.

"Is that a light up ahead?" Tedda said with a quaver. She felt not so much terrified—it was wonderful to be in here—but disoriented as if she were on a carnival ride.

"Yes, good old fluorescent light," Wally assured her. He took her hand from her waist, and then let go of her hand.

She walked ahead of him in slow, wondering steps, down a sort of ramp made of this same tunnel dust, and onto a firm concrete floor. "Wow," she said. With Wally standing patiently beside her, she started to get her bearings. It was almost disappointing, so ordinary: a complex of tunnels carved out of stone; fluorescent lights overhead, strung on thick black or orange cable running to some power source that hummed annoyingly and loudly in accompaniment to the lamps' buzzing. One or two fluoros flickered nauseatingly, apparently near the end of their charge life. It made Wally's face alternate in sickening shades of light blue and faded green, and she imagined she presented a similar coloration to him. It was neither hot nor cold in here (up here, down here, she wasn't sure) but a slight breeze stirred lukewarm air that smelled faintly of machine oil and chalk. An orange golf cart sat to one side by a small loading ramp whose edges were marked in alternating yellow and black warning stripes. Tools sat around; gray metal boxes smelling of enamel and turpentine hung bolted to the chiseled rock face. "So where are we?" she asked.

"We are in the auditorium," he said stepping down past her with his hands in his pockets. He shrugged lightly, apparently not feeling intimidated by their surroundings. "I'm told the space we occupy at the moment would fit into the distance between a hydrogen nucleus and its electron jacket."

She gasped, trying to imagine such a thing. She couldn't. Even the distance he mentioned—for example, almost the entire mass of an atom exists in the nucleus, which is less than 100,000 as large as the atom, and the atom itself is infinitesimally small. "I am having a hard time getting my mind wrapped around it."

"I understand," he said. "Maybe this will help. Imagine blob of mass and energy, which will be the nucleus of a hydrogen atom. The electron of this atom will be a basketball over 100,000 kilometers away—two fifths or nearly halfway to the moon. On that scale, a bucket of hydrogen would occupy a volume the size of the solar system."

"Ah yes," she said, suddenly remembering she'd heard things like this before—but where? And why? And it seemed urgently important. "What is the problem with it all?" She held her fists to her temples and squeezed her eyes shut, concentrating, but her memory wouldn't tease out any more information.

He regarded her curiously, with a kind of veiled respect. "The problem is that the other side, East Gotha, is doing the same stuff we're doing. It started out innocuously enough. Someone invented a way to make space compact by quantitatively reducing, in a limited space, the so-called strong force, which holds subatomic particles together. They did this by developing a kind of monopol graviton magnet that pulls black monopoles in one direction, leaving their opposite the white monopoles, which causes an imbalance that collapses the local universal scale by one or more quantum levels. Spies from the other side stole the information, and now they are building a similar storage facility, and it's become an international or global defense issue. Let me show you." He led her to the golf cart. They climbed in, and he whirled the machine around in a sharp turn so that they headed out into the corridors.

Wally explained more as they drove, with engine whining and batteries cooking off an alkaline smell. "A very strange thing that seems to happen is the process of Rules gets out of control, and features we want may multiply many times over. We don't know how to stop it, and there doesn't seem to be a rhyme or reason for it. We might want one little corridor in a specific place, and maybe 100 iterations of it turn up. That's why there is so much here. We originally planned on a set of ten galleries bounded by one main street running all the way around. We have no idea how many miles of corridors there are, and we haven't been able to explore even a tenth of it all." They turned this way and that among corridors that always seemed to look the same: straight tunnels with chiseled, irregular wall surfaces, and ghostly interactions of shadow and light under cold fluorescent tubes. "As I said," he explained, "it started out as a storage experiment, possibly for acres of archives that could thus be kept in a space that would fit under your bed. So now, the next thing to explain is that, in creating this artificial volume of space, it's necessary to generate high amounts of energy to pull away the black monopoles. So far, it's not an efficient or cost-effective system, but as with all things, there is hope the scientists can improve it."

"Are you working on that, Wally?"

He shook his head. "No—I'm a high level systems programmer with a background in three-dimensional modeling. This project goes far beyond the skills I learned in college, but it's a fascinating field and I'm learning huge amounts of stuff day by day. Hey, so as I was saying, once they figured out how to create an artificial mini-world space, they figured out how to populate it with objects. It turned out to be a relatively simple process, based on the real world. It's called modeling, and they use Rules to create sets and subsets of objects. Rules are complex sets of instructions that mirror how the world behaves. Take a simple example. If I stress a banana, it breaks in half. I then have two halves of a banana. The trick is not to write a rule for breaking bananas, but to write a general rule for how solids of various types behave under various stresses, so there are many possible outcomes for the banana; maybe it gets smaller rather than breaking; or it becomes a handful of nuts. Not literally; those are metaphors, but then much of it is metaphor. There are a whole bunch of high-end mathematicians working on this, and they've given us programs, algorithms, for all this. That's our job here in the auditorium, besides maintaining the micro-space. We apply the rules in a kind of real-world programming that's similar to those energy transfer games. Think of the several steel balls suspended from an A-frame that one sees on people's desks. You lift one ball and drop it. It stops dead when it hits the next, stationary ball, and all the balls in turn transmit the potential energy through the row, until it turns into kinetic energy at the other end, and the last ball on that end leaps away. Think of Jules Verne's novel Journey to a Comet, in which someone throws an object into a body of water chilled to right around freezing—a reaction sets in as the near-ice crystallization of the water is nudged one smidge further, and an entire lake surface instantly crackles as it turns to ice. That's how the rules work in our femtoworld. More specifically, we can create a tunnel like this by just applying a Rule, and the tunnel crackles into existence. Energy with just the right instruction set ripples through, shaping things as we wish. It's not an exact science yet, but we've done wonders."

As they drove, Tedda noticed walls resembling shelves in the distance. People seemed to be busy stacking objects there. Several tow motors raced about in clouds of bluish exhaust.

Wally explained: "That was the original idea. The fatherland has invested large sums of money and resources in this project, and they are storing copies of our entire culture's documents, arts, records, you name it, on shelf systems down here. Originally, the idea was just to create a virtual world and store virtual objects—copies made from solid, hadron objects— but the project quickly found that something more than virtual reality was able to be built down here. Without the Rules, this would have all become a meaningless mish-mash of random space, like ice floating on top of a river in winter. Instead, we forced intelligent construction into this temporary micro-universe."

Wally drove in silence a while, and then stopped as they came to a dead end. "Listen," he said, sipping quietly at a bottle of water.

She listened, and heard what sounded like echoes of distant hammering. It sounded like hammers in a distant cavern full of water, where the sound reverberated many times on the cave walls.

"That's East Gotha," Wally said. "They are trying to tunnel into our space and deliver a bomb that will blow us to hell. Now you begin to understand the urgency of our mission. We've stopped expanding our own side in these micro-worlds. We are waiting for them to try and puncture into ours from theirs, and we hope to blow them out before they do us in."

They sat for a few more minutes in helpless silence, listening to the persistent hammering. Sometimes the hollow, metallic blows seemed frighteningly close, other times vague and far away like distantly echoing thunder. It was the sound of East Gotha applying its own rules, popping out new corridors, new halls, new underground caverns, in the hope of getting close to the West Gotha side and finding a soft spot that could be exploited to insert deadly mines.

Chapter 19

Are you starting to feel comfortable with your new life?" Lindy asked early one morning as they headed back to the fortress after a long night in the Bit Cave. They walked uphill along the dark street that had high stone walls on either side, and no street lighting. The brightness of the university campus was falling behind them.

"I think yes." Tedda took a deep breath and exhaled, watching her breath come out as vapor. It was still dark out, and lights gleamed in many university windows. The wet walls gleamed with reflected ice on the sidewalks. "I'm beginning to feel more focused. That make any sense?"

Lindy shrugged, walking along her scarf over her lower face and her hands jammed deep in the pockets of an old army coat that swung as low as her ankles. She had her dark hair pinioned inside a faded wool beret.

Tedda felt livelier than she had in a long time. "I have this feeling that something is wrong down there, and that I can help them somehow."

"Isn't that why the fatherland supposedly plugged you in?"

Tedda laughed. "I imagine they know what they are doing. Don't you?"

Lindy seconded with a less animated laugh. "Glad to see you're on a roll. So what do you think you can do for them?" Her face looked shadowed under the walls.

"They have a proliferation problem with their algorithms. I'm going to think about whether that is related to the energy input when the Rules shape things. In other words, they pull out the black flavor monopoles, and then tell the gray flavor monopoles to act in certain ways under the sea floor or Bottom so that the quarks will swarm this way or that, and in turn the subatomic particles line up and form a stone wall or an iron bar or a pond full of water. They can even replicate finer and more complex artificial structs like a golf cart or a fluorescent light." She trailed off, lost in a flood of equations—balances, relationships, imbalances, potentials, transformations, a wealth of such underlying music that defined the scaffolding of reality. "They just can't seem to tell the process how hard or easy to go at it, when to stop, or how many scooters or caverns to make."

Lindy added: "They also hear the East Gothans doing the same thing on the other side."

Tedda had a growing surge of insight. "Not sure. If it's a mirror image, that would be curious. But it seems we are on the defensive, while they are the aggressor in this business. You know...what you said...and I heard that banging, ringing, as if they were having an anvil concerto...I wonder if rhythm, wavelengths, timing, focus, concentration have something to do with it." She answered her own question: "Of course they do. Everything hangs together, Lindy. Sometimes the hard part is getting one's arms around the whole thing. Until that works, nothing falls into place. Once you go around it a couple of times, the larger parts start falling into place, and then the smaller ones, until the whole picture makes sense."

"So what's you guess?"

"West Gotha invented a peaceful technology, for data storage and tunneling, which was stolen from us and now seems to be being developed into a weapon to invade and attack us. So we must react by developing the same thing, only a little bit more powerful, to stop them. Maybe we can deter them."

Lindy said: "Maybe the whole thing was a bad idea, and we should let the particle sea fill in the tunnels, let the connections close up forever, and we forget it like it never happened."

Tedda shook her head. "You can never turn back progress. If you lose your nerve and back away, you enemy will double his efforts and clobber you."

"You sound like a Cheddar Billo propaganda soundtrack," Lindy said, grinning. Cheddar Billo was a quaint myth from the pre-Moss days. Then, realizing the treason she'd spoken, her smile faded and she looked straight ahead. She walked a bit faster, avoiding Tedda's curious gaze.

Chapter 20

If they (whoever that was) were still feeding her drugs, then some of what happened made sense. So Tedda thought. Like, she'd wake in the middle of the day and find herself in a weird dream state, on her knees before Confessor Grün in that strange, narrow room or house without the front wall. The floor was concrete, but damp and mossy, and crawling with worms. She could smell the slime on the worms' bellies, and moisture trapped in the fur of a racing spider's tail half, or grass bending under the weight of water droplets nearby. She could smell the loam, a comforting smell, except for the moldy smell of mushroom breath coming from gopher holes in the ground. The reason she saw those was that her head was resting on Confessor Grün's hard, broad knees and his heavy, steely hand rested on her head. Her face lay sidewise, paralyzed, her senses stripped and alert, and that was how she came to observe the dance of insects in the wet lawn across the gravel path while Confessor Grün spoke with her in that powerful, throbbing, soothing voice. He would ask questions and she would answer, but she wasn't sure what he said or what she answered. He appeared to seek something, and she appeared not to be delivering whatever it was, and he appeared to be damming in a great deal of anxiety and frustration within the walls of his infinite cleverness and patience. This happened several times.

Chapter 21

What happened also was that Major Grün took her for rides on his horse. He appeared to be related to the Confessor by the same name, either a son or nephew. Why was she not tired, having worked all night? Major Grün laughed at her question. "This is a form of sleep. No, you are not in your bed dreaming. We are giving you a little psychotropic help from our highly developed formulary so that your body thinks it is sleeping while in fact I am enjoying these rides in the park with you."

"Why?" she might dreamily ask, holding on to his strong, lean back (in thick wool green winter army uniform, with brown belts and dangling revolver) as they rode on the clatter-hoofed white battle horse through a park. The park was veiled in haze, with the sun trying to poke through like a lemon slice visible in icy water in a glass frosted with condensation. Trees stood about like fog-draped ghosts. Birds chirped hollowly. A woodpecker drilled distantly, in precise, punctuated rattles. Water dripped, spiders wove, birds fussed over nests, worms wriggled, mushrooms gave off their fungal breath, and the horse's nostrils snorted steam while his steel shoes clap-clap-clapped on gravel paths.

"Have you ever made the acquaintance of a Captain Alton Hedrock?" asked Major Grün.

Tedda's eyes were half closed as she bounced almost painfully on the saddle. She felt the hard leather pressing into the softness between her legs. The slamming of her cheek against his hard spine was cushioned only by the thick olive-drab wool tunic he wore.

"If he contacts you, it is imperative that you let me know. Do you understand?"

"I don't know who you mean, but if anyone contacts me I will pass it along to you," she said in a slurry dreamy sleepy voice that seemed to be coming from someone detached from her. The horse cantered at a majestic pace of spaces and silences, slamming steel, clip-clop and clip-clip, echoing among the hills in the park, where foresters with their huge saws cut up fallen trees, sipped warm beer, and stopped to wave as the Major rode past. The Major waved to them, saluted them, called them by name, as if he were some feudal lord parading on his manor grounds.

This happened more than once.

One time, they dismounted and sat in the shadows of a huge tree. Its roots were very hard and gnarled and uncomfortable, but the moss between the roots was tender and thick. There they sat, and Major Grün ran his hands along the planes and curves of her body while she tried weakly to push his hands away. "It's important for the fatherland to have your help," he said, "and just as important for you to understand how much I desire you." Grün took her chin roughly in his fingers and forced her to look him in the eye. She did, with lolling eye and gag reflex making her choke. He said: "I wish you could understand that there is a fine line between treason and being duped, and you have been walking that line ever since Captain Hedrock of East Gotha walked into your life."

She stared at her tormentor with glossy eyes. "Hedrock, my husband." She remembered the beautiful man with the easy grin and small mustache, whom she loved. She did not know where that bit of nonsense came from but she felt the pain of Grün's fingers tightening like a vise on her chin, and she saw the pain and rage in his eyes. His mouth opened and he gritted his teeth as if he wanted to maul her face with his mouth. From the crazy scintillation of his eyes, she believed Major Grün to be capable of something like that. Luckily she passed out and woke in her bed, and the memory of his mushroom breath faded as she got up to brush her teeth.

Chapter 22

The Bit Cave, for all that it consisted of an island of light and cubicles amid a vast, amorphous darkness, had its own sort of districts and regions. Tedda would approach each day from the rear entrance of what had once been a huge auditorium, whose seats were now all gone.

On her left was the very hushed and conservative realm of the mathematicians or quants, who were very cliquish and had their own social order. Mostly they seemed to be pudgy middle-aged men with fleshy lips and cynical eyes. Their conspiracies seemed Byzantine, their betrayals of each other subtle, their schemes and jockeying endless.

On her right as she approached were the young software engineers, with hardware, systems, and com handshakes mixed in. This seemed to be the fun section, where giggling could be heard at sudden moments, or even someone crying and overturning his books and papers in a fit of frustration. At times like that, the mathematicians across the aisle would prairie-dog, raising their heads to eye-level in order not to miss a good row.

On the far left, beyond the mathematicians, and divided from them by a main cross-aisle, were the project leaders and administrators, like Wally.

On the far right, beyond the engineers, was everyone else, including accountants, Tedda, clerks, lab assistants, technicians of varying specialties, and even the customary fatherland detective spy, one Werner von Werner, who hardly ever spoke with anyone, but seemed aware of every conversation, every wink of the eye, every subversive gesture. Lindy whispered to Tedda: "They have microphones and sound pickups and minicams all over the place. An ordinary screw in the edge of your cubby divider might be an electronic spying device."

In the middle of these four tribes was a neutral area with tables and chairs, where people went to relax or have lunch. Lamps hung down low over the tables, and several people plaid cards at every opportunity, it seemed. There was another island outside the four tribes, just off to the right equidistant from the programmers and the clerks. There were two tables there—a long one, and perpendicular to it, like the middle bar in a letter 'E,' was a shorter table. Several lamps hung over these tables also, and here people had set up board games that they could play for days on end. They could leave their chips and paper money and dice and markers in place, and return in between shifts to play another half hour at a time. There were stacks of old-fashioned cardboard boxes under the table, with various such games.

Tedda found herself getting hooked sipping hot tea and watching anywhere from four to six people play a board game called Monorail. "Aren't you ashamed of yourselves for sitting here with this old thing?" she teased them. A chorus of laughs and snickers and disavowals came back at her. "We get tired of the virtual stuff," someone said. "Once in a while you have to go back to basics. It doesn't get any more basic than this."

It seemed at the moment an exciting play was in progress. The board itself was simple. Resembling a certain famous real estate deal board game, this one involved traveling through an exotic, faraway city on an advanced rail system. The object of the game, from what Tedda could see, was to own as much of the capital assets as possible. You started from a rail yard with a stack of paper money and a game token. The game tokens were all the same—a really cool electric locomotive about the size of a noodle. Each player had a different color locomotive, and each player owned a trolley line named after the color of his token. Thus, one player owned the Green Line, another the Red Line, another the Yellow Line, and so forth. Say you owned the Green Line—the object was to add to the Green Line's properties. Once you owned at least one property on each of the four sides of the board, you could charge Monorail Fare if anyone landed on any square you owned. As you accumulated cash, you could add frills for which people had to pay. Everyone started with Third Class service. You could build your way up to First Class service (very expensive!). Also, travelers had to rest in hotels, and that got expensive. So it went, and Tedda found herself getting sucked into the game during her spare time. She enjoyed the young programmers and engineers, male and female, bantering, flirting, dissing each other, having popcorn fights. Even the detective came snooping around now and then. Often the area smelled of fresh popcorn, a little burned around the edges, or coffee, also burned.

Tedda had her own little cubicle off to one side in the cats and dogs department, as it was known. She met angry stenographers with advanced degrees, who were bitter at not having done better. She was surrounded by crippled army veterans, a man horribly disfigured in a fighter plane fire, a track star doing religious studies because he believed in prophecies, a pair of women raising children together as single mothers while constantly complaining of a dearth of good men, and so forth. Wally stopped by from time to time to see how she was doing, and she was doing just fine.

In fact, she almost couldn't keep up with herself. She had to be teased from her cubicle for tea and popcorn, and a game of chess or checkers, or Monorail. She'd sit in her cubicle with pencils and paper, with her computer and printer, and write programs that calculated the dimensions of tiny spaces, the thresholds of energy levels at which changes of state took place, the quantum strata, and more. She thought she was beginning to come to a more or less intuitive sense of how the black monopoles worked. Actually, she began to be driven by worry. She told Wally about this one day as they sat having hot tea alone together out of earshot.

"What's troubling you that you called me out here?" he asked.

She pushed a stray wisp of hair from her eyes as she showed him a tattered printout spread all over her lap. She indicated features with a mechanical pencil amid the tight jumble of tiny black ink speckles. "Wally, the problem I see is that there may be a critical energy shed coming as we continue to grow this maze."

He blurted absently: "What, you think it might blow?"

She rested her hands on the paper on her knees so the pencil hung loosely. "I don't know if I'd put it quite that way, but yes, at this point anything is a possibility."

"And why do you figure this?"

The pencil started moving again as she pointed to patterns and tendencies. "Wally, if you track the growth of this maze, it's out of control. It's governed only by the fact that there are brown-downs almost every day, especially around air attacks, when the city reduces the energy grid to minimal output. Nevertheless, there is still volume growth in progress."

"So our maze is getting bigger?"

"Yes, and therefore the overall energy demand is increasing."

"What if we slowly lower it?"

"You can't shrink this thing. You can't lop off sections. There's nowhere to go. Once we've created this thing, which we have, the only way to kill the natural growth momentum is to totally shut the power down."

"And then?"

"The entire universe of that maze would vanish as if it never existed."

"And the other side?"

She hesitated. "Wally, there's more."

He stared at her intently.

"I'm afraid their activity is feeding it too. Without meaning to, both sides have been contributing to the steady proliferation of physical features by means of these Rules and the subatomic energies that drive them."

He looked sick. "People's jobs and careers are on the line here. You don't have a family, do you? Well, I do. They won't want me reassigned to a field battery if this project gets shut down." He rose. "Don't tell anyone about this, okay? Let me know what you figure, and we'll take it from there." He added weakly and insincerely: "Let's not start a panic." He added: "Watch your back. You have more riding on this than you know."

Chapter 23

Tedda's partners in the Monorail board game included Wally and a strong female player, with a Latina accent, named Dominica. This woman was dark-skinned and dark-haired, with a full body and smooth, youthful cheeks. Dominica was the soul of kindness and competence, and Tedda felt a growing liking for her. Dominica would say "Play your best hand; you're doing fine" and then clean up as she took tokens and money and reduced Tedda to penury. They all laughed at Dominica's uncanny ability to excel at that board game. Tedda found herself drawn not only to Dominica as a friend, but to this strangely appealing, addictive game. Sometimes Lindy came by to watch, but Lindy rarely ever picked up tokens to play.

Tedda found that the game was fun. The board was worn, its edges frayed and showing the brown cardboard inside. Its surfaces were painted in happy pastels—a mild sky blue, a mild bilious green, tomato reds, all edged in quaint black borders. When a good game was in progress, workers young and old would cluster around, and a chorus of groans or cheers accompanied each play. Stacks of wrinkled play money would change hands amid stacks of sandwiches, open soda cans, and discarded cookie wrappers. A cola belch was not unusual among the spirited players as they bantered while throwing dice and moving their pieces.

One day, the fatherland detective, Werner von Werner, approached Tedda. She was finishing a cup of peach yogurt, and sat alone at the Monorail table while the players had just left to respond to some technical crisis (there were at least two or three a day).

The detective introduced himself. He was a middle-aged man with smooth, ruddy skin and a round head of very tightly cropped fine white hairs. The first pink splash of baldness was seeping through the hair on top. He always dressed conservatively, in a white shirt, dark red tie, and charcoal suit trousers. Usually, the matching jacket hung draped over the back of his chair in a special cubicle with a door near Wally's cubicle.

"How are you today?" he asked, sitting down nearby. He had soft pink hands that he folded in his lap while steepling his thumbs. His eyes were blue, Tedda saw, and his soft features seemed to harbor some repressed steel-spring energy—maybe rage, she guessed. Whatever it was, and however mild he looked, he projected an inner tension and severity that made her uneasy.

"I'm fine." She sucked on her spoon and tried to emanate waves of repulsion at him, hoping he would go away.

"I guess you know of me. I'm Werner von Werner, the political officer on this project. I haven't had time to welcome you directly, but I find that it's important to chat a little bit."

"Okay, Werner, chat."

"Thank you. I guess you understand you are here under duress."

"Yes. Supposedly I ate babies or something equally horrible."

"Yes, something equally horrible, but it wasn't cannibalism." His demeanor was mild but firm.

"You know a lot about me." It was a question.

"I know what I need to know."

"More than I know about myself."

"Yes. Try not to be uneasy. I don't mean you any harm."

"For some reason I get nervous just being near you."

"Thanks for your honesty."

"I love the fatherland and only wish to do good." Tears welled up on her lower lids, making her eyes swimmy, and she thought she was about to lose it. She put her yogurt aside and covered her eyes with her hands.

He gently pried one hand loose and looked at her closely with one light-blue eye. "I am certain you are a patriotic woman. I just want to ask you if you have a real sense of what is going on here."

She blurted: "We made a mistake developing this technology."

"You think V.R. is a mistake?"

"This is not V.R., mister. This is something totally unrelated."

"Oh?"

"Not a technical heavy, are you?"

He shrugged lightly. "I know what I need to know. Don't waste time trying to second-guess me. Just answer my questions."

She felt outflanked on posturing, and switched to facts. "This isn't Virtual Reality at all, though I suspect it started as something along those lines." He looked at her intently, without speaking, and she continued: "This is something else."

He volunteered: "Intereality."

"Is that what they call it?"

He shrugged lightly, flicking his eyes upward a second.

"Intereality," she echoed. "An interesting term. What does it mean? A person from inside that cloud of miniature world over there could step out here and pop into a full-blown person in our world. That's intereality, I suppose. Good term then. In V.R., it's all a metaphor and you can't pop back and forth. There is a real world and an imaginary world. Here, it's different. Far more powerful. We can apply physics and Rules and all sorts of esoteric science to create a tiny artificial space, which then gets out of control and starts growing. Even if it's many miles across in all directions, it's still invisible because it fits into the space between a nucleus and its electron swarm."

He looked at her as if he had not heard a thing she'd said. "What were your parents' names?"

She stared at him, rattled. Tedda and von Werner were back in the world of posturing and feeling. She felt him bullying her in some subtle but raw, powerful way. Tears sprang up again. Had he said 'were'? Did that mean her parents were dead? And she couldn't even picture them vaguely, much less know their names. "I have no idea," she blurted, and started bawling with a bottomless sense of loss.

"Thank you," he said and rose, leaving quickly.

Lindy came by a few minutes later to comfort her. Lindy handed her a handkerchief that smelled of Lindy's body heat and cheap but sweet perfume. Tedda sobbed into the handkerchief, welcoming its warmth from where it must have spent hours in Lindy's ratty pockets. Lindy rubbed Tedda's back while Tedda bawled face-down into her hands on the hard table.

Chapter 24

On another of those dream days, when she awoke like someone pickled in amber wine, there was a loud knocking on the door. She sat up in bed, having been sleeping naked, and held the sheet up to her chin. Trembling, she glanced over at Lindy. Her roommate's small shape lay twisted and still amid her gray blankets. Lindy's snoring was light and even, and she apparently did not hear the pounding at the door. Tedda shrank back against the wall in terror, still holding the sheet to her chin. She could see the door visibly moving as feet kicked it and fists pounded it. Still Lindy slept.

Suddenly all became still. A man's sharp voice barked through the wood. It seemed to be Grün the Younger, rider on the huge white horse. He too fell silent. She heard him say "Well?"

Reluctantly, afraid not to obey, she rose from the bed. She quickly slipped on her underpants, slip, skirt, and a turtleneck sweater. Striding to the door, she hesitated a moment, then lifted the crossbar. She stepped back as the door swung open. For a moment, she saw only Major Grün standing there in his jodhpurs, holding a riding crop in one hand and tapping the palm of his other hand with it. His brown boots looked muddy, and his herringbone civilian suit looked rumpled, damp, and smelled faintly of horse sweat and horse manure. His hair was mussy, and his eyes looked foreboding. In that moment, she realized she had made a terrible mistake to open the door, but what choice did she really have? In a few moments, they would have battered the door in to get at her.

She feared rape as she saw the four or five burly infantry rejects fill the air space in the door—men who might have served but had been physically or psychologically wounded and now only ran errands or drank in the stable or hung about looking sullen. She saw their dirty knuckles and twisted fingers on the door jamb, saw their intent faces, their eyes boring into her, their hands grasping toward her. She shrank back, tripped, and they were upon her in a moment. She had time only to glance over once more to see the sleeping figure of Lindy, whose arm rose and fell gently as she lay facing away toward the wall. Then the men pinned her down, one on each limb and the fifth cradling her head between his thighs as he knelt beyond her. He pulled her chin up toward him and stuck something wooden in her mouth. Something to pry her teeth apart and keep them that way. She struggled, tears filling her eyes, and anger making her bite down on the mouth bit. Before she closed her eyes and passed out, she saw another glimpse of Major Grün. Two white-coated medical orderlies entered the room. One carried a metallic case in one hand and a very painful, ugly-looking complicated naked steel clamp in the other. The other man carried a fine, piercing light in one hand and a small forceps in the other—too small for vaginal operations, so it must be the mouth or the other end. She felt her clothing being pulled off her. For a second, while she was suspended in air as her clothes pulled away and she felt a chill breeze on her bare, goose bumpy skin, she struggled. Then they pinned her down again so that her soft flesh was crushed painfully against the hard wooden floor. She saw a very ugly, large syringe rise into the air, with brownish fluid in its cruel glass window. A squirt in the air, and then it plunged into the skin of her neck, right into the big arteries pounding away under the soft skin there. She closed her eyes and began to see lights. She felt sharp pain in two places—her mouth and her anus. Wires of fire seemed to be snaking up into her bowels and down her esophagus. She felt herself gurgling and choking frothy warm fluid that she assumed must be blood. *I don't want to die,* she cried silently, *oh please, I want to live!*

She had that horrifying glimpse again, of herself astride the other woman with a knife, like in a violent and nightmarish painting by Breughel.

With that, she passed out and slept deep and hard. It was a dreamless sleep, except for a monotonous series of brief waking moments in which she seemed to be an underwater thing, an eel, in a sunken building, and she darted snake-like here and there, grabbing bits of stray food floating in the dim sunlight from somewhere far above, before retreating once again into the darkness of her lair, an ancient coal bin.

When she awoke, a rich but melancholic sunlight filled the room. The building smelled of beef gravy and sour bread. She heard the inmates babbling and fighting down in the echo chambers of the first floor. Lindy was somewhere down the hall, singing a cheerful song interlaced with broken whistling. Tedda's mouth felt dry, and she reached for the water glass by her bedside. The water tasted metallic, almost like blood. She made a face and spat it out, back into its glass, and she saw rusty sputum full of old blood roiling like tomato-marble. She cried out in shock and dropped the glass, which shattered on the hard floor. She pushed the blankets away and looked down at herself. She was naked, and her arms and thighs had faint discolorations. She felt stiff and sore. It had not been a dream. Hearing voices in the hall, with the door slightly ajar, she pulled a blanket up.

Lindy breezed into the room, carrying a stack of freshly laundered, dried, and folded clothing. "Oh, hi, you're awake."

Tedda tried to speak but only a croak came out. She sat up and ran her fingers comb-like through her hair.

"I thought you were never going to wake up," Lindy said. "I wonder what was in the stew this morning when we got home. "I slept like someone on drugs."

You probably were, Tedda thought as Lindy merrily put her clothes away in her locker.

Tedda cleared her throat. "I dropped the glass."

"Oh," Lindy said, glancing at the floor, "I'll get a broom and dust pan. You okay?" She stepped from the room, still in earshot.

"I had another of those dreams I've told you about."

Lindy came back with a worn broom and black, dented dust pan. She squatted by the bedside, cleaning up. "I told you, they keep us doped up sometimes."

"Why?" Tedda said, swinging herself into a sitting position to get dressed. Her rear end burned for a moment, and she squirmed until it no longer hurt. She put a finger in her mouth and twisted it around, searching for any kind of foreign object, but felt only soft, wet tissue and teeth with old dental work needing repairs. Her teeth felt sort of numb, but that was the only anomalous thing she could sense. She wasn't even sure about that.

"Who knows?" Lindy said as she rose and took the broken glass outside. Tedda rose and walked to the window, stepping into her clothing as she did so. She lifted the window and leaned on the sill, enjoying the comforting trilling of birds and the last golden blast of sunlight on opposing windows in the quadrangle even as the sadness of evening descended. She leaned out and spat more rusty sputum, watching dizzily as the clotted droplets twirled heavily on their way down into bushes and darkness.

Chapter 25

Wally came and apologized for his outburst. "Sorry about the other day." He awkwardly shook her hand, wrapping both his huge brown paws around her hand.

"It's okay. I went home early and slept a long time after an uncomfortable conversation with Werner von Werner."

"Ah yes, our political officer." Wally sat down and carefully unwrapped a peanut butter brittle candy bar dipped in milk chocolate. He offered a bite, she declined, and he bit in. Chewing a large mouthful, as if it were medicine for some ailment, he said: "I think there is a lot of political undertow here, and someone is afraid that you may upset their apple cart. That's why they're doing to you what they are doing."

Her heart sank, and her stomach lurched. "What—who is doing what to me?"

He stopped chewing, wide-eyed. "They didn't tell you?"

She shook her head slowly.

He put his hand over his mouth, either to try and recapture his words, or to cover the chocolate dribbling down his chin. He pulled a handkerchief from his pocket and mopped his lower face. Recomposed, he leaned forward with his hands folded prayerfully between his knees, and his shoulders slumping regretfully. "I was told they are moving you into the stacks near Bottom."

"What?" Was that life-threatening, she wondered. "That sounds awful."

He shrugged. "Well, it could be worse."

"You mean I'm going to have to live inside that—that model?"

"Not live, for now anyway. Work. When you report for work each day, you won't come through here anymore. There is a special entrance for heavy equipment and cargo."

"Oh, thanks a whole bunch! Who the hell is doing this to me, and why? What does it mean?"

He shrugged again. "I think they are just trying to move you someplace where you can't make trouble."

"Am I making trouble?" she fairly yelled. She sat with her arms akimbo, glaring at him.

"I'm just the messenger," he said with defensively upraised palms. "Don't shoot me."

She glared at him, noting he'd said she would only go into the Intereal during work hours, but he'd left open the question of whether they would permanently move here out of the Fortress and into the Intereal. "Who is doing this to me, and where can I appeal?"

He rubbed his palms on his thighs as if trying to warm them. Then he rose. "I'll see what I can find out. Meanwhile, I suggest you empty your desk and get ready to move. Do you need a box or anything?"

"No, I don't need a box. All I have is a few pencils and a stack of paper with calculations on them."

He nodded curtly. "They absolutely want everything of yours to go with you." Before walking away, he did something very odd. He winked at her. She wasn't sure if it was just a wink of reassurance, or if it meant something entirely different was afoot. She stared after him in a mix of powerful emotions—anger, pain, even humiliation; even separation, for she had come to treasure her friendships with the humorous and vibrant denizens of the Bit Cave. Now the small island world of stability she'd built here was being torn from her. She felt a deep, visceral sense of betrayal and abandonment, being torn from the womb of this sheltered place of night work with its board games and seeming immunity from the bombs that continually rained down on West Gotha from her gray, industrial neighbor to the east.

Chapter 26

Moping?" Lindy asked. They had already discussed the whole thing on their way home from work before dawn. It was clear that Tedda had suddenly become a liability, and must be removed as far as possible, but why?

"Huh?" Tedda had been lying on her bed, chin on her palms, while she stared into a rainy day that matched her mood. The sky outside was gray, and the leaves in the tree outside glistened with water. Tedda heard dripping in various places outside, and the disconsolate cooing of a dove or pigeon hiding in the building's worm-eaten eaves outside.

"You look as if you lost your best friend."

Tedda shrugged. "In a way I have."

Lindy plopped down near her, a thin rail wrapped in ragged clothing, mostly earth tones. "How do you figure?"

Tedda shrugged again. "Board games."

Lindy did an eye-thing. "Oh, I see what you mean. Yes, it's a lot of fun. Maybe you'll meet new friends down there."

"Too bad you're not coming along. Next thing, they'll separate us completely."

Lindy grinned. "I wouldn't be surprised if they shift me down there too."

"Oh?"

"Yes. The project is grinding to a stop. It's hit a snag. I'm not sure what it is."

"Overheating."

Lindy's turn to say "Huh."

Tedda rolled over on her back, gesticulating as she spoke. She felt more animated. It was like getting this off her chest. "I've been sensing something wrong, and I've done the math backwards and forwards."

"Yes?"

"The rapid proliferation of tunnels and cells and objects, coupled with a certain presence of background radiation and its equivalent (charm, chatter, whatever they call it) from the black monopoles, all suggest to me that the system is being overloaded."

"That's all over my head."

"No, listen, I'm just thinking out loud." Tedda tried to take it to the next step, but couldn't. Her mind wasn't ready for the leap. Instead, the two women sat together on the floor by the window, smelling the fresh air blowing in through leaky seals, and sipping fresh hot green tea. Wind kicked up outside, banging on the window, rattling the glass in its frame. The heater sighed on and on in the room, warming the air and making it dry and cozy.

With gusty wind and rattling windows as background music, and the ever-darkening sky as a rain storm moved in, the two women retired to their separate beds at opposite sides of the room. Lindy was soon snoring lightly, turning away in her customary sleeping position. Tedda fell into a shallow and turbulent sleep, in which she had terribly nervy and vivid dreams. She heard herself, woke herself, several times when she started up, crying out in fear.

Her dreams were muddled, but full of weird kinetic high energies. It was like being in a too-hyped cartoon world running on 240 volts after drinking ten cups of coffee. It was jittery. Tedda tossed this way and that, or dreamed that she did, for she rose and fell on waves of passing calculations, ten, fifteen feet, more than anyone could bounce around in a bed in real life.

The solution came to her, as these things do, with a brilliant flash of sickening, alkaline light, and deeply, invasively ringing bells rocking the frame of her bones. Before she sat up with a start and had to catch her breath, drenched in sweat, she had a realization.

The Other Side (East Gotha) and Tedda's fatherland (West Gotha) were mirroring each other. The two nations were locked in a deadly competition that went on and on with a life of its own. Now they were playing with the newly discovered monopole subfloor of existence, and even though each side's calculations suggested they were well in hand, far from tipping over the critical edge of any energy levels, what if the combined presences of their monopole activities was causing critical mass?

Startled, she awoke—thinking this had significant implications, but what would those be? She sat groggily on the edge of her bed, tangled in the sheets, and couldn't get her mind to return to the brilliant focus it had enjoyed moments earlier.

Chapter 27

Tedda set up shop in a weird little corner of what she came to call the Intereal. On the one hand, her rectangular room at the end of a long, dusky corridor was cozy once the fatherland got lights and furniture in there. It was dry, and there was no moisture dripping from the walls, nothing like that. On the other hand, it was just plain claustrophobic. She spent hours sitting hunched over her desk with one hand holding her forehead, and the other holding a pencil, as she scribbled out dense sheets of tiny, crabbed calculations and notes joined by serpentine lines and arrows. She would sometimes lose her concentration for no apparent reason, and sit up with a jolt, maybe with a shout. It was the loneliness, the dry silent blanket of nothingness, that permeated this deep coalmine of artificial reality. That must be it—the loneliness, the near-death presence of nothingness. She'd sit holding her hands over her mouth, and tremble. She'd wait until her wildly pounding heart calmed, and the tears dried up in the corners of her eyes. She really missed the boisterous, fun people in the Bit Cave. She missed playing board games, laughing, smelling popcorn, drinking tea, exchanging jokes by e-mail.

She continued her daily routine, otherwise, walking with Lindy to and from work. Their conversation became a tiny bit more strained, for reasons Tedda didn't fully grasp. Was Lindy somehow uneasy to be too close to her, now that this thing had happened? It was a faint, subtle change, and Tedda told herself, *maybe I'm just imagining things. Or maybe she just feels bad for me.*

Part 4 - Buy Rails, Hotels, & Souls

Monorail Game

Chapter 28

One of the programmers, a young man named Rory Crane, came to visit her one day. Rory was a slender, blond-haired man roughly her own age, almost a male version of Lindy in that he favored slightly too large sweaters, and slightly too small jeans that rode up around his ankles. Aside from the jeans, he dressed in ill-matching earth colors. His sweater, when he came to see her, was a faded ruby-red, with many fraying wool threads sticking out from complex linear-braided designs. "Hey."

She turned. "Rory." He stood with his hands in his pockets, sort of awkwardly hunched. His ink-blue eyes batted slightly, and he had a shy smile. "You almost scared me. What are you up to?"

"A couple of us miss you up there. I think we all do. Like Dominica." Dominica came a moment later, and gave Tedda a hug, but let Rory do most of the talking while she sat pleasantly nearby.

Tedda put her pen down on the large printout before her, and rolled her chair around to face him. Her mind was aswirl with calculations and theories, and she rubbed her hands across her face as if clearing away cobwebs. "Grab a seat, Rory. I think that's all there is." She pointed to a rickety old wooden chair with torn green leatherette seat.

"Thanks." He pulled it over to him with a scraping sound across the raw concrete floor, and sat straddling it with his arms crossed over the backrest. "So how are you doing here in your dungeon?"

"Ha!" She rose and went to the small canteen they'd brought her. It was little more than a cardboard box beside a hot water machine for making coffee or tea. She had a basket of cellophane-wrapped cookies and crackers. "Want some fattening junk food?"

"Sure. Toss me some of those chocolate cookie things." She did, and he caught them in a swift, sure motion. He said "These are some of those field rations that are so chemical, even the ants won't attack them."

Dominica blew Tedda a kiss and walked a way in a jangle of wrist bracelets.

Rory and Tedda made small talk, while she brewed tea. They took their steaming mugs of tea outside to a mezzanine overlooking warehouse space below them. Except for two men working distantly with a tow motor, unloading bales of cable and other heavy objects, the space was empty. It was a sort of lonely panorama. In fact, she felt glad for Rory's company, and pressed close to him, enjoying his body warmth as they chatted. She felt strangely affectionate toward him, as if they'd known each other for a long time. It wasn't a sexual tension, although they stood within the aura of one another's body heat, and she smelled the clean, soapy warmth in his sweater. "Would you like to really play the Monorail game?" he said at last, with a strange light in his eyes.

She stared at him probingly, examining the frank yet still veiled come-on, the dare-you insouciance, in his eyes. She realized he had no untoward intentions upon her, and the almost haughty tilt in his head, smile on his lips, shine to his face, were all about the fact that he knew she would not say no.

She laughed out loud into his face. "Okay, you've got me. I'm stuck down here like a rat in a hole, and I'm desperate for any kind of action."

"Okay," he said, stirring his tea and staring down into his cup with a mysterious look. "You need to be careful though. This is very dangerous."

"What, playing Monorail?"

"This isn't the old board game."

"Oh? You mean—?" It dawned on her what he meant, and she felt a rain of anxiety needles in her stomach.

"Yes, it's another Intereality."

"Too much!"

"No kidding!"

"I mean—."

"Yeah." They stood regarding each other with mutual awe at the thought. These crazy programmer kids had used, no stolen, the fatherland technology in some war-weary springtime of the soul, maybe before being drafted to die on some muddy battlefield, and they had created a game world using the Monorail concept.

"What do you call it?" she whispered.

"Monopol City."

"No, get out."

"For real." Suddenly he looked a bit spooked, hopping from one foot to the other and looking right and left while keeping his hands jammed in his jeans pockets. "You could get us all burned if you rat."

"I wouldn't tell a soul." She reassured him: "I'm in, okay? Trust me. I'm just glad to be part of something." She added some more reassurance: "Look, I'd be as burned as you, right? You know how the fatherland works. They take no chances. We'd all be scraped, maybe sent off to the front."

"Yeah." He relaxed a bit. "Sure." He relaxed some more. "Okay." He raised his palm, and they high-fived. "Cool," he said. "Okay."

"When do we go in or whatever it is?"

"I'll come back for you soon. In the meantime, don't tell Lindy. Will you promise that?"

Tedda felt a pang. "Why?"

He regarded her frankly, painfully. "She is very dangerous. That's the problem. That's one of the problems. It's for her own good, actually. Will you trust me and not say anything to her? Otherwise, we'll all be toast."

"I promise," Tedda said. She watched him put his half-finished tea aside and walk off with a final wave. So Lindy was not all that she might be. How to handle this, since they lived together and spent so much time together? Maybe it was a matter of putting things in compartments, and not mixing them together. She would simply shut part x of her mind partially off when she was in one place, and partially shut of part y when she was in the other. How else to handle this new, looming disconcertment? Why could the world not be simple and straightforward? Still, it hurt to think that her closest friend might somehow be untrustworthy, have an agenda, betray her.

Chapter 29

Rory came to visit again not long after. This time he was alone. Tedda was glad to see him. He sat down on the floor with his back to the wall and his knees under his chin. His eyes had a relaxed, understanding twinkle. "How is your exile coming along?"

"Dreadful," she said. "I miss you guys terribly."

"I can imagine. If it helps any, we miss you a lot also." She basked warmly in those words, as he continued: "I've been authorized by the Monorail Players Association to let you in on a secret."

She giggled. "The MPA? Is there really such a—?"

He put a finger over his lips and looked furtively left and right. "Shhh. This is serious, Tedda. We could get in a major jam. You have to swear you'll keep it secret no matter what."

She shrugged. "Sure." She could almost guess what it was she must keep secret, but when he told her, it surpassed her expectations and left her breathless.

"You know the Monorail game we all enjoy so much?"

"Yes?"

"You know how we software engineers are. In our spare time, we have created our own Monorail City game."

"No." She pictured the tattered, worn game board with its pastel squares. She visualized how the dog-eared play money lay in untidy piles amid skyscrapers of soda bottles and stacks of sandwiches while the young programmers and techs bantered and rolled the dice.

Before she could coax her imagination further along, he rose. "Want to see?"

"Yes," she said dreamily.

"You'd better bring a jacket. It may be cold."

"Very well." She took down her brownish corduroy jacket, the one with the tan leather lapels with moss-green velour rectangles worked in, from its hook behind the door. Holding the jacket draped over one arm, she followed him out into the corridor.

"Where is Lindy?"

Rory shook his head. "She doesn't know about the game. Please—for her own good, and yours, and all of ours—don't tell her."

"Why?"

He didn't answer.

They walked under the sterile lights along empty corridors. Once or twice, they ducked into a doorway or into a side tunnel as they heard the sound of human activity nearby. Aside from the whirr of air conditioning motors in hidden ducts, and the buzzing of fluorescent lights, the only major sound was a distant, pile-driver pounding of the enemy side's Intereality burrowing. They ended up leaving the femtoworld by the step-down collar. They were back in the hangar near the Bit Cave.

He said: "We use the same step-down collar. The management doesn't know about it. It lets us have our own little play world next to the official one. You're going to love this, because we've made our Monorail game three-dimensional, live, and real-time."

"No!" Intrigued, she followed him through a narrow concrete tunnel that made her claustrophobic. It seemed hotter, too.

"Are you ready?" he asked, and then, without waiting for her reply, he pushed open a door leading to a descending stairwell. She inhaled that raw, almost damp concrete smell she remembered from construction sites over the years. Sand and grit rasped under her feet. Stray wrappers lay kicked and jammed into corners. A dead little lizard lay dry, brown, and flattened on a splash of dried mud grains.

Rory explained: "We kids, playing around, have created an embedded, encysted Monorail City world. We figured if the game is so much fun—what if we could descend into the game, become directly part of it, enjoy it from inside instead of from above? Besides, some of us are doing doctoral papers, and we have experiments to run. How do the rules play out?"

"The rules?"

"Well, yes, you know, the way we make virtual stuff happen inside this raw intereality environment. We write rules for how we want certain things to occur, above and beyond the normal way hydrogen, helium, and the other elements aggregate in our own universe. Remember, there was no Big Bang here. We've pinched off a segment of our own universe, tamed it, created a sort of femto-small sheltered bay in which the wildness of the ocean doesn't smash its big chaotic waves. There is chaos here, but it's just the eddies of the big waves in the macro-universe we inhabit. It's almost a challenge to stir things up, get life going, so to speak."

"Life?" she echoed. Suddenly, she had a dread suspicion. "You've populated this little play universe?"

"Not exactly. It populates itself. We just set the rules in motion and it all happens. We don't create or populate anything—the people just occur, though sometimes we can help nudge the circumstances along. By the way, we call it interchangeably Monorail City or Monopol City."

They came to the bottom of the shaft. There, on a smooth concrete floor that looked as though it had been flooded recently with rain and sand, he paused. He had one hand on the emergency fire bar of a door opening to someplace unknown. He looked at her in surprise. "Yes. Haven't you seen any of the Monopol City denizens outside your office?"

She shook her head slowly. "I didn't know there were any."

"You have a lot to learn," he said. "Life is just a more complex instruction set. The basics are ingrained in the mathematical laws that govern how the elements interact. Life, as evolution tells us, is inevitable. It's just a more interesting level of complexity. Complexity means that more events happen in less time in an interactive manner, and it's not just more events, but different events—in other words, not the same lapping of water against a stone dock in a river, but all the events that transpire inside a mouse or a person or a diatom in a given second. The point is—we can write rules. Here, see for yourself." He flung the door open, and Tedda stepped into a gripping, complicated world that communicated its vibrancy and love of life—but above all, doused her in a shower of rain and fresh air.

"Welcome to Monopol City," Rory said.

Chapter 30

As he threw open the door for her, she gasped at the overwhelming sheet of sensual impressions that sucked her into Monopol City. This wasn't just a game or a city—it was a world. She could see that right away.

It was raining lightly, but the air was damp and filled with noise and steam. It was cool here, without being really cold. She absently slipped on her jacket, welcoming its warmth, yet feeling almost warm again to take it off again.

"It rains for an hour or so once or twice a day," he said, "almost like in the tropics back home. We had to build in the variability for game purposes. Think of this as a subtropical city surrounded by ocean on most sides. It's connected to a distant mainland by long tidal flats and marshes over which just a few roads and rail lines run. Few people feel the need to venture that far, since this is a city of a million people that offers anything you can imagine."

The city loomed above all around—its skyscrapers, its rooftop neon drowning in fog and colored light, its lightning-filled clouds roiling black and gray, its passing airplanes above and cars sloshing over wet asphalt below. The city wanted to take her in its arms and dance with her, pull her out into the unknown. It filled her lungs with the smells of wet tires and spilled gasoline and damp loam. The city filled her ears with the sounds of rustling leaves and laughing pedestrians and blaring trains and hammering pistons.

She shrank back into the musty concrete stairwell, and Rory took her gently by one elbow. "Don't be afraid."

"It's so real," she croaked breathlessly.

"We do good work," he said. "Our rules are complicated enough, not just in their basics, but in their iterations and complex loops. If you step in front of a car down here, you could die. If you don't wear your galoshes, you might catch cold. It's as real as real can get."

She let him guide her slowly out onto the sidewalk. She pulled her jacket tight around her shoulders and shivered nonetheless. "So where is the monorail?" she asked, trying to sound light-hearted when she was scared to death.

He pointed through a break in the skyscrapers, just in time to see a tube of yellow light pour around a corner ten stories up, coming from behind one building and laterally vanishing behind another two or three seconds later. "That's it up there," Rory said with quiet pride. "The programmers who specialized in it did a great job, didn't they?"

"Yes," Tedda said dreamily. She flinched every time a truck roared by in a spray of water, or a four-engine, straight-wing propeller plane droned by overhead, or a taxi fled past with horn blaring, or a fire engine penetrated even all that noise with its klaxons. "It's so noisy," she observed.

He grinned. "We put everything into it. All that sugar, all that soda, all that energy, even some illicit pills and things we smoked. All our energy, and now we have a secret playground that the Fatherland doesn't know about."

She felt a pang of fear. "Are you sure?"

He nodded. "Worst comes to worst, we pull the plug and it's all gone like it never happened."

"You mean the power source."

He nodded. "A flick of the main breaker switch, and the university blacks out for a half hour. When the juice comes back, Monopol City is just a memory of a handful of programmers."

"All of them are in on it?" Something was bothering her, but she couldn't quite put her finger on it. Not the fatherland. Screw the fatherland. Something else.

"Not all, Tedda. That's why you must swear to me you'll keep your mouth shut about this."

She nodded. "I'll bet a few of them are spies. They'd report this in a heartbeat."

"Yes, and the consequences—"

"The consequences," she interrupted, "are far more than you realize."

He looked at her numbly. She didn't know where this was coming from. She felt almost like another person as she said: "What nobody realizes is that there is an overload building. I tried to tell the people in charge, and they exiled me down into the femtosphere. There is an overload coming because both enemy sides are trying to do the same thing in the same space. It can't be done. It's almost as deadly as colliding matter and anti-matter, but think of it as apples and oranges trying to co-exist in the same bowl, and in the same space."

He gripped her upper arms and shook her with gentle urgency. His teeth were gritted, his eyes manic. "Tedda, for God's sake, what will happen?"

"Don't you know?"

He shook his head, let go, stepped back with his hands dourly in his pockets.

The dark sockets of his eyes reminded her: "It creates a vortex, a pinprick in space that opens up to swallow the entire overload and fix space and time again at some fundamental level. It could suck the whole planet in and destroy our world."

He had tears in his eyes. "Then why won't they listen?"

"That," she said, "is the real question. Who is running the show and what is the agenda?" Privately, a part of her knew: It was the dictator Moss, and he was too megalomanic to care. "Come," she said, offering her arm, which Rory took under his. "Let us enjoy the game while time remains for our world." She brightened, looking up as great searchlights beamed up from the ground among the skyscrapers with their Gothic and Art Deco cornices. Discs of light played back and forth under the whorls of sullen cloud.

Chapter 31

The layout of Monopol City was fundamentally the same as on the cardboard game board.

There were, in fact, exactly 36 metro stops on the main line, which roughly formed a square (8 stops on each side, plus the four corners).

Each side of this square was approximately three miles long, so that the perimeter was 12 miles (that being the length of the main line).

The main metro line ran around the perimeter of the central city with its population (signs said) of a million souls.

The central city therefore contained approximately nine square miles of parks, skyscrapers, avenues awash in neon and pedestrians, streets lined with the bright plate glass windows of stores open almost day and night, as well as the darker, seductive windows of bars and entertainment venues.

The people of Monorail City, unlike those of the real world, were not on a perpetual war footing.

In Monorail City, life had a light-hearted, happy cast overlaying all the usual dark and light aspects of human life.

Newspaper machines on every street corner told of the scandals of entertainers, the venality of politicians, the terrible accidents that freakishly took lives in the air and on the ground.

The people Tedda saw passing by were busy, ratty, tatty, smiling, grimacing, they were in a hurry and resembled blurs at times, while at other times they seemed quite distinct. They dressed differently, as if the Jazz Age had decided to stay on.

Perhaps they had no world wars here.

What a concept, Tedda thought, as they walked through a drizzle that coldly peppered her eyes and cheeks.

Rory bought them each a newspaper from a stand run by a blind man with sunglasses in the night, just so they could shield themselves from the drizzle.

"These stay here," he cautioned. "Nothing goes up into the real world when we leave, okay?"

"Yes, sure," she said giggling. "What if we lose our way? What if we get stuck here?"

He shrugged. "That would be fun for a while. Remember, a momentary power blip, a browndown for a few seconds, anything at all, and this place vanishes. Did I tell you? We vanish with it."

She yelled: "You didn't tell me that. Now I'm scared."

"Don't be. We could get hit by an Eastern bomb up there any minute and be dead. What's the difference? Dead is dead."

She held his arm tightly. "Of course.

Chapter 32

Rory took her into a tavern that smelled of beer and cigarette smoke. She liked the twang of country rock that echoed among dingy old speakers set in the ceiling corners. She liked the dim lighting, the neon signs all around, the lazy way men and women sitting back on bar stools watched a pool game in progress. The four pool players moved about the green felt almost as if it were a femtoworld all its own, with its perfectly shaped and symmetrically colored balls. They were playing straight pool, which was about as eventful as Sunday softball at a neighborhood park. She found it relaxing. Then, to her surprise, just as Rory handed her a cool mug dripping with beer suds, several familiar faces walked in. Several wore sunglasses and hip attire. They were her friends the techs and programmers from Wally's shop. They all grinned and high-fived and got beers.

Several of the young men stood in a circle, grinning, and as Tedda worked her way through the crowd, she noticed that they sidled off to a side corridor near the bathrooms. For a moment it looked as though they were going to share some illicit drugs, and they waited each time a local patron excused himself to wade through. Then she saw their grins, and the bar lights glistening on their smooth young faces, and neon reflections glittering in the black planes of their sunglasses. Dominica was among them, laughing and clapping. One of them, Jakko, had a stack of Monopol Dollars he was handing out. "Just printed it all up this afternoon," he said with faux gangster cynicism. They pressed a wad of M$10s into her hand, a thousand monopols worth. She rolled the money up and stuck it in her pocket with a guilty feeling. "Relax," someone said, "this whole thing is only a game."

Wally leaned his big frame sideways through the crowd and said with serious mien: "Hey, listen, this is as real as our own world. If you cut these people, they bleed. Bleed enough and they die. If they cut you, you bleed."

"Easy," Jakko said, "we're just kidding around."

"Play money makes one feel strange," a woman quant said.

"It's real to them, play money to us," Jakko said. He looked to Tedda like a natural born card sharp.

Feeling giddy from their beers, they headed to the downtown area. There, billboards loomed, here and there above the skyline, in appropriate colors: Green Line, Red Line, Blue Line, Yellow Line. That made it look a bit more like a game town rather than the very real, bustling city it seemed to be.

The rain let up, and a warm dry wind blew through the streets. Papers twirled like dead brush, rolling down the drying sidewalks. Ripples moved across puddles. Wally explained: "This is actually a sort of desert city, a Las Vegas by the sea, if you will. A San Diego with the sea before its face, and mountains and deserts at its back. As on much of the California coast, mornings and evenings the wind comes in from the sea bringing a thick marine layer with drizzle. As the day warms up, the wind turns, and warm dry air pushes in from the desert."

"So there is ocean nearby?" Dominica asked.

A female software engineer said: "We should come by day next time, and bring our swim suits."

"That's right," Wally said as he lumbered along, still carrying a beer mug he'd abducted under his coat, "There is ocean to the north and east, desert out on the west and south."

"Do they have any other towns or cities?" Jakko asked.

A young woman tech said: "I still think we made all this up, and it seems a bit silly to ask what they have."

Wally glowered: "They are as real as we are."

A male quant who looked very professorial said: "Get it through your heads. This is a real world. It's a miniature, contained universe. We didn't create it. We just pinched it off from our own when we compressed its fundamental forces. It's an incredibly miniaturized slice formerly of our own universe, with its subatomic particles jammed way closer together."

"But is it a universe, or just a piece of one?" a male tech asked.

The quant replied: "There is a new theory that if you inject enough new Go matter—that's the subquark stuff—or energy into a femtoworld, it will go critical. It could blow up and annihilate a huge chunk of the parent world."

"Oh the hell with all the details," Jakko said. "Let's party and have fun!"

They let out a group cheer as they walked down a dark, deserted back alley, and Tedda heard a crash of shattering glass as Wally discarded his empty beer mug. Several of the men lined up to pee on a dingy brick wall, the backside of a factory with broken windows and bent security mesh on them. Several of the women lined up afterward and did the same, proving that women can do everything men can—if they handle the plumbing a bit differently. Tedda was more demure and squatted in a dark corner between a wall and a wire fence, feeling cool air moving below her, only to scream and jump up when fronds of long wet grass rubbed against her fanny. Everyone laughed.

They entered into the bright center of a cosmopolitan city that was not at war and obviously was a center of artistic and musical accomplishment. Greenish copper mansard roofs reminded Tedda of Belle Époque Paris (Paris being in the West Gotha sphere of influence) and the custard walls of buildings reminded her of baroque Germany. After all, Tedda thought, this place was driven by rules the Bit Cave had culled from the best of their own world. She had a different sense of what would happen if this place went critical. The explosion the quant had mentioned was possible— something like matter and antimatter annihilating each other—but Tedda had a different idea. She didn't know why. Had she been a quant in a previous incarnation?

They rode together on the marvelous monorails and trolleys and elevated trains that rumbled through every section of the city. It was basically the same system they'd enjoyed on their game boards above in the macroverse, but more complex. It wasn't just a square like on the game board, but a complex of whorls and loops that ran through the city at street level, at fifth story level, through the skyscrapers at tenth story level.

Along the way, a new friend attached herself to them. She introduced herself as Hadley—an athletic, brisk figure, an attractive woman with sandy straight hair dangling around a pleasantly oval face. She wore a long Hadley came out of nowhere and seemed to know a lot about these visitors to this world. When Wally tried to brush her off, she showed him a small gold badge. Wally backed away. Hadley gravitated toward Tedda, oddly enough. Hadley's wiry figure moved inside a mannish wheat-colored pants suit with white shirt and desert tie. She wore a moss-green brimmed hat, and Tedda almost felt her making advances, almost imagined her having a small mustache pressed tight against the rim of her upper lip. "Do you recognize me?" Hadley purred as she pressed close to Tedda, who backed away. "I know about you," Hadley said quietly so only Tedda could hear.

"What do you want? Who are you?" Tedda asked.

"Transit police." Hadley rocked on her heels while gripping her thumbs in a pair of suspenders. Her head bobbed left and right with the moss-green hat on it. "I'm the law around here, and I need to keep up with what's going on."

Jakko laughed as he held up a wad of money. "Can we offer you something to get lost?"

Hadley's black-gloved hand swept backhand, knocking the money out of Jakko's hand. On the return arc, her palm slapped his face. Money twirled gaily as the train rattled on. Behind them, M$10 bills filled the air over a grassy baseball park.

Hadley said: "Attempting to bribe a police officer can be a felony. I'm going to assume that was less than a grand, and I'll let you go with a verbal warning regarding an attempted misdemeanor. Do I make myself clear?"

Jakko's sunglasses hung around his neck, and he stood with one hand on his cheek and a shocked expression.

"That'll teach you to be a wise ass," Wally growled. The others laughed.

Hadley waggled a finger, then took Tedda aside. "You don't know who I am, do you?"

Tedda shook her head. She shrank back, feeling the woman's steely grip on her upper arm. Her thumb dug into a nerve point there, just enough to cause a moment of pain. "Ouch!" Tedda said. Still Hadley hung on, now massaging the nerve point to ease the pain. "I care about you!" the female detective muttered with gritted teeth and impassioned eyes. Tedda pulled back and shook the hand away. There was something deeply disturbing, almost passionate in the way the woman was trying to insinuate herself, almost (though Tedda pushed the very thought away) sexual, seductive, forceful, intrusive—and pathetic.

The train rolled into a brightly lit station. "Come on," Jakko said, "let's get off this damned thing." His sunglasses were back on his nose, covering his ego-wounded eyes. The happy go lucky Jakko laugh was absent.

They all got off, while a crowd of locals of all ages and descriptions got on—well-dressed, orderly, without the hunger and anxiety of crowds in the Gothas East or West. Tedda felt Wally pulling her away by the back of her jacket as she locked eyes with Detective Hadley. Hadley made no move toward her, but leaned back against the train window and rested her arms—in surrender? Exhaustion?—on the metal hand rails under the windows. A crowd of party-goers from the bar district and the ball park blended together, packing the car with bodies, banner, twirling spinners, and Tedda lost sight of the woman. Wally pulled hard, and Tedda fell backward into his arms just as the doors closed. The train let off a warning squawk, oily smelling vapor rose from underneath as the air brakes loosened and the engine kicked in, and the train sped off down the track like a row of red books standing on edge. Tedda untangled herself from Wally's massive arms and stood dusting herself off.

Monopol City—its heart, its throbbing music, its celebrating nightlifers, its elegant parks with their paths and fountains, its bustling avenues and swarming boulevards—took them in its arms. This was no toy town patterned on a cardboard game board. This was a powerful and cultured city in many ways superior to the thin gruel of perpetually war-drained West Gotha. This was how life could be in peacetime, in a world dominated by common sense and decency, without the all-pervading fatherland secret police and uniformed thugs on every street corner. Why not, instead, have a poet or a minstrel on every corner, and health care for all, rather than the endless blood sacrifice of the military? Just walking in a place like this made so much more sense than the dreary atmosphere of the Gothas.

Tedda felt intimidated and alarmed. She felt exposed and overwhelmed. Wally seemed to sense her discomfiture, and quietly put his large hand on her shoulder. She bet he could feel her trembling. She wrapped her own arms around her upper torso and shivered in her jacket. She felt some sense of safety in numbers as the Gotha invaders paraded happily down the wide sidewalks, watched by men and women sipping demitasse and listening to violin music at sidewalk cafes (a Jakko touch, perhaps; for all his gaucherie, he had a flair for the absurdly elegant). The tone changed just as quickly, putting them into the throbbing, screaming midst of a throng of samba dancers with all the urgency and abandon of three a.m. in Rio during Carneval. The Gothaneros joined in, forming a conga line, and Tedda suddenly laughed, joining them. She felt a quant man's stiff fingers on her hips, and held the bony hips of one of Jakko's fellow code boys as they swung left and right through shifting arrays of masks and laughter.

Some number of beers and dances and bratwursts and potty stops later, Tedda found herself drowsing with a smile on her face in the back of a taxi that smelled of leather coats, spilled champagne, and ground-in mustard. She heard the continuing laughter and music, and the comments of her fellow Gothans, through the haze of her intoxication. Wally sat on her right, Jakko on her left.

"She's coming around," Jakko said. "Hey, Tedda, welcome to Monopol City."

"Just in time to get back home with us," Wally growled.

She sat up and rubbed her eyes. Her head felt muzzy. Someone offered her a small flask of brandy, from which she took a fiery sip that made her cough. For a moment, the inside of her nose burned like the Schwartzwald on fire. Someone else handed her a thermos of black coffee, from whose lukewarm depths she drank thirstily until her ears whistled like caffeine steamboats.

"What's going on?" she said weakly, handing the thermos back over the seat.

"We're almost there."

"You were going to run off with two tango dancers," Jakko said. "We had to pay them the rest of this fake shit money to make them go away."

Wally growled: "Couldn't afford to get separated. We theorize there is a limit to how long a person can say down here before they start getting absorbed into their Go-plane."

Jakko nodded. "You get your Go-dots sucked down into theirs, and you become part of their landscape. I wouldn't like that."

"You'd lose your whole world," Tedda whispered. She wasn't sure if that fear were really true. Now why did she think that? Was she really a quant, as she suspected? Why had they filled her with drugs and made her forget so much?

"Watch out," Wally said suddenly.

The taxi slowed, and the one behind nearly hit them. Tires squealed as the three baby-blue Monopol City Cabs slowed and then stopped.

Tedda saw where Wally pointed: the door in the wall leading up to the Gotha world stood open. In fact, it leaned slightly as if its hinges had been forced.

The street was empty except for a large gray truck parked about two blocks away. The truck looked dark and abandoned for the night, like all else on the street, slumbering in its own shadows.

Wally seemed like a changed man. "Everybody out," he barked. As he stepped from the cab, he had a black automatic pistol in one hand and a small radio in the other. "Secure the door!" he shouted. Two techs dropped their pretensions at innocence and raced to the door brandishing weapons. That left Tedda and a half dozen others milling about on the opposite sidewalk. Wally waved to the taxis, which Tedda quickly surmised were driven not by locals but by West Gotha agents. The three drivers lined their cars up in a barricade line at the curb outside the door. Wally held the middle of the street like a giant anchor while waving directions. He ordered his five men—the two techs, the three drivers—into defensive positions behind the cars.

Wally turned to the civilians, Tedda and Jakko among them. "We can't stay here any longer than we have to. For the moment, cluster over here and stay in the shadows. I'll call you once we've secured the doorway back to our world." So saying, he strode across the street with his gun aimed squarely at the doorway. He shouted to his men: "Cover me while I go in and clean it up."

Out of the corner of her eye, Tedda saw Jakko looking scared and pale as a ghost. Beyond him, down the sidewalk, she saw a figure in a long coat approaching, hands I pockets. It was Hadley.

Hadley pointed silently to Tedda and flicked her left index finger for Tedda to come toward her. Hadley's right arm was out now, in the dark at her side, and Tedda could almost swear she saw a miniature assault rifle in Hadley's hand.

"There's that Monopol cop again," Jakko muttered. Someone else muttered: "What does she want?" Another said: "Do you think the city cops busted our people?" Someone else said: "More likely East Gotha." Someone said angrily: "You think she's an East Gotha spy?" Someone else grumbled: "I'll bet they drilled down into the city here and put their own agents on the streets."

So it went, and the possibilities opened up before Tedda's eyes. She saw Hadley beckoning to her, while Hadley glanced often at the open door across the street and hung back into the shadows. Hadley's eyes were wide with anticipation, as if something were about to happen. But what, Tedda wondered. Was Hadley in on something, or just aware of it and trying to save her?

Tedda's attention focused on the door, from which a wan yellow stairwell light fell innocently out onto the sidewalk. She heard a shout, then gun shots. She heard a rapid succession of popping noises.

Wally staggered out, clutching his mid section and looking down at the growing reddish black stain on his torso. "They shot him," one of the agents behind the car yelled. "Stick with me—let's take them out before they close the doorway and we're stuck here forever!"

Three of the surviving five men took positions and carefully, professionally, worked their way closer. Covering each other, they waited while the other two climbed into the rearmost taxi and backed out of sight.

"What are they up to?" Jakko said, shivering as he held himself in his arms.

"Going to get help?" someone guessed, but someone else said "From where?" and a third person said: "I'll be our side has some kind of secret office here in the city." A fourth said: "Then the other side probably does too." Someone else said: "Maybe that's what all the drilling we heard was all about."

Through all of this, Wally's body lay in the street.

Tedda heard the whisper of an approaching motor. The next thing that happened was over in seconds. The taxi came scooting down the sidewalk. It slowed as it approached the door. It came so close that its handles scraped the wall and trailed showers of sparks. The car blocked the doorway and both men inside unleashed a blinding wall of machine gun fire that must be tearing up the stairwell and anyone in it. The man in back changed to a grenade launcher and unleashed several deafening concussion grenades. The car lurched forward several feet and stopped. Its two occupants jumped out holding assault rifles. Meanwhile, the other three agents joined them as all five rushed into the teeming smoke. Tedda heard more gunshots. The doorway was so heavy with gunsmoke that Tedda couldn't see inside. Even across the street, several of the waiting tech workers coughed.

Where are the local police? Tedda wondered. Why were there no passing cars, no shocked pedestrians, so wailing sirens? Then she remembered that, for all of its sophistication, this was still a construct world. Surely they had set up rules for police and emergency crews, but perhaps someone had gotten into the guts of the game and turned off the switches, counters, flags, whatever that drove that part of the generating code. But that didn't make much sense either—this wasn't a virtual world, driven by executing computer code, even free-wheeling compilers that generated reality on the fly. This was a solid, created construct whose creation rules winked out in favor of real-time execution rules just like in the real world. Once set in motion, this world just kept on rolling according to the inverted pyramid of simple rules. First atom hydrogen, one proton, one electron; second atom helium two protons, two electrons; and those alone constituted a vast percentage of the entire universe. Same thing with numbers: 1, 2, 3... from such simple building blocks, and the simple rules governing their separation and interaction, all quickly and easily evolved into unthinkably complex rule sets for a world.

When the smoke cleared, Tedda saw several more bodies lying twisted like dead fish in the street. Tedda and her companions shrank back against the shadowy wall behind them as the magnitude of their side's defeat became evident. From the inside of their own stairway came several lumbering towbots—humans inside robotic armor derived from and originally designed to function as factory towmotors, but quickly drafted into further service as fighting machines. The human stayed inside, like the squishy oyster body in its shell. The human, so the joke went, was the good jelly at the center of the fritter doughnut. And, it now seemed apparent, these were East Gotha donuts. Tedda could see no other explanation.

Hadley came at a dead run, gun in hand, coat tails flapping.

Tedda's companions screamed and dove out of the way. Hadley flung herself through the air and tackled Tedda, driving her down and further along the sidewalk.

Just then, the three large tankbots across the street opened fire and started raking the sidewalk with bullets. Tedda heard the screams of dying techs and quants fading as bullets bounced and rattled all around. Hadley had the strength of several men as she dragged Tedda further along the sidewalk, through a row of bushes, through a hole in a wire fence, and into the darkness and safety of a brickyard. "You'll be safe here for now," Hadley breathed. "They're operating out of that truck down the street." She opened the clip in her assault rifle, checked it, and clicked it shut. "I'll be back for you. Stay put." Hadley crawled back out through the fence, through the bushes, out onto the sidewalk. "If I don't make it, head for the city. My people will find you in the Green Station."

"Hadley!" Tedda called out after her. She had a million questions. But the long-coated female soldier was already running at a crouch through the rubble and drifting smoke. Tedda pressed her face against the fence, but ventured no further, while watching for her rescuer to safely make it.

Across the street, the three lumbering tankbots were busy with some task of their own, whose reason soon became apparent. No! Tedda thought as she saw that they were getting ready to dynamite the doorway back 'upstairs' (metaphorically) to West Gotha.

Hadley vanished into night and fog.

At the same time, one of the tankbots let out a shout and pointed after Hadley. While two of them continued about the business of unpacking boxes of explosives and stringing electrical fuze cables, the third tankbot started lumbering down the street after Hadley. The operator inside, invisible to Tedda except for a faint smudge of face visible in neon blue light inside the helmet-cab, had his guns up and was ready to fire. Tankbots had multiple arms, some symmetrically paired left/right, others just appliances on some part of the body. This one had twin gatling guns, one on each forearm of its firing limbs. Already, the gun tubes were turning with an audible whine, and twirling as coolant air surged among the independent gun barrels. The tankbot released several test bursts, and amber rivers of fire spewed like firehouses along the street. Then the shooting stopped. The tankbot must have received orders not to shoot for fear of hitting the truck.

The truck's lights came on and its engine fired up. Tedda heard the ratcheting sound of its mechanical brakes being released, and saw a gout of diesel exhaust as the vehicle bucked into motion. It was a tall, narrow deuce and a half with a high box in the rear, with an odd roof—not rounded but pitched. The front wheels turned and the truck bucked again. It was clear he wanted to turn around and head up the street—perhaps to pick up the drivers inside the tankbots and then roar out of sight as their handiwork played out and the doorway exploded in ruins.

In the reddish light of the truck's taillights, Tedda saw the lean figure of Hadley, coat flapping, as she ran by the cab and unloaded a burst of fire into the cab. Tedda saw the driver's head slam against the shattered window, and then glass and head hung out of the window in a gout of gore. Hadley laid down a chatter of rounds into the front wheel, which went flat and the truck pitched slightly forward to the left. Shots erupted from the passenger side, missing Hadley entirely as she ran at a crouch back to the rear. She shed her long coat as she did so, exposing a plain inner tunic of dark green wool covered with crisscross leather bandoliers and pouches. Without stopping, she chattered up the rear wheels, which puffed gray smoke and dropped several inches flat onto the rims, so that the entire vehicle rocked.

Tedda saw the rear panels swing open. She caught a glimpse of an electronic maze lit by myriad green and red lights inside. She saw the massive shape of a fourth tankbot waiting to be lowered on its hydraulic tailgate lift. She saw several shadowy technicians with guns in the truck. They looked down left and right, searching for their assailant. The tankbot's face burst into blue light. Tedda could make out the pale, underwater, almost fish-skinned face of the operator, who frantically ran through his pre-ops check even as the tail lift whined and the tankbot slowly sank toward street level.

At that moment, Tedda saw a shape under the truck. An arm hooked out. An object sailed upward, making a backward arc, bounced into the truck while its pin sailed away, and rolled down the slight incline toward the banks of winking lights. Tedda heard the shouts of men jumping from the truck. Just as the grenade blew, the new tankbot touched ground. The roof was blown off the truck, and its equipment was shredded by steel shrapnel. The explosion blew the top of the tankbot off from behind. It was amputated from the chest up. The upper half of the operator was gone from the waist up, and his lower half lay draped over the yawning opening of its insides, bent at the knees, with the belted trousers hanging outside, still full of leg meat and some amount of intestine hanging down like coils of sausage to the ground. Tedda had never seen such gruesome violence, and right now she was too numb and overwhelmed to reflect on it. The technicians who had jumped from the truck turned and tried to fire under the truck aimlessly, but a steady chatter of fire from under the truck cut them down quickly, one by one. The tankbot down the street was tracking the muzzle flashes from Hadley's gun, and started laying down sheets of fire. Tedda thought she saw Hadley roll over and take cover behind the truck's massive wheels. Tedda crawled forward, keeping behind a concrete block wall inside the bushes but outside the chain link fence. She squatted behind the wall, carefully peering out of the bushes and down the sidewalk toward Hadley's position.

Then the explosion in the stairwell rocked the street. Luckily, much of the blast was contained inside the stairwell. Still, the noise was deafening. Tedda fell down and smacked her chin on the concrete sidewalk. The shockwave buckled the street and the sidewalks as if someone had yanked on a carpet with both hands. Debris collapsed inside the shaft and the lights went out. Dust roiled outward in total darkness. The air was filled with a singed, bitter smell.

As smoke and dust drifted down the street and started to clear, Tedda saw a startling sight. One by one, the two tankbots by the building disintegrated. They seemed to turn into a thousand mosaic pieces that fell to ground like snowflakes and then even those winked out of existence. The tankbot down the street did the same. The bodies in the street disappeared, including that of Wally. The broken tankbot behind the ruptured truck chassis winked away along with its dead operator.

Tedda rose to her feet, staggering as she headed down the street. She stepped over the bodies of her dead companions—some of whom vanished while others remained. She heard weak cries from Tedda, and focused on getting to her.

As she approached the truck, or what was left of it—cab blown off, middle of cargo area buckled so that the rear end with its eight huge tires seemed to point upward slightly—she saw Hadley crawl out from behind the tires. She was clearly wounded.

Tedda rushed to her side and helped her up. Tedda stripped away the tangled leather bandoliers and made Hadley lean against the big tires. "Where are you hurt?"

"Here, I think." Hadley pressed her hand to her side. When she briefly took her hand away, her palm was black (a trick of the light, making red seem black). "Here too," Hadley said, putting her other hand over the same shoulder. "I got it in the left side and left shoulder."

"How long can we afford to be stuck down here?" Tedda asked.

"Don't worry about it," Hadley said. To Tedda's startled look, Hadley blinked with great soulful eyes. "You're covered."

Tedda gave the shoulder and the side a cursory look. "The shoulder wound is just nicked bone. The other one is internal, and could be serious."

"Ouch!" Hadley cried. "Ouch! Dammit! *Hooh!*"

"Let me take you to the Green Station," Tedda said.

Hadley nodded. "Good plan, but I can't walk far." Already, she slumped down, her butt riding down over the tire until she was seated with her back to the wheel. Her head slumped to one side. Her eyes were open, and she used her good right hand to point up the street.

Tedda knew what to do. She ran up the street toward the still-smoking ruin. The massive building stood erect—a great shadow of brownish brick. The force of the explosion must have pointed up the stairwell. Tedda wondered if the pressure had erupted into the femtoworld above, or even destroyed the Bit Cave and that whole building with its lobby entrance. Or perhaps the entire explosion, on this femto scale, had been so minute that it seemed like a momentary pin light, inaudible in the West Gotha world.

No time to ponder much. An attacker staggered out of the shadows on the sidewalk about 50 feet head, dragging an assault rifle. Along the way, Tedda saw an East Gotha assault micro much like Hadley's lying in the street. She scooped it up as she ran, figured out the mechanism along the way, released the safety. Meanwhile the other had spotted her, and swung around into hip firing position. A burst of bullets flew wildly through the air, missing Tedda though she could hear them singing in the wind near her ears like mosquitoes. She dropped to one knee, took aim, and put a brace of bullets through the person's midsection. He crumbled into dust as he fell.

Another rule, she thought. Jumping into one of the abandoned taxis and starting its engine, she asked herself: *How do I know that?*

As she drove up the street, bouncing from the sidewalk into the street, she realized: *the drugs are wearing off.*

It was an exhilarating realization. Bit by bit, in faint echoes and hollow visions, the puzzle of her lost memories, her vanished past, began to reassemble itself.

Principal in that array of tantalizing glimpses was the image of her lover's face, her husband's, that of Alton Hedrock. She drove down to the truck, got out, and walked around to Hadley's side. The woman sat weak and slumped from loss of blood, but as she looked up into Tedda's eyes, Tedda knew the truth.

Tedda knelt beside the dying woman and held her hands. "You're from him, aren't you?"

Hadley nodded. "He loves you."

"He's a scoundrel."

"Yes, but the two of you made a deal to save the world. He loved you that much, to betray his own side."

"And you?" Tedda asked. She sat beside Hadley and cradled her head.

"You know what I am," Hadley said. "I am a rule."

"What's going on?" Tedda asked as gently as possible. She stroked Hadley's hair.

Hadley coughed, spitting up blood. "They kept you, brought you, as bait to draw out Hedrock. They're on to the whole thing."

"Who is?"

"The Moss syndicate that runs the Gotha world." Hadley coughed again, and more blood came up. She was weakening.

"You mean both sides of the Gotha equation?"

Hadley nodded. "East and West. People die for the fatherland myth, and the corporation gets richer." She choked a bit, more on body fluids than emotions. "It's a huge betrayal, and you and Hedrock were going to" (she paused) "save the world" (another pause) "but—"

Tedda hugged her close and said: "But what?"

Hadley took a breath and let out a long shuddering gasp. She looked up into Tedda's eyes as if she wanted to tell her something important, but was only able to utter a rattling sound from the throat. Her eyes glazed over and she slumped against Tedda's breast. Tedda felt the dead weight of her and felt a wave of pity. She started to hug the body close and grieve over it, but the body suddenly became light and fell apart into a million mosaic pieces of stained glass and then dust that vanished. Nothing was left. Only a faint breeze briefly spun on the street and made sand dust rise in a funnel before that died down. Several yards up the street, Hadley's discarded coat collapsed on itself and vanished. Only the assault micro was real. Tedda picked the gun up in one flowing, exhausted motion as she headed back to the taxi for her drive to Green Station.

Chapter 33

As Tedda drove back toward town, she saw one reason why no police or emergency crews had come. There was a pretty obvious reason why this part of town had been abandoned to its anarchic fate. The outer edges of Monopol City must be breaking apart, and Tedda did have some foggy notions about why that might be.

Tedda drove around yawning jagged black fissures in the street. Finding the way was otherwise pretty simple. She noticed now that the outer edges of Monopol City had lost much of their glow. Only the central part with its parks, theaters, avenues, and of course the main Monorail line remained fully animated.

There was some sort of national holiday in progress, and the inner streets were barricaded. Tedda abandoned the taxi and made her way on foot. She carried Hadley's assault micro under her jacket with the carrying strap over her shoulder, under the jacket. The earlier rain was gone, and a kind of humid heat filled the air. Tedda stripped off her jacket and carried it under one arm, with assault rifle wrapped up inside. With its spidery folding stock and components, the rifle was luckily compact enough. She had about two dozen rounds left in the magazine, about half of its full load. The ammo alone weighed more than the weapon.

Much like on the game board, the stations of the main line were arrayed in a great square throughout the city. She spotted the high, illuminated billboards advertising each station in glowing neon in the appropriate color: Green Station, Blue Station, Red Station, Yellow Station, White Station, Orange Station. There were more as the row of distinct signs faded into distance and fog (*and mosaic breakup?* she wondered), but these were all she could make out. Mulling such thoughts, she threaded her way among conga lines and samba dancers, costumed party goers, and elegant men and women sipping demitasse while violinists played cloying love songs.

As she sauntered tiredly along carrying the heavy weapon, she noticed too late that several men and women had fallen in line behind her. When she walked right, they followed; walk left, and they followed; speed up, same; slow down, still there. She was just about to turn around and tell them all to fuck off, when she became aware that one had walked up real close and stuck something in her neck. She reached up to touch the thing, whose bite felt like a bee sting.

Dancers reveled around her, laughing and singing, clapping their hands and regarding her with increasingly bizarre faces. Concentric circles began to rotate hypnotically in their happy eyes, and their teeth gleamed like ice bergs, until she fell over the edge and into the sea...

Chapter 34

When she awoke, it was in a creaking, cheap cot in what looked like a rented room.

Torn shades covered the two windows, which were framed in crudely shellacked red wood. The walls were covered with various shades of bilious green wallpaper ornamented with purple grapes, brownish melons, and a variety of other fruits.

Several men and women surrounded her. They looked at her intently, and spoke to each other in some foreign tongue.

She couldn't speak, and her limbs had been tied or taped down.

She knew she was heavily drugged, because her own body didn't make sense. She wanted to move this arm or that hand or that foot, and something else moved, or else nothing moved. She wanted to speak, but gibberish came forth.

Then came the men with the forceps and the needles.

That again! Now what?

She tried to scream, remembering the pain, the spitting of blood, her beet-red stools for days.

This crowd of people held her down.

All she could do was twist left and right, but not very well because her body did not seem to want to obey her.

One of them held up a finger, warning her to be still. He made facial expressions signaling that everything would be okay if she just relaxed.

A woman made motions suggesting she relax. Meanwhile the work began in earnest.

Tedda felt her rear end ripping and tearing as if claws were forcing it open so fire could be stuffed inside.

Likewise, cold forceps pulled her mouth open in four directions, so that she was afraid her lips would tear.

They must have given her the needle, for she felt herself fading.

As she faded, that old image came forth again: herself astride the other naked woman, as in a pencil sketch about hell, and she holding the woman's head up by the hair while getting ready to plunge a huge knife into the woman's gut. But why?

She had murky, nauseous dreams in which they took apart her head and put it back together again, but argued about which jaw went on top and which on the bottom.

They stuck things in her and pulled things out.

They used wrenches to tighten her teeth down and loosen them up, and either way, her teeth ached.

She did have the vivid impression that they were undoing whatever the other crew had done to her in the room while Lindy slept and Major Moss watched, holding his riding crop.

Chapter 35

Tedda awoke alone in this derelict hotel room.

She was naked, and her clothing lay neatly folded on a chair.

There was a white enameled bedpan with blue insides next to the bed, and she vomited into it.

Retching repeatedly, she lay helplessly looking at her own distorted reflections in the white enamel top of the bedpan. She saw the same blood as before. Her teeth ached, and her rear end felt as if she'd sat in acid. Still retching, she reached down weakly with one hand, and probed with her fingertips to see what they had done to her bum hole.

She grimaced, touching raw surfaces. They had apparently put lots of salve on, for her hand came away feeling greasy, and smelling faintly of lemons and some sickly flower smell. The smells made her vomit again and simultaneously cry.

A tray with a plastic water bottle and a plastic glass wrapped in sanitary cellophane stood on a stool. With trembling fingers, she fumbled until she got her self a glass of water to drink.

Again, she let a gob of spit escape into the water, and watched the twirling, rusty-colored galaxy of blood.

She threw the water against the wall, refilled the glass, and drank it all down.

Clutching the half-full bottle, she gingerly got herself sitting up, and started to think about dressing.

As she did so, she sobbed quietly to herself. Blinded by tears, she keened softly as she picked up her stockings and pulled them up her legs. She felt violated and angry.

She'd seen so much that she was past being hurt or outraged. Part of her wanted justice for all this, and part of her just wanted revenge. A larger part wanted this all to be gone and never come back, but she knew the nightmare she was trapped in must lead her to yet further surprises. She used an edge of the bed sheet to wash her face gently with water from the bottle.

Her mouth hurt and felt swollen, and her gums were on fire. Her teeth throbbed, particularly the molars.

She found her jacket, but the weapon was gone. She also found a box of painkillers, with directions to take two every two hours. She took four and washed them down with water.

She eased out of the room, cautiously looking up and down the dingy hall.

Seeing no other soul, she quickly went to the nearby stairwell, and clattered down a rickety flight of wooden steps.

She exploded her way out of a nondescript wooden door below and found herself in someone's grassy back yard.

She heard some kind of plaintive accordion music, heard people speaking a foreign tongue, heard chairs scraping and laughter.

Children' toys littered the lawn, and chairs stood about on a dismal concrete patio under a bare light bulb.

Still spitting blood, she hurried out of the yard and into a street full of people.

There, looking alike any other drunk, she blended in rather easily.

Chapter 36

She came to Green Station. Her shoes gritted on the sandy concrete here (*must be near the beach,* she thought) and loose papers blew about as she climbed the steel staircase to the overhead platform. The painkillers had her numbed up, and she was feeling little pain, although she felt herself stumbling a bit.

She could smell the sea now. She walked across the concrete platform and leaned out over a parapet. Resembling a California sunset lingering late into the night, orange clouds livened the western horizon. Wide ocean surfaces reflected sunlight up into the sky and bounced light down from clouds. It would all start breaking apart soon, she thought, unless something could be done—but what? What had she and Hedrock schemed to do? What had Hadley said: they were going to save West and East Gotha. But how? She must find Hedrock and ask him.

She looked about on the platform. Two rail lines ran through the station, one for each direction. The One Line went one way, and the Two Line went the other way. Looking about at the surrounding skyscrapers sleeping in their bluish fog, she reflected that no doubt in the corporate board rooms, high rollers were buying and selling Monopol real estate just like in the game. She wondered how often the various rail stations and lines changed hands. Who built and lost empires here?

No sign of Hadley's agents. She looked idly at the boy on the far wooden bench, the young woman teasing lipstick on her mouth in the reflection of a glassed-in metro schedule, the older businessman in black suit squinting into the pages of his Monopol Commerce Journal. She examined each of the thirty or more fellow travelers waiting to go in either direction, and none noticed her.

As she waited, she inhaled deeply and enjoyed the peaceful air of Monopol City, even though it echoed with the frenetic festival beat all around. Up here, it was quieter, actually. So she found as she turned her attention to the distant sea. Even at that, she thought she detected some odd straight lines like fissures in the whorls of distant pink and orange cloud still glowing with lost evening sunlight.

Her body ached from the pain, and her soul ached from all the death and destruction she had witnessed.

Nothing I can do about it. Tedda closed her eyes and inhaled the night air as she leaned across the parapet with arms loosely folded. Smells of loam and grass, maybe even swamp reeds with that pungent iodine whiff, rose up into her nose like life-worshiping incense. The death of the Hadley rule played again and again in her heart. *Enjoy it while I can.*

She barely heard the train arrive behind her. It stopped, its doors whooshed open, and passengers got on or off. A female announcer said something like "Green Station; Green Station; last turnover before Red and Blue. Passengers are reminded to carry their tickets with them and be ready to show them to any Transit Agent who may ask for proof of purchase. Train boarding now for Blue Station. Blue Station is next."

"Hello," said a man's voice, and she turned. It wasn't Hedrock, but he looked familiar. The smiling blond man in the finely knitted chocolate and maize herringbone suit held a field-gray raincoat draped over both wrists, and rocked lightly on tan leather shoes. "I'm Eduard."

Tedda laughed weakly. She sat leaning over her folded arms. "You must be joking."

He laughed too. "No, I'm not kidding. Don't tell me you've met my sister."

"You aren't joking," Tedda said. She felt a ball of anxiety in her gut.

Seeing her expression, Eduard paled. "Don't tell me something has happened to her."

Tedda made fists, winced at her own pain, and felt tears welling up. "I'm sorry. I don't want to have to tell you this. I held her in my arms as she died."

He lost his humor and looked crushed. "I see." He sat down heavily on one of the glossy, blond wooden benches. He held his head in his hands and sat like that for a few long minutes. She sat beside him, putting her arm around his back. He shook slightly, as if sobbing. Then he appeared to be hardly breathing. She grew alarmed. "Are you okay?"

He was silent for another minute. Then he looked up as if he'd awakened from a long sleep. He looked about as if checking for danger. Then he looked at her. "Are you okay?"

"I was asking you the same question."

"I'm a rule," he said matter-of-factly. "Rules tend to be all right. When we aren't, it usually means we no longer exist."

"I'm afraid I don't understand."

He looked directly in her eyes, with that same direct, cool gray look as his late sister. "You should. You worked for the central fatherland government. You helped create us."

"What?" She was upset at the thought that she might have participated in such questionable experiments and technologies.

"You don't remember," he stated as much as asked.

She sighed. "I'm afraid I can't remember, because I've been drugged. I'm not sure I want to remember."

"You might not," he said dubiously. He had a quality of naïve innocence that made his personality different from the harsher, more direct tactical personality of his soldier sister. "In any case," he said, "I am here to help you."

"Do you know anything about the people who have now twice spread me open like a cow to be butchered, and stuck all kinds of things in me?"

He pursed his lips with sorry recognition. "Your own West Gotha people wired you because they've been tracking you in the hope you'd lead them to Hedrock. Our people were forced to remove the West Gotha hardware. I'm sure it hurts like hell, and I'm sorry."

"You're really East Gotha?"

He nodded. "You are supposed to hate us, but it's time to get over that. You knew that before all this started. You were a leader."

"What do you want to help me with, besides surviving?"

"To get back to West Gotha. To work with Hedrock to save your world."

"How exactly were he and I trying to accomplish this?"

"Do you remember any of your published papers, Doctor?"

"Doctor!"

"You don't remember? You are a quant, a professor of mathematics. You practically invented the femtoworld."

She shook her head. "Does Hedrock know all this?"

He nodded. "He loved you enough to marry you, though he seduced many women during this spying."

"And how do you know him?"

Eduard looked at her wistfully. "I am a rule based on him. My sister was, too."

"I am sorry you lost your sister." Tedda's eyes grew moist and itchy again. She could still see the fading light in Hadley's eyes.

He nodded. "I was able to process through most of my grief a few minutes ago. I will grieve more when there is time."

"Sort of mechanical, are you?"

"Rules can be anything we set them up to be. My sister was a soldier. I am a guide."

"A guide? So you will guide me where I need to go?"

"Yes. And I have a message for you."

They rose. He led her to the One Line train step. She'd already seen a few trains head off toward the Blue Station, Yellow Station, Orange Station, and beyond. "Hedrock says he loves you more than ever, and is determined to stick with your plan even if it means you die together."

She nodded slowly. "I saw some of that passion in your sister's eyes."

His turn to nod: "She was a lot more like Hedrock than I am. She was passionate and fiery. I'm afraid I am rather easy going." The train pulled up, and doors opened. Some passengers got on while others got off. Eduard guided her into a clean, gray-rubber-lined coach where they took seats on orange and yellow padded benches. An attractive 40ish woman sat opposite with large bags from shopping in women's clothing stores. The other passengers were the usual mix of businessmen going home with their suits, coats, umbrellas, and hats; schoolchildren heading home, yawning, far too late; men, women of all walks of life; and not a single soldier or militia person among them. Eduard spoke softly so only Tedda could hear: "You should remember something about rules. There are two main kinds. One is the rule that is attached to a living person from which the rule is spun, and connected by a deep empathic Go-level channel; and the other is the free-floating rule, whose source person has died or never existed. Kind of a samurai rule. My sister and I are connected to Hedrock, so we are the more durable rules. We just vanish if our owner ceases to exist, or if we are killed like my sister was. The other kind, the free-floaters, they also cease to exist if they tried to relocate from one femto-plane to another."

"I don't quite get you," Tedda said.

"I know. Sorry. It means that, since I'm a connected rule, I can go with you to the Gotha worlds. If I were a free-floater, I would simply vanish."

Tedda recalled the way rules vanished, and tilted her face up to signal enlightenment at what he was saying. She could see again the mosaic pieces of Hadley falling like the finest powder and vanishing before they hit the street, leaving just a momentary twinkle here and there. She prodded: "So what else can you tell me?"

Eduard said: "Both East and West Gotha drilled down into this femtoworld."

"Who created it?"

"Your side."

"Meaning."

"West."

"I see." She found this shocking. It went against all her lifelong conditioning to not hate the rule sitting beside her.

"Get over it," he said with surprising firmness, almost with the true Hedrock fire. "The days of Leader Moss and his syndicate are coming to an end."

Leader Moss... Now what did that mean?

"I see you are still grappling with information," he said. "They kept you pumped full of drugs, which must be wearing off. I should warn you, though—some of it may kick in again when we get to West Gotha."

Her lifetime of conditioning kicked in with alarm bells again. "What are you going to do there?"

"Relax. We are going to shut down the huge energy field that Moss and his gang have had running for at least three generations to separate our world into two halves that hate each other for no reason so that the war industry can profiteer. And of course the Moss clan owns much of it on both sides of the wall."

"And how are we going to stop this?"

"You had published papers saying that this intereality project could lead to an uncontrolled reaction that would make the whole earth explode."

"I see. It's coming back to me a little bit." She held her head between stiff fingers and closed her eyes, trying to concentrate. There were vague snippets of thought, images, but nothing coherent. "Tell me more."

"You and a few colleagues invented the intereality principle. That involves taking data basing a million steps further by creating miniature rooms or worlds in which a mix of real and virtual objects can be stored or manipulated. At its simplest, it means taking matter and reducing it vastly in size by removing some of the Go energy underlying everything, thus reducing the distance among baryonic particles (subatomic protons, neutrons, electrons, and their fragments). You could theoretically do a lot of things—like create a miniature city, Monopol City for example, on an overcrowded world. You could perhaps even store a million people on a generation space ship, using a far slower time in the femtoworld, so that they could travel a thousand years but only age a day. The possibilities are limitless. Using subtle quantum properties, you could reduce a group of mining engineers and their equipment on Earth, and relocate them almost instantly to a receiving station on Mars, using deep Go channels. You opened up a whole new universe of possibilities. And then you discovered a serious catch."

"What's that?"

"There is a balance-imbalance principle you discovered, or bal-imbal, as they call it in the trade. According to this balimbal principle, these artificially reduced worlds are never stable. They will either expand or contract in some time period based on a complicated mix of factors that scientists don't have a handle on yet. So a world like this will either implode and vanish, or else it will cause a runaway chain reaction that could be more powerful than a million hydrogen bombs or like the antimatter bomb that both sides have been working on for years."

"Another way to destroy the world," she said bitterly.

"All for the benefit of the Moss clan," he added.

"So what is the biggest triggering factor?"

"Energy pooling. The problem is that the earliest experiments at your laboratories, in creating a small room or maybe a warehouse, grew into this Monopol world, to which the Bit Cave engineers of West Gotha added another layer of energy by spinning off a game world. The problem is that East and West stole each other's technologies and duplicated each other's research, and they wound up with a number of separate femtoworlds that merged (without human interference) until this whole city and its oceans and deserts and outlying communities were created. According to your own calculations, the tolerance limit is rapidly approaching, and then the whole thing blows. It might blow off a mile-deep layer of the earth and totally destroy mankind."

"But Eduard," she said, "I already see signs of decay. If anything, this world will implode."

He looked startled. "If that's the case—and I can't see it—then we are doomed. Our whole world here is being starved of energy. Isn't that so? They use nuclear reactors to generate the energy it takes to keep these miniature worlds alive. It's like throwing a billion or a trillion balls in the air and juggling."

She could see the picture. "Yes, I suspect you are right. One side or the other has turned down its reactors. For some reason or another, perhaps for safety reasons, this Monorail world is being powered down until it shrinks out of existence. Sad, isn't it?"

He continued her line of thought: "All these lives, all this civilization, this splendid peace, and it's fading like a dream."

The train stopped at Blue Station and they got off. He led her through a series of lesser and lesser streets toward some hidden East Gotha gate upworld. "Funny," she said, "I don't see any more of those cracks in the texture of the world."

"I don't either. I've never seen them. Are you sure you weren't dreaming?"

She shook her head. "I'm afraid maybe it means I am being absorbed here, since I've been here too long."

"Ah, yes. Well, you won't have to worry about that much longer, because I'll have you back home before long."

They stopped at a nondescript door on a back street lit by street lamps and ambient night light. He jangled a bunch of ordinary keys on a little chain, until he found the right key and unlocked the door. Pulling the door open, he gestured for her to go inside. She stepped into a concrete block stairwell much like the one that had brought her here, and which the tankbots had blown up. He flicked on a light switch, and fluorescent light bars popped on above. With her eyes, she followed the succession of crunching, groaning, and popping fluoros up a seemingly endless series of steps. He pointed upward. "Your home is up there. Don't take any right turns, because those will put you into East Gotha space, and you might be arrested by the authorities there. Remember, Hedrock is wanted by both sides." He indicated the stairway with his eyes. "Ready to start climbing?"

"Thank God you are along to protect me."

"Let's get going then."

They started up the plain staircase with its white-painted tubular steel railings.

The stairs turned left, left, left, until she began to tire from climbing. Eventually, gasping for breath, they put their arms around one another's back for support. Tedda's aching spots began to burn, and he gave her some anesthetic salve which she applied while he looked away. Where there were right turns, they hurried past for fear of making a mistake in their fatigue.

Finally, they came to the top flight. There was no place higher to go. A battleship-gray steel door marked only with the stenciled red letter B offered the only way forward. Eduard grasped the handle and turned. It opened, and she stumbled into the hangar housing the Bit Cave. Eduard followed close behind. He said to her: "Tedda, you know that Hedrock must still be alive." She stopped and stared at him, trying to fathom his meaning. He extended his arms outward and explained with a bright expression: "A rule is meant to exist in his or her world of origin. A free-floating rule can travel down to a lower plane without harm, but not upward or upworld. The very fact that I am still alive tells you Hedrock is still alive. And he is probably well, knowing what a slippery character he is."

"Why do I care?" she snapped, resuming her climb.

"Because you love him, and you'll want to find him."

"And why do you care?"

"Because you are our world's only hope."

Chapter 37

As she entered the Bit Cave area, for a moment Tedda thought nothing had changed. Heart pounding, she walked from the exchange area out to the work area. Eduard trailed close behind. She half expected to see empty cubicles, and maybe some flowers in memory of those who had perished.

People sat at their desks and worked as if nothing had happened. A few looked up and nodded or smiled or waved hello. Lindy stepped out from behind her cubicle carrying a thick printout, and looked surprised. "Oh, Tedda, where have you been? I was looking for you so we could go to lunch."

"I was—busy," Tedda said cautiously. "What time is it?"

"Almost time to go home. I figured you must have been wandering around in the halls near your office. Say, who's your friend?"

"Eduard."

Eduard said politely: "We work together—down below."

"Oh." Lindy shrugged, accepting that information. "Okay. Let me know when you are ready to head home." She strode off with her printouts.

"My roommate," Tedda told Eduard. "I see some of the people that were killed below. Am I dreaming?"

Eduard whispered: "Rules. They are replacements. Your fatherland doesn't want to let on that anything has happened. It's knee-jerk secrecy. The first instinct is always to lie, to deny, to cover up. Truth is the last option when all else fails."

Tedda nodded to Jakko, or his rule, and he waved back. He looked preoccupied—a far more serious and toned-down Jakko than the joker she'd left among the street of bodies in a Monopol City suburb.

Out lumbered Wally (or his rule). "Hi, Tedda. Glad to see you made it back. Who is your friend?"

"One of the techs down in my area."

He nodded and said to Eduard: "Next time, wear your badge or the guards are likely to lock you up."

"Oh darn." Eduard made a pretense of patting the pockets of his herringbone jacket. "I'll have to go back and get it."

"Get a visitor pass for now. Tedda, you'll need to vouch for him."

"Sure, Wally. Do you happen to have one handy?"

"Here." Wally rummaged in his upper desk tray, found a plain badge with *Visitor* printed on it, and threw it on the desk. "You can turn it in for me."

"Thanks."

Tedda and Eduard stepped into an empty cubicle that she chose at random. She sat on the desk, he in the chair. "What now?" she asked.

"I've never been in West Gotha," he said.

"And I've never been in East Gotha."

"I think you have. You just don't remember."

She held her head in her hands and shook it. "What am I going to do? What?"

"I think we must figure out how to get your identity back. We must get your memories back, and maybe that involves getting you back to your work place. You were in charge of a large building of laboratories and test facilities on the edge of the city. Maybe if we go there?"

"How would I get in?"

"We have to try something. Even if you just see the building from outside, it might jog you into remembering more. We could try taking it one step at a time, one little memory after the other, until it's all back."

She embraced him, kissing him on each cheek. He squeezed back affectionately, with that mild lack of arousal she'd been noticing. He reminded her almost of a neutered cat. Apparently the real Hedrock was an acrobat of sensuality and seduction. This derivative of his must have been designed not to wrestle her into bed at first sight. She grinned privately at the thought. She could not even remember what Hedrock looked like, and she only vaguely felt herself feeling heated up at the thought of an amorphous someone whose name happened to be Alton Hedrock, to whom she apparently was married and with whom she was supposedly trying to save the world. It all sounded so crazy that some of it might actually be true. Curiosity was beginning to be her dominant passion—a sure sign that some of the fatherland's medicines were continuing to wear off.

"Should I tell Lindy that I am working late and she should go home by herself?"

"You mean Moira?"

This struck an odd, disturbing note in her. "What?"

Eduard looked confused also. "I think she is called that. Moira Lindy. She is Wally Tonsonby's assistant in real life. I remember that from my formation. Your name is actually Amy Tedda, but secretly you married Alton and are now Amy Hedrock." He looked apologetic and pained. "I'm sorry, it's just disjointed information I can't explain except to regurgitate."

"Oh God." Tedda sat down hard. "Amy Tedda. Yes, that's me. Amy von Tedda. My family owned large land holdings that were confiscated by the Moss Syndicate decades ago. There was a lot of bitterness in the family about it, but then as the Moss Group took over the global trade, nobody could stop them, and there was a lot of bitterness everywhere, so my family weren't alone."

She closed her eyes and shook, trying to hold on to the edge of the desk beside her as fragments of memory roiled up. "I was being taken to prison for murder, and the person I murdered was Moira Lindy. Much as he professed to love me, and I believe he did, he couldn't stay out of other women's knickers. I think he was still spying for the East while I was working on him, trying to convince him to take my warnings back to his superiors in East Gotha. I caught him in bed with her, and I ran her through with a kitchen knife. He managed to escape, but I was tried and imprisoned for her murder. I was being transported in a prison van, when we were washed away during a flood, and I ended up breaking free and wound up at this institute."

She broke free and ran, out into the graying dawn. She ran, a lone figure fleeing uphill on the cobblestone street between high walls where she and Lindy walked every day. The university on her left, the walled fortress of her prison on her right, she ran up the hill, curving right where the high grass blew in the wind by the old fortress gate. She ran into the fortress grounds, across the ancient green parade fields that were now parks. She ran among the whispering trees whose huge crowns bent down sadly. She ran down the crunching pathway along the white wall until she came to the Confessor's recess in the wall. There she stopped, heart beating wildly, and leaned against the wall to catch her breath. She heard him stirring inside, making questioning groans. "Is someone out there?" his deep voice rumbled.

She forced herself around the corner and entered the long, narrow room with its high ceiling. Before her eyes adjusted to the gloom, she saw what looked like a waxy moon gleaming. As she approached, the moon seemed to rise. It was the Confessor, raising his head from a sleeping state to look at her. He smiled with mysterious warmth. "Come in, child. I am always here to hear your confessions."

She stood before him, knees trembling, but regarding him with the utmost courage. She understood that this thing imprisoned in here, wrapped in silk robes and attached to the wall like a slug though it had a human torso, was a rule. "I have come to ask about Moira Lindy," she said.

"Ah yes," Confessor Grün said. He leaned back under his robes and folded his arms. She noticed he had long fingers with mandarin-like fingernails that had never been clipped. "Did you come to confess the truth and seek fatherland's absolution?"

"No, I came to find the truth, but I'm not sure I'll find it here."

The Confessor slapped a panel at his side, probably to summon help. "You must kneel down and show respect."

"I'm happy standing. Now why don't you tell me the truth for once? What is this place? Why am I here?"

"Why, this is West Gotha, my child. You are a loyal and patriotic citizen of our beloved fatherland."

She advanced on the thing. "You have kept me here, drugged and oblivious. Why?"

"Tedda!" said Lindy's voice behind her.

"Stay back, Lindy," Tedda said. She pointed at the Confessor. "End this now!"

The Confessor grinned smugly. "My dear, nobody can end what is happening. We are about to finally defeat East Gotha and save the world."

"And rule the world," she said, "the Moss Syndicate wants to rule the world for its own purposes."

"How dare you!" the voice rumbled, and the Confessor's face contorted with outrage as his eyes grew wide.

"Tedda, no!" Lindy screamed.

Moving slowly as if in a dream, Tedda looked back at her roommate. Lindy could not possibly know the truth, or she would already have hinted at something. No, they must have her more doped up than they'd had Tedda.

"Please," a man's voice cried out. It was Eduard, who had found them and now stood frozen in the doorway for a moment, a shadowy figure arrested in motion, with one hand on the stone lintel. "Come out of there."

"Stop, Tedda!" Lindy cried.

"How dare you!" the Confessor boomed.

Tedda stooped down to pick up a melon-sized boulder.

Eduard rushed into the passageway and restrained Lindy, who kicked and screamed in her efforts to reach Tedda.

"You cannot win," said Confessor Grün, reaching toward Tedda in his (or its) black silk robes while its long-nailed fingers writhed in eager anticipation of wringing her neck or gouging her eyes out.

Tedda raised the stone high. Confessor Grün shrank back and tried to shield his face.

Chapter 38

Tonsonby joined Leader Moss, who had invited him to have tea in a high lookout just big enough for a square table, a few chairs, a few leather pieces against the aluminum and glass walls overlooking gorgeous vistas of the city. Orderlies and servants came and went through the flower-lined and long-windowed passageway connecting the sky patio with the main bulk of the administrative headquarters. The tunnel actually connected directly to Leader's spacious offices, where he held court or dallied with young female staffers or whatever a beloved and high-ranking member of the Moss Syndicate did.

Tonsonby had come to despise the Moss Syndicate, but he resolved for the sake of family ties and creature comforts—not to mention the bodily safety of his wife and children—to play the game and continue making Leader happy.

Moss gloated as he stirred his sugared tea. "So, Tonsonby, you have come to redeem yourself."

"If you will permit me the honor," Tonsonby said. He always had a fearful tremor in his knees when he was around Moss.

"Good," Moss said, licking his spoon and setting it down. He sat back and looked out over the city. "Soon, I will launch that MIRV with its many warheads, and knock East Gotha out. Then our troops will swarm across and take the key points, and this entire multi-generation war will be over. A great victory." He raised his glass.

Tonsonby raised his glass, and they clicked glasses in a toast before drinking the steaming liquid. "A great victory, my Leader."

"I am pleased to hear that you have a solid lead on Hedrock's whereabouts."

"I do, Leader, and it's only a matter of time. All my people have been committed to the task. All my resources."

"The fatherland is grateful. You lost him when he drove his truck over the cliff and landed in the houses below, but your technicians were able to triangulate the signal that his organization beamed to kill our MIRV rocket."

"Yes, Leader."

"Excellent. Now, I'm curious. What was the give-away, the clue, the hint, that broke the case for you?"

Tonsonby sipped his tea with some relish. He had done well with this, and could afford a little pridefulness of his own. "They masked their signals well, as we knew they would. However, as you say, there was one tiny detail that they overlooked and this gave them away."

"Yes? Yes?" Moss leaned eagerly forward.

Tonsonby enjoyed telling his story. "Leader, as you know, we watch a lot of people."

"Yes, excellent. Well?"

"When the van went over the cliff, it automatically sent out a repair station alert signal. It's a feature we build into our military vehicles to alert the operator to a tire going flat, let's say, or the need for an oil change. Saves resources. Oddly, this signal went to a different sort of place."

"Yes? Yes?"

"We were able to locate the target and found it was a secret repair depot registered to a blind corporation, owned by someone we've had our eye on for a long time—a scion of an old West Gotha family that lost its properties in the ongoing war. We sense feelings of resentment, however unfairly, against our patriotic government."

"Go on."

"This turned out to be a possible enemy agent we identified as Felix. You may recall the dossier."

"I vaguely recall something about a spy network headed by someone codenamed Felix."

"To jog your memory, Leader, Felix is the oldest son of a long-established family that continues to send sons to the military academies and daughters to the nursing corps. Felix has been spending a lot of time circulating around Amy von Tedda and her clan, if you get my drift."

"Oh, clearly," Leader said gleefully. "Well done!"

"So, one thing leading to another, we were able to trace Hedrock's possible movements through the city and we think he is going to appear shortly at a safe house run by Felix and his gang. If he does show up, we might have him in our clutches as early as tonight."

"Wonderful! If you succeed, expect to be a brigadier general this year."

"Leader!" Tonsonby felt truly touched, and his resentment evaporated. He thought what the extra money and authority might mean to his family in terms of added rations and privileges.

"It's a trifle," Moss said dismissively. "See how we take care of our own, particularly when they do well. And you, my dear Tonsonby, have done very well indeed. Get me Hedrock on a platter, and I'll be grateful."

Chapter 39

Tedda's aim was true, as she raised the stone high and tossed it with all her might. Confessor Grün shrank back and tried to shield his face. The rock embedded itself in Confessor Grün' face, which spattered apart in all directions like a smashed egg. As Tedda, Lindy, and Eduard watched, the Confessor Grün rule shimmered into many tiny mosaic pieces that drifted apart and then all at once fell to the ground and vanished. Tedda had a disgusted glimpse of the robes opening, revealing a large, grayish spiral like s mollusk inside its shell. It was attached to the wall, and where it had been, was a round wet spot that slowly dried up. Only a dry, foul mushroom smell lingered.

"Murderer!" Lindy screamed hoarsely. Her voice tore at Tedda's eardrums in this confined space. Eduard slowly let Lindy go. Tedda strode past her, saying "Let's get out of this foul place."

Eduard followed to make sure Lindy wouldn't become violent. Lindy ran alongside Tedda speaking in gleeful, cruel tones. "I know why you are in here. It's for killing a woman, isn't it? You bitch. You drove your man mad and when you found him playing around, you killed her. What did he see in her that he didn't see in you? Bitch!"

"Shut up, Lindy," Tedda said, "you don't know what you're talking about." She resisted the urge to yell back that it was Moira she had killed, and that she felt sick about it, but what was done was done and they must all live on as best they could. She said simply: "Whatever I did, and may I remind you, miss righteousness, whatever you did, we did in another time and place."

Eduard caught up with them. "You're right, Tedda. Lindy, the worst thing you can do is beat each other up over imaginary wrongs."

Lindy turned on him with fierce eyes. "Imaginary! You have a nerve talking."

Eduard said calmly: "Do you know whom she is accused of murdering?"

Lindy shook her head in confusion and denial. Her eyes suddenly radiated dread and anticipation as the veil of falsehood began to crack.

Eduard said: "Does the name Moira Lindy mean anything to you?"

Lindy shook her head, but her eyes widened as memory apparently poured in. She raised her hands to her face and began to scream loudly. "No-o!"

"I'm sorry," Eduard said dutifully. "The truth can only help us, even if it is painful."

"I didn't want you to know," Tedda.

Lindy regarded her with unbelieving and speechless outrage.

They all heard a shout, and turned, just in time to see a terribly upset Wally Tonsonby. He must have looked into the Confessor's slot, guessed something had happened, and cried out in horror. As he turned, he slipped on wet loam and fell to one knee. Lurching up, he ran toward them pulling a revolver from his pocket. "What's going on here?"

Tedda realized it was the same weapon his rule had brandished down in Monopol City before dying in a hail of bullets. She faced Tonsonby and said: "You aren't just a technician or a lead software engineer, are you?"

"I don't know what you are talking about."

"I think you do," Tedda said. She did flinch then, because he cocked the hammer with a click that seemed to echo across the park under the wind-blown trees. For a long moment the four figures stood looking at one another. "Are you going to kill me?" Tedda asked. He stared at her, and she continued: "If the fatherland wanted me dead, they would have killed me long ago. You need me for some reason, don't you?"

Eduard cleared his throat. "They want to hunt down Hedrock. That's what it seems to be."

"Who is Hedrock?" Lindy said, her eyes still slits of hurt and fury, her fists balled at her sides.

"Your lover," Tedda said. "My husband."

Lindy's eyes opened wide in horror. "You—bitch! That is ridiculous. This gets more crazy by the moment."

"Easy," Eduard whispered to Tedda, "spare her."

"What are you talking about?" Wally said, aiming the revolver at Eduard.

Eduard regarded him coldly. "You're most likely a rule just like I am. Like Lindy here. Shoot me, and you accomplish nothing."

Wally looked from one to the other, and slowly uncocked his revolver and put it back in a secret holster at his back, under his jacket. "One of you killed the Confessor."

"Just another rule," Eduard quickly countered, before Wally could single out Tedda as the likely perpetrator.

"I've reached the end of the line," Tedda said. She was amazed at her own calmness and coldness. "I am tired of being screwed around with. I'd rather be dead than have to go near another horror like that snail thing in the hole there." She indicated the now-lifeless Confessor slot in the long white wall. Then she turned to Eduard. "Will you help me find my way back to my laboratory so I can read my papers and figure out what is going one, what I have to do next for our country?"

Eduard regarded her sympathetically. "I'll be glad to help, but I have only a vague idea where it is." He pointed away from the fortress, out over the university, and toward the cloudy horizon where East Gotha lay. "Somewhere out that way near the border."

Tedda looked at Wally. "Do you know where my laboratory is?"

He looked slightly confused. "I don't know now." He seemed to try to think. "I have a car, and we could take that. I guess you are right. The fatherland must need you, if they have gone to all this trouble to lock you up and keep you alive and even give you so much freedom."

Lindy said: "If she gets out, I'm going along."

"No," Eduard said quickly, "for your own sake, please don't do it."

Lindy pointed at Wally and yelled: "If you don't take me along, I'm going straight to the top. I'll turn you in as a traitor for letting this woman out of prison. They may spare her, but they'll execute you."

"Easy," Wally said.

"Lindy," Eduard said, "you don't understand. You and I are rules. That means we are people spun off from other people. We are created to do a job, to accomplish a purpose."

"What kind of nonsense is that?" Lindy looked close to tears.

Tedda started to explain: "Lindy, I think they wanted you close to me to keep an eye on me."

"Oh shut up!" Lindy yelled in Tedda's face.

Tedda tried once more: "Lindy, I'm accused of killing Moira, your source."

"Shut up, liar! Bitch!"

Eduard said: "It's important that you understand this, Lindy. Rules are not VR programs nor artificial beings. We are real people, spun off as part of the environment around us. We are copies, in a way, but we are each totally original, just like our source people. We don't die like they do, and the rules for our survival are a little different.

"If we stay in our realm of creation, like I was created or born in Monopol City, we live normal lives and die like any flesh and blood. This is all driven by the Go-dot subquark layer of reality, which is the basement of the basement of the basement of the house, so to speak. Its rules aren't magic but science; a science far ahead of its time, though Dr. Tedda took us on a great leap forward.

"My source and Wally's source are still alive, Lindy, but yours isn't. That's the problem. If you leave here, then I'm not even sure you can get back here even if you believe us and try to turn around."

"Lies," Lindy said. "I've been cooped up here for years, and I'm sick of it. Like this bitch here, I've had it. I'd rather die than stay here another day. I think it's terribly unjust that she killed someone and gets to leave here, but I only killed the man who was raping me, and I have to stay here forever." She bawled heartbrokenly: "They don't even tell you how long your sentence is. That's part of their cruelty. I can't stand this anymore!"

"Don't," Eduard cautioned.

Wally relented. "Okay, Lindy, you're in. Let's go."

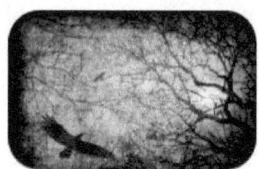

They walked together down the cobblestone walkway.

"Sh!" Wally said at one point, spreading his arms.

They stood silently and listened.

All Tedda heard was the brushing back and forth of long willow fronds dappled with sunshine.

"I thought I heard hooves riding on the hill there," Wally said, pointing to the far end of the fortress. "Never mind, I must have been hearing things."

Chapter 40

Still hurt from his multistory drop in the van—and only saved by the intervening trees and then the roof collapsing, while he was secure in his harness and bucket seat so that his bones were not mashed in a welter of blood—Captain Alton Hedrock limped along the deserted nighttime streets of West Gotha. Military patrols, seeing his West Gotha uniform, asked for his papers, and he showed them. They seemed puzzled that he wasn't riding in a staff car, but he explained that there had been some informalities and exigencies (he winked, indicating some sort of embarrassing dalliance) and they let him go. He figured the van had sent its signal, and Felix would know what to do. He could have telephoned Felix's organization, but thought better of it. Why invite the West Gotha dicks to zoom in on him? Felix would know what to do. Dreamily, he thought of how nice it would be if Amy would hide him for a few weeks until he healed. What a bit of heaven it would be to have some time with her. Then he remembered that she had not been seen for a while, and the thinking was that the Moss Syndicate were holding her prisoner somewhere.

He took a taxi part of the way, then walked the last few blocks through narrow city streets that seemed more Parisian than West Gotha. He smelled wine, sausage, and heard laughter, violin music, conversation—now if only life could be like that. Or was it the pain killers he'd been popping?

As he approached the safe house owned by someone in the Felix-Amy sphere of operations, he felt the small handgun in his side pocket. He turned its safety off and then on again. Better safe than sorry or dead.

He turned the corner and walked the last hundred feet down a neat, dull street of concrete and windows. He knocked on the door as prescribed. No answer. He looked right, then left, and punched the finger-code into the key pad. The door next to the key pad swung open. He limped inside, glad to be safe, and looking forward to a hot shower and a beer, then sleep. "Felix?" *No answer.* He stormed forward, turning on the light and pulling out the gun at the same time. *Nobody.* He stood holding the gun and listened suspiciously. *Silence.* He laughed to himself and put the gun in his pocket. Eagerly, he limped to the refrigerator in the clean little kitchen and opened it, hoping to find a cold beer. The fridge was empty.

Hearing a noise behind himself, he turned.

Two men stood there. One was just a big dumb guy they'd hired. The other was that stupid Tonsonby. Both brandished small hand guns and had the situation rather under their control.

How did they get onto and into this safe house? Hedrock eyeballed the two, and the lay of the land, looking for a way to hurt them, kill them, startle them, anything to win his way out of this losing position.

"I want to take you alive," Tonsonby said.

"I think there is a misunderstanding. All I wanted was a beer."

"We'll get you all the beer you need."

"I don't understand," Hedrock said thinking of the handgun he'd just put in his pocket. "I have my papers here in my pocket." He reached down.

Tonsonby yelled "No, don't!" but the big stupid guy with him fired. Hedrock saw the repeated muzzle flashes. He even saw Tonsonby yell in anger and turn and shoot his own ally, who went down looking stupid and died faster than Hedrock could.

"Fuxl!" was the last thing Hedrock heard as he lay bleeding on the carpet. It smelled funny, of rug cleaner, in that odd sweet little way Amy had. He decided to think of her, now that the darkness was closing in.

Chapter 41

They strode out the gate together, to a huge fancy car. It was glossy green with white trim. The roof was white, and aerodynamically shaped like the rest of the car. It had wrap-down fins and long red taillights. "My pride and joy," Wally said. "It's a 1959 Mercury. Just had it repainted recently. Check out the chrome." He pointed to the gleaming silvery strips along the doors.

They all got in, and Wally started up the powerful 8-cylinder engine. Lindy rode shotgun in the front. Tedda sat behind Wally, while Eduard sat to her right. Wally rolled the windows down. "Automatic," he told them. As the car jumped forward, he reached under the seat. He steered with one hand, while groping with the other, and the car made a quick, powerful turn around the green island outside the gate. As the car rumbled downhill of the cobblestones where Lindy and Tedda had walked every day, Wally said "Ta-daaa!" He produced a plain brown flimsy cardboard package. It was a box, which he handed to Lindy. "Go on, open it."

Lindy's eyes lit up in wonder and delight.

"What is it?" Tedda and Eduard both said in the back seat. They were unable to see what she was staring down at. Lindy smiled for the first time, and held up a pair of white fuzzy dice with black dots. "Fuzzy dice," she said, "like in the movies."

"Go on," Wally said, "hang them on the mirror. Got to do this right."

Lindy dutifully shifted her butt to the middle of the front seat and busied herself. The tip of her tongue protruded as she fastened the dice under the wide rearview mirror. "Does this mean we are going steady?" she said grinning.

"If you want," Wally said. He put his arm around her shoulders, and she pressed close against him.

Tedda and Eduard exchanged questioning, worried glances. *He is trying to make it easy for her,* Tedda thought. Eduard's look suggested the thought *I think she may know.*

It was a long drive, taking much of the day. Tedda was surprised at how large West Gotha really was—the city, the countryside, the continent, the world. The air grew clear and sunny. They drove through rolling fields. Farmers waved from amid their hedgerows and village lanes. The road was little more than a two-lane blacktop, but it was marvelously straight. The macadam was black and fresh, and the median line pure white and clean as if it had all been painted recently. The sky was clear blue, except for some fluffy mint-white cumulus clouds. Tedda spied the soaring black figures of many birds, large and small. Some birds were so close that she could see the greenish-red gleam of their feathers, the whites of their eyes, the dark dot of the bird's throat as it opened its beak to chirp hungrily.

Farm tractors stuttered back and forth along brown furrows. Fields of green corn and lettuce and tomatoes stretched far to the right and left. The road headed straight on, passing through towns with smoking chimneys atop matte orange clay roofs. Herds of cows wandered in meadows gleaming with puddles of standing rain water. The healthy smell of fresh manure arose from various domesticated animals. Wally and Lindy enjoyed their closeness, and muttered softly between each other.

They made a few short stops at various gas stations and diners. In one place they had a potty stop and bought gasoline. Eduard took Tedda aside briefly and said, eyeballing the distant Lindy who was walking happily hand in hand with Wally: "Doesn't she get it? Can't we stop her?" Tedda's mind wasn't entirely clear again, as if the very air here was drugging her again. Or maybe it was all this fresh, thick air like cold dairy milk. She could only shrug and walk away from Eduard's concerns. Eduard's voice floated after her: "There will only be three of us coming back, Tedda."

In another place they munched smoky hot dogs on buns, smothered in relish, ketchup, mustard, and onions. Wally and Eduard each polished off a large frosty looking golden beer in a brown glass bottle, while Lindy drank health tea and Tedda opted for crystal clear bottled water.

Late in the day, they were cruising along with the windows open, singing and laughing, while the radio played old rock tunes from long ago, appropriate to the style and era of car.

"Are we getting close yet?" Tedda asked. "How far out is this laboratory of mine?"

Eduard shrugged and withdrew into himself. He looked tired, and seemed to want to doze. Lindy, too, yawned. She said: "Too much fresh air." She glanced back fondly at her roommate, conflict forgotten. Tedda smiled back at her, glad Lindy had found romance with Wally. Tedda impulsively reached forward and patted Lindy's hand, which lay on the seat behind Wally's neck. Tedda was glad later that she had done that, though Lindy pulled the hand away and looked out the window toward the opposite side.

"Something is coming up ahead," Wally said cheerfully. "Must be the lights of East Gotha. I think we're almost to the border. Your laboratories and offices were somewhere near the border on our side, I remember that much. Look for a big sign that says Tedda Industries, or something along those lines."

"Yes!" Tedda said excitedly. "I remember something about that. I have a picture in my mind. I think there were long white buildings and a blue plastic sign with huge letters that said something like von Tedda Industries Gmbh, or something along those lines."

"It is getting a little cold," Wally said. Now he too was yawning. He rolled up the window and turned on the heater. The cabin filled with a dry warmth tinged with a faint, comforting aroma of light machine oil. Wally turned on the radio, and searched for some music, but the stations were growing increasingly staticky. In the end, he turned the radio off.

"Look!" Lindy said. "An aurora borealis."

Tedda leaned forward and frowned. "What is that thing, Wally?"

He shrugged. "Looks like a force field. Could East Gotha be beyond there?"

Eduard sat up, shivering. He was pale, and hugging himself. "It's not an aurora and it's not the border. It's the end of the world."

Tedda and Wally looked at Eduard. Lindy turned and looked over the back of her seat at Eduard, then resumed her forward looking position.

"What's going on?" Wally said, slowing. He had beads of sweat popping out on his forehead, and drew shuddering breaths.

"Maybe we can still turn around now," Tedda said in alarm, clutching the door handle with her left hand and the back of Wally's seat with the other. Her hands were trembling.

"Wally?" Lindy asked, looking at him with alarmed curiosity.

"This isn't the top world," Eduard said. "I should have figured that out already. That is the end of this femtobase. We're cooked."

"Wally!" Tedda cried, beating on his shoulder. "Stop the car! Turn around."

Like a drunk's, Wally's head slumped forward and his foot grew heavier on the gas pedal. The car speeded up. Tedda heard the powerful engine purr, and the wheels hum on the smooth road surface.

"That looks like the ocean out there," Lindy said. She sat stiffly back, a pale image of fear. In the back, Eduard sobbed quietly. Tedda remained simply confused and frightened.

The wall of greenish-orange light, rippling and moving silently, approached quickly. Behind them, Tedda caught one last frightened glance of the normal world: a truck parked in a bean field; a rusting pump on a crumbling concrete apron in an abandoned gas station; a crow, fluttering to a landing on a tree branch as night fell.

The car sailed into the rippling barrier, and the light in the car turned dim orange, then dimmer dark green like under the sea. Only it wasn't the sea. It was the dying light at the edge of the world.

Lindy turned into a mosaic and crumbled away into nothing. Tedda started to scream, but then Wally winked out of existence. Tedda found herself looking at the massive steering wheel with its creamy white plastic hand guard all around. Hearing a sobbing noise on her right, she glanced over just in time to see Eduard vanish like a cloud of dust motes in bottle-green evening light.

Chapter 42

The spy named Felix arrived in his car at the safe house and knew, just from the way the lights were on and the curtains on the second floor askew, that he was too late. "Damn!" he said, pulling out his automatic. He jumped out almost while the car was still rolling—though in reality he pulled the hand brake and it was just rocking on its chassis as Felix ran across the street, through the door way, up the stairs, and into the apartment, the safe house—just in time to see the big dumb guy roll over on the carpet in his dying moment with blood spurting from several torso wounds. In the kitchen, by the open fridge, lay Captain Alton Hedrock on the floor in a pool of blood and it was immediately clear from the wounds on his head and torso that he was dying.

Still standing was Major Tonsonby, whom Felix knew quite well as a distant Moss family member and army intelligence officer. Tonsonby held a gun and now turned in shock to aim it at Felix.

Felix was quicker, unloading his own gun first. Tonsonby dropped his weapon as he sailed backwards against the wall with blood and gore splashing from various parts of his body. Felix made sure Tonsonby was finished before Felix turned his attention to Hedrock—but it was immediately clear as he leaned over the body and started CPR that Hedrock was already gone.

Chapter 43

Too horrified even to scream, Tedda sat with her mouth open and her hands pulling her cheeks down under dazed, grieving eyes of disbelief. With nobody's foot on the gas pedal, the car rolled slowly to a stop in the edge of the sea. There, the motor sputtered and died out.

It wasn't a sea of water, but a sea of free-floating Go-dots. The beach was the end of matter, which Tedda understood as that powerful layering of energy types which the human mind perceived as being both matter and energy. Here, that energy ran out. The car came to within inches of the churning, darting froth of decaying higher-order energy whirling on the deep pool of matterlessness where, literally, nothing mattered. For a while, Tedda sat staring out over the utter blackness in which not a star winked, a sea of nothing on which whitecaps of stray attenuating reality did their final dance, just like whitecaps offshore on an earthly sea.

Slowly, after a time, Tedda climbed over the seat into the driver's side. She was afraid to set foot outside. Whimpering with fear, she cranked the key. The starter whined and whined but wouldn't start. She smelled gasoline and realized she'd flooded the carburetor. As she waited to let the gasoline evaporate, she thought about what had happened. Lindy had evidently chosen to go. She must have known what was coming, and perhaps at some deeper level she knew the truth about herself. She'd always seemed to know more than Tedda. Wally—that was a surprise. It meant that his source had died already, and stepping through the energy barrier of this femtoworld had been his death sentence as a rule. Eduard—that was the biggest surprise of all. His passing meant that Hedrock was dead. Quite possibly that meant there was no hope to execute their scheme (whatever it was) and rescue the world from oblivion at the hands of the reckless and self-serving Moss Syndicate machine.

Carefully, she turned the key, and felt the engine slowly shudder to life. A few times before it kicked over, she thought it was going to die out again. But it started up, and she put it in reverse. Leaving tire marks in the sandy soup of outermost reality, she backed up. She got far enough from boiling, vapor-drifting edge to make a tight u-turn. Gunning the motor, she approached the barrier and sailed through.

She emerged unscathed on the long, empty blacktop heading back toward the fortress. She had never felt more lonely, and she almost looked forward to seeing the Jakko rule or anyone pretending to be a live human being, if she made it back. Tired to the edge of exhaustion, she forced herself to drive on and on. She ran out of gas within view of the city skyline. She could make out the towers of the university, and even the keep at the fortress where she and Lindy had roomed. Being out of gas, and having no money, she plodded along on foot.

She walked, one step after another, one step after another, until she found herself staggering up the cobblestone street between the fortress and university walls, and in ten minutes she was passed out face down on her bed.

Part 5 - End Game: A New World

Monopol City

Chapter 44

Tedda woke in the late morning. She sat up slowly, groaning, and realized she must have slept pretty much in the same face down position in which she'd landed on the bed. Her legs felt stiff from the long walk, and she felt emotionally drained from all that had happened in the last few days.

With an effort, she swung into a sitting position on the edge of the bed. Everything was very still. The sun shone in, its harshness broken by the huge trees outside. It warmed the bare, almost black floorboards. She spent a few minutes wriggling her toes on the warm floorboards and watched dust motes twirl in the lazy light. She reached under the bed, and found her plastic water bottle. It was three quarters full. She unscrewed the top, and drained the entire bottle. She tossed the bottle aside, belched, wiped the back of her wrist across her mouth, and sighed deeply. Her sigh ended abruptly as she looked across at the empty bed there. The blankets were still disturbed where Lindy had climbed out into the world yesterday, but most of her immediate effects had vanished. Tedda sat and bawled out loud for a few minutes, until her hands were dripping with tears. Slowly, her grief and exhaustion turned to anger.

She stormed to the sink and washed herself. She threw gouts of cold water repeatedly on her face and studied herself in the mirror. She patted her face dry with a towel. She changed into a fresh dark blue sweatshirt with long sleeves, dungaree pants that loosely fit her thin frame, wool socks, and soft ankle-high hiking shoes.

As she left the room and started down the stairs, she realized that part of the peacefulness she had been enjoying was from a new sense of emptiness and abandonment in the building. There was evidence everywhere of many people—a lost comb, an empty candy bar wrapper, a book of hymns lying open on a chair, a dirty towel unevenly hung on its rack in a bathroom as she passed. There were dozens of touches like this, but not a human voice anywhere. Not a soul was in evidence. She checked around the basement, hoping for something to eat, but the cafeteria was dark and shuttered. All the inmates were gone as if they had been raptured to their next life.

Tedda emerged from the building more puzzled than ever. She stood on the steps pulling her hair back with both hands and looking about. There was no sign of human life. The stillness was profound. She stepped down to the sidewalk and happened to glance down.

There she saw something that explained much. Kneeling down to look more closely, she drew her fingertip along a jagged black line running through the concrete sidewalk and right through the loam and grass on either side. It was the same phenomenon she'd seen in Monopol City. This world, too, was breaking up. She'd seen no evidence of it during her trip outward yesterday, but there had still been people here too. She remembered it had been quieter, as if some of the rules had already disappeared, but today was already drastically different.

She did not have much time to worry about the cracks appearing in the world. Through the wind sighing in the tree crowns, she heard the cantering hooves of a heavy horse. Walking to the edge of the building, she peered up the road and saw the distant white speck of Major Moss and his horse approaching.

She started to run—in the only direction she knew—toward the medical unit from which she had first set foot in this world. It was way at the other end of the fortress plateau, half a mile from her room with Lindy, half a mile from the place where she had destroyed the Confessor rule, and probably a mile from the opposite end of the diamond shaped plateau along which the white war horse and its rider now approached.

As Tedda ran, she recalled the gently sloping hillside, and there it was. As she ran around to the front of the medical prison, she looked up to the window where, not long ago, she had recovered from her near-drowning ordeal. She realized with a shock that someone was looking down at her: Nurse Amit.

Tedda smiled and waved. Nurse Amit blinked at her and stood with folded hands, but did nothing to help. Her lips were pursed, and her eyes seemed cold and calculating. "It's me, Tedda! Remember me? You promised to take care of me if I needed help."

Nurse Amit made motions of waving Tedda away. She signaled for Tedda to return the way she'd come. Seeing Tedda's distress, she changed her tune and signaled that she would come down as quickly as possible to let her in.

Tedda began to panic, for she heard the pounding hooves of the white war horse coming much closer now. No way the nurse would make it down here in time to save Tedda from the rider.

Someone else was in this part of the park: Watka, the drunken NCO. He stood on another slight grassy rise, facing away and waving a half-empty vodka bottle. He raised his arms from his sides and sang at the top of his lungs. Tedda had time only to glimpse the loose, baggy, dirty uniform, the muddy rubber boots, the askew garrison cap with its fatherland emblem in front, the open coat, and the long, stringy hair.

Hearing the rider draw near, she whirled to face her fate. Major Moss looked majestic and in control as he rode close. He wore a gray field cape over his fully decked out green uniform. He had clean, shiny belts and all his medals were in place. His high brown boots shone, and he wore a peaked cap with fatherland eagles and, on the bill, plenty of gold laureling on a red velvet background. *How magnificent he looks,* Tedda thought as he unsheathed his cavalry saber.

They don't need me anymore with Hedrock dead, she thought. *I might as well go out with dignity.* She slipped off her jacket and let it drop to the grass. She raised both hands to fumble with the collar of her sweatshirt to expose her neck. When that felt constrictive, she took the sweatshirt off and held it over her bare breasts for modesty. She bend her long neck forward, head out, face down, facing the oncoming saber blade. She glanced up once, and saw a look of pure power craziness in his eyes as he raised the saber that would take her head off in one slicing motion.

Watka continued singing and raising his arms to the stars.

She felt the ground shake as he drew near. She could see foam and sweat dripping from the horse's underbelly. She could smell the loam on Major Grün's boots and the cigar smoke in his cape. She felt the wind of the saber passing over her.

She was still alive.

Puzzled, heart pounding, she looked after the horse's powerful, huge hindquarters. Grün's cape lay parted over its bobbed stub of a tail. Its steel-shod hooves cut up flying clods of soil.

In the same instant, all this happening in a blur, she heard a scream and saw the saber slice through the neck of Nurse Amit. Her body collapsed, while her head rolled away. There was a gout of blood in the air resembling a comet tail

Major Grün barked an order at Watka to compose himself properly, even as Grün wheeled the horse about for a new charge, again directly at Tedda. Seeing the bloody saber aiming at her like an airplane wing, and the magnificent way in which Grün leaned to one side while cantering the horse slightly to the opposite in compensation, Tedda felt as if she were part of a ballet or symphony in which she was to play an important part. Once again, she kept her quiet dignity while lowering her head to expose her bare white neck.

She glimpsed the rising saber, the contraction of the green-uniformed upper arm in preparation for a downward blow, and composed herself for a dignified fall. She kept clutching her sweatshirt modestly to her breasts and hoped they would be covered when she fell.

A shot rang out. Another. Another.

The horse thundered past.

Tedda felt the wind of the twirling saber knocked free into the air, and the passing of Grün's dead empty hand that dangled from a crisply ironed sleeve below much gold and red uniform hashing.

She had no wind to scream, but stepped back and clutched her sweatshirt all the closer. The saber came to a stop tilted blade-down in the loam. The crumpled body of Major Grün lay in a broken pile on the hard stone walkway. The magnificent white horse galloped away. In the next instant, Grün's body vanished, and the white horse just seem to grow white, and silent, and then invisible as it too vanished.

Coming toward her was not Watka, but Captain Alton Hedrock. "Tedda! Are you all right?"

She recognized him. "Oh, Alton! What has happened to us?"

He took her in his arms, and she pressed herself against him. There was something odd in his demeanor, almost stiff and a bit distant, but he hugged her affectionately. "I'm glad I was able to save you. You are too beautiful to let a swine like that take you away. Also, I need you."

"I need you too," she whispered. She raised her hand to touch his cheek, and wanted him to hold her, but he pulled away. "Tedda, you don't know, do you?"

"Know what, Alton? You're scaring me, even after all this horror."

He appeared reluctant to go on. "Okay," he said, glancing about at the empty lawns and hills.

She looked about too, and saw that Nurse Amit's body where it had fallen. "Look," she said, "Amit was real."

He nodded. "Maybe you can get some of the orderlies to come out and pick the body up. Give her a decent burial."

"She's from upstairs, yes?" Tedda looked upward, thinking it was a metaphor, a borrowing in the I.R. world from the V.R. world.

"Yes," he said, "they are real up there. He added: "Most of them."

"What do you mean?"

"I'm not Hedrock, Tedda. I'm a rule."

Dreamily, she accepted this new sadness. "I was wondering just now why Eduard died, and I thought it was because Hedrock is dead. Now that you explain you aren't Hedrock, I'm less confused. What does it mean, though?"

"Hedrock died trying to buck the system on both sides to make the world whole. He was in West Gotha, trying to bring the Moss Syndicate down, and in East Gotha, trying to take power away from his bosses. In the end, it got him killed. I am the only surviving rule. My name was Edgar, but I am going to style myself Alton Hedrock in his honor."

"Did you know Hadley and Eduard?"

He nodded. "They were my sister and brother."

"Oh, I didn't realize."

"We're not clones or twins or anything like that. We are rules, created from the natural fabric of a femtoworld and pushed along on a very predictable and focused path. We become a unique individual, but we bring with us strong elements of our source."

She laughed. "Hedrock was an individualist, wasn't he?"

He nodded. "Hedrock caused a lot of mischief. He was very attractive to women, and he used them right and left—until he met Amy Tedda." He smiled wistfully. "I can see why."

"I loved him, didn't I?"

He nodded. "When the drugs totally wear off, you'll remember everything. Some of it is good and some not so good."

"Did I murder Moira?"

He shook his head. "The fatherland and the Moss Syndicate made you think that so they could fill you with guilt and self-loathing. It made you more pliable in their hands so they could pursue their goal."

"And that goal was to use me to snare Hedrock."

"Yes." He regarded her with an oddly warm light in his eyes that made her squirm. "I can see why Hedrock broke all his own rules when he met Tedda. You are beautiful. Your chemistry speaks to my chemistry."

She put her arms over his shoulders. "Are you more like Hedrock, like Hadley, or like Eduard?"

He put his hands on her waist, and it made her crazy. He said: "I like to think that, aside from my own unique nature, I have some of the best of all of them in me."

Their faces flew together, their lips locking in a hungry sucking kiss that went on and on. She closed her eyes and let herself drift to a joy she could not remember, lost somewhere beyond the fatherland drug haze clouding her memory. Their tongues explored each other, and they held each other in a warm embrace. She felt the strength in the sinews of his back and his steely arms, while he explored the exquisite softness in the curves of her body, which she knew she would offer to him if they ever had the time, the place, the opportunity.

He pulled away. "I want to be with you, and I have a plan for this. You must help me. The odds are stacked against us, but it's important that we try. If we succeed, we may save a world or two. And—"

"Yes?" She waited breathlessly.

There was sadness in his eyes. "We may never see each other again, so it is important that I tell you I love you. You will remember Alton Hedrock when you are free from what the fatherland has done to you, and I want you to remember me as a man who gave his life's love to you."

She held him close, cradling his head in her palms while resting her arms on his shoulders. She nuzzled her face against his. "I will give you all my love, just the same, so take that with you. We are all we have, you and I, each other. I love you, Love."

"And I cherish you, Love." One more long kiss and embrace, and they had to tear apart. He took her hand and said: "Come with me. Before you go upstairs, I want you to do something." He led her back down the cobblestone street, into the lobby, down the elevator, and into Monopol City.

The deterioration was evident, in that the skyline had shrunk and a telltale greenish-amber aurora danced on the distant horizon. "It will be just a matter of time before this whole world implodes on itself and winks out of existence like one gigantic, glittering, fading rule that blows away as if nothing had ever happened. All the concerts and symphonies and monorails and samba parties, all the composers and thinkers and other great minds—all will be lost. There is just one faint hope, and you must take it with you upstairs." He took her around a corner, down an alley, up a street, and around a small square. Beyond the fountain and the tiny park in the square, apartment houses reached skyward. He took her hand and showed her: "59-510 Rue d'Argent. Number 59 Silver Street, Fifth Floor, Apartment 10. We have a safe house. It used to be East Gotha intel, but those guys are gone and it's now just anyone from upstairs trying to help out or hide out. You'll find me here if you come back."

What? So we can die together? It seemed a dismal hope, but she did not express her dismay. He took her back to the secret door, up the elevator, and out the lobby.

He took her into Bit Cave, which by now was an abandoned hall whose ceiling had started to cave in upon the cubicles. "West Gotha was building the database area they had you working in," he explained, "which you could call the B world. You thought of it as the top level, but it isn't. You're going to the top level, though. It's the top source level."

"So Monopol City would be a C world?" she asked.

"Right. Now you know—there is a really real source world, A, which you are going to visit shortly. So if that's A, then within that is the fortress, which is B. Your banishment is C, as is the toy world the techs created— the Monorail world. Two C worlds. So tiny the whole thing sits on a little chip. It was meant as a diversion to enhance their fun with the board game, but they were able to use the technology they worked with seriously so many hours a day, and create something they thought was fun." He led her to through the collar, and down near her former office. In a hidden and top secret hallway closet, which the techs had protected with a simple padlock, lay the entire Monopol City in a tiny container—not a chip, not VR, but a Go-dots electromag device. Unable to find the key, Alton smashed the lock with a stone lying nearby. They entered the simple, almost empty closet. There on a metal rack surrounded by winking computer lights and components, sat a tiny gray thing—a sort of chip, an inch long, ¾ inch wide, and ¼ inch thick, containing the whole Monopol world. Tedda could sense that he was short of breath, and weakening.

Alton Hedrock explained: "I can't go up, since my source is dead. I can only go down, which prolongs my life. I have some unique strengths as a next generation rule. Killing my source doesn't kill me, but if I go downstream, I can't come upstream again. Also I have to go very small, to conserve energy. That's why we have to part here. You, Tedda, have to take this and go to the institute." He handed her a note he'd scribbled. "Wait until I'm in, and then take the chip with you."

She stuck both in her pocket, sensing the lack of time and the urgency, and didn't bother reading the note. They kissed and embraced passionately, until he pushed her away. His eyes were full of regret. "My dear Tedda, I will pray that we meet again. There is very little chance of that, but I have hope."

She accompanied him to the university. They walked to the door of the lobby together. The lobby was, as always deserted and dimly lit by indirect light from elegant Deco wall sconces. Light glowed softly on hazel wood wall paneling, on a glass clock lens, on an abstract mural in muted green and blue and yellow spatters, on a quarter acre of rouge carpeting. After a last kiss, a last impassioned look into each other's eyes, he hurried away to the elevator. She lost sight of him as he rounded the corner. She heard the soft *ding* of the alarm signaling the door's opening. She heard the sliding of the door, first open, then shut, and a final *ding* as the elevator slid away into Monopol City. By the time she returned to the Bit Cave to remove the chip, he would long be sauntering along the crumbling avenues under the Blue or Green Station, thinking of her, wishing things could have been otherwise. Perhaps he knew she had other business up in the A world, once her memory returned and she realized whatever it was they had made her forget.

Tedda ran alone up the cobblestone street, turned right into the mossy stone gate of the fortress, and jogged through the tree-overgrown park toward the medical institute. She saw that Nurse Amit's body had already been removed. She carried the chip and the note safely stashed in a deep pocket. She noticed black, dull fissures in the ground, that had not been there just a few hours ago. Both the B world (fortress) and the two C worlds (Tedda's office of exile as well as Monopol City) were in the process of breaking up. How long this would take, there was no way of telling. The process might linger endlessly, but more likely would speed up. As he carried the chip and the note upstairs through the C and B worlds, they expanded proportionately, just as he did.

Orderlies and guards opened the gate to let her in. They seemed to know where she was going. An elevator opened up, and Tedda looked anxiously upward as the car moved up. She understood: the elevator was not only IR reality, but VR metaphor. Once that door opened, she would be in the A world. There, the truth about herself would be finally revealed.

Chapter 45

The elevator door rumbled open, and Tedda stepped outside. She was now in the A world—the source world of all that she had known below.

As she stepped outside, heart pounding, she had a sense of the anticlimactic. The hallway she stepped into was drab and cramped. An maintenance worker in khaki pushed past here, with a mop and bucket that smelled foul. His sense of stressful urgency set the tone for the way the wartime world of West Gotha closed in around her with its cares and woes.

She came to a familiar-looking door. A large number 909 was embossed on the door in grayish-blue lettering upon routered particle board. It was the room in which she had wakened after her ordeal with near-drowning. It was the room in which Nurse Amit had first appeared and led her down into the fortress. She tried the door handle, and found it unlocked. She pushed the door open and looked cautiously into a large, sunny room. She stepped into the room, which seemed to swim in a sort of vapor of light, a faintly steamy or smoky whiteness that reflected blindingly in the polished floor boards. The light came in from several windows under the gabled roofs. She had been in here at one time. She recognized the plain gurney with its straps and black plastic body cushion. It was parked against a wall.

"Lost something?" a woman's voice said with languid sharpness.

She turned and saw a nurse standing behind her with hands folded over her belly and a frown. The nurse's face looked familiar, but Tedda couldn't place it. She told the nurse: "No, I think I found something."

The nurse pointed silently up the hall. Curiously, Tedda followed the direction with her gaze, then regarded the nurse. "What are you doing?"

"She's in there," said the laconic young woman, younger than Amit, lighter-skinned, but with a darker aspect. "The one you are looking for." The nurse made no effort to walk with her or guide her, but just kept pointing up the dark, almost smoky corridor. She added: "The guards were all rules, and they were terminated. For the moment, it is safe to go down there."

Tedda walked cautiously down the hall, looking left and right at the doors. The numbers were all 900's but in no apparent order. Tedda looked back, and the nurse had vanished.

The corridor ended on a stairwell leading straight down under one overhead window with some stained glass squares in it. Tedda retraced her steps, thinking that whatever the nurse had pointed to, it must be before that stairwell. On her right, she saw a door numbered 990—her former room, but with the two latter digits transposed. Did that mean anything? She turned the handled and walked in. Room 990 looked very much like Room 909, except that there was a hospital gurney in the middle, and a patient lying asleep on the gurney. Tedda felt a pang in her gut as she stepped cautiously closer. The woman lay bundled under gray and green military-style wool blankets. Her face was toward Tedda, with cold silvery light filling the air behind her from the windows, so Tedda could not quite make out who she was.

Until she got right next to her.

The woman sleeping under an array of I.V. drips and hanging bags was Amy von Tedda. Instantly, that told Tedda one of them must be a rule, and the other real. They couldn't both be rules, Tedda thought with pounding heart while holding her fingers over her mouth as if she were about to involuntarily scream or even throw up. Eyes contorted in sorrow, she thought: *If I were a rule, I would not have been able to come up to Level A. Or how does that go again? As long as my source is alive, I am able to travel and exist freely?*

As Tedda looked down on the sleeping woman, she knew the truth in her heart. She, not the sleeping woman, was the rule. *If she dies, I will fall apart like a puff of dandelion spores. But isn't that how life is for everyone?*

Tedda took out the note Edgar, the last Hedrock rule, had given her to give to this sleeping woman. She opened the crumpled paper and read the penciled scrawl. "He said to tell you he never really loved a woman until he met you. Have the rule Tedda take you out of the hospital. The right people will be waiting to take you to a safe place. Maybe there is still hope to save both Gothas. Best wishes/the rule Edgar."

As Tedda crumpled the note and put it back in her pocket along with the chip, the door opened behind her. It was that nurse again. "Hurry. I can't help you. You must get her out of here." The nurse rushed in anyway, and severed the IV lines with her belt-pack scissors. Get her away from here, and these drugs out of her system so she can wake up and think again."

"I thought I was her," Tedda said weakly.

The nurse barely looked up as she expertly bunched up the sheets to roll Amy von Tedda off the gurney into Tedda's waiting arms. "Honey, you have rule written all over you. Now get this woman out of here. And take good care of her—she is your source." She pointed to a camera in the ceiling. The camera pointed straight down and looked dead. "We shorted the system out. It will come back on line in a few minutes, but you'll have time to get out, and I'll have time to blend back in."

"Yes. Thank you. Can you show me the way?"

"Hurry." Reluctantly, darting fearful glances all around, the nurse helped Tedda get Amy out of the room. "Down the steps now, and good luck to both of you."

Amy moaned and gripped the stair railing while Tedda staggered a bit trying to manage the woman's near dead weight.

"Good sign—she's starting to move around." With that, the nurse took off running. It was an incongruous sight, Tedda thought. *Probably an East Gotha spy, trying to do her duty while staying incognito.*

"Come on, lady, let's get you moving." With that, Tedda pulled one of Amy's arms around her neck and hoisted her upright while trying to rush down the stairs. For a moment she thought they would both go crashing down, but she caught herself on the railing, rested a moment while catching her breath, and then started back down.

Two or three flights down, they came to a glass door locked to the outside. There was an emergency bar for fire exits, and Tedda kicked it open. Amy actually lurched out on her own power, straight into the arms of two waiting men. Tedda was alarmed, and Amy uttered a faint, drugged shriek. The men reassured her as they took her to a waiting black car. "Hurry," they urged Tedda. Tedda ran along and jumped into the passenger seat in front, while the two men had Amy between them. The car was already moving while the doors slammed shut.

"We work for Hedrock," the driver said. It was Watka, cleaned up and looking very sober and younger in a dark business suit.

Chapter 46

As the black car containing Watka, Tedda, Amy, and the two agents barreled through the rainy streets of West Gotha, Tedda had her first opportunity to see her source world. It looked like a grim, threadbare place. It didn't have the orderliness, self-confidence, and culture she'd found in Monopol City. Parts of this place actually looked bombed out. She saw flashes on the horizon that she weren't sure were lightning or enemy missile strikes. At the moment, the legendary rumbling of artillery was still—the fake effects designed to fool her, which she'd heard in the B world, the fortress world.

Watka said: "We'll get you to a safe house where we can detox the great lady and then she'll make a new plan. With Hedrock gone, she'll be heartbroken, but she's now the leader of our movement to save the Gothas from destruction."

"I thought you were an old drunken NCO," Tedda said, squirming and not sure if she should admire him or be outraged.

He grinned at her, quite a handsome looking man, she thought. "Fatherland Academy of Performing Arts," he said, "professional actor. I thought I did my part pretty well, particularly being around when Moss Jr. was around so that he wouldn't feel he could get his paws on you."

"A Hedrock rule shot him."

"Oh good," Watka said happily, "but unfortunately Moss—or Grün as he was known in the fortress—also was just a rule. The real Moss Jr. is alive and well up here, and about to cause a world war that may well end life on this entire planet."

"So are you now in charge, that Hedrock is gone?"

Watka nodded. "Temporarily. Nobody can replace Amy von Tedda as leader. She managed to tame the savage animal, the seducer, the East Gotha master spy. Who else could have done that?"

"They were in love."

"Oh yes, they were." Watka reflected on that. He said thoughtfully: "I brought him over from the East. I was actually his spy master, his handler. I was afraid he was a loose cannon, at first, but then I began to see his potential. He could have been a great leader, had he lived. I introduced him to Amy von Tedda, whom I knew from social circles where I was cultivating a lot of potential contacts."

"So you have been spying for the East?"

"I was, but like a number of other high level officials, I am now working for the downfall of both sides. You rules have been instrumental in breaking ground for a new world order here."

"What do you mean?"

"Power," he said, "power is good, but when it becomes concentrated too narrowly, that is bad. We had a convenient system of sharing power here among the Junker class. Then, in the last few generations, the Moss Syndicate has taken all power to itself. They dispossessed most of our Junker families, like my own and the von Teddas. A similar thing has happened on the other side with the Grün Syndicate."

"Grün!" Tedda said. "You mean, like Confessor Grün and young Major Grün down in the fortress?"

Watka chuckled. "Do you get it yet? It's all one big syndicate, one organization masquerading as two enemies. Moss and Grün are the same families, give or take a few cousins and uncles on either side."

Tedda sat back and let that soak in. "But the war; the battles; the people dying, what about all the suffering?"

He laughed. "It's all a huge dark joke, my dear. It is a war between the Moss and Grün sides of the same family. Now it has gotten totally out of hand, with Leader Moss in possession of a huge new weapon that has the potential to break the stalemate and actually let the Moss side win. We can't allow that to happen." He added: "Besides, this two-headed syndicate has ruled long enough. The degeneration has set in. The next generation are all half-crazed wastrels who spent their youth doing drugs and playing around. They aren't fit to continue ruling. That was the final insight of Captain Hedrock and Amy von Tedda. It has spread through the top echelons of government like wildfire. I'll tell you more a little later. We'll stay at the von Watka estate for now."

He wheeled the automobile off the road and onto a gravel driveway. A great iron gate with family crests swung open at the hands of half a dozen men—possibly rules, Tedda thought—in white wigs, tri-cornered hats, breeches, and silk frock coats. The car crunched up a long gravel drive at whose end sprawled a great gray mansion with a pillared portico in front and a central cupola bell tower. The car crackled among fountains and leafy labyrinths. Tedda saw rose gardens and tea pavilions. At the end of the road was a circular drive. Watka spoke on his car phone. "No activity at the main door. I forbid it. Meet me around the back." So saying, he turned away from the great circular drive. He took his passengers along the side of the house at a good steady clip. Tedda saw park-like meadows and trees extending as far as the eye could see. Watka rounded the corner and pulled up by a service entrance. There, several men in hunting gear and women in nursing uniforms stood waiting. The men of Baron Watka's private hunting army opened the doors, and the women helped Baroness von Tedda out. A stretcher was waiting, and Tedda watched them carry Amy von Tedda to a private infirmary in the great house. Whatever misgivings bothered her deep down, Tedda was glad to be safe for the moment. If she felt a tugging at her heartstrings, it was for Edgar—or Alton Hedrock as he styled himself.

Chapter 47

Watka gave Tedda a tour of the great house. It was soon apparent that he wanted to seduce her, and she avoided all hints of encouragement. She tried not to offend him, but made it clear that she was in love with the afterimage of Hedrock.

"But he's dead and gone," Watka said as they tramped through the upper, third stories. She glimpsed the servants' quarters, hunters' quarters, armory, all very antique with some of the weapons muzzle-loaders accompanied by powder horns and flints. She saw torsos of armor, swords, and shields with family crests on them. "This estate has been in our family for nearly 600 years," he said. "I could set you up in a little cottage with a servant or two."

"No thanks."

"You'd be the most comfortable rule ever created."

"No thanks." She was offended by his highhandedness. It was evident that he did not see rules as having quite the same value as source.

He trapped her in a doorway with his arm, and radiated charm at her. "I hope you'll change your mind once you've gotten used to the comforts of this place."

She pressed past him and they came through a series of kitchens: a bakery, a beanery, a place for churning cream and cheese, a place for gutting fish or smoking game, and so on. He trapped her again with the same great charm: "What do you want, Tedda? What is your heart's desire?"

"To be with Hedrock."

"Crazy!" he said, slapping himself on the forehead. "You are a rule, and he is a dead source. You can't have him, because it's impossible."

"Then clone him," she said petulantly and pointlessly.

"Not the same thing!" he said chasing her as she walked briskly back to the central staircase and descended to the second floor. "Clones are cooked and booked from DNA. Rules are spun in motion from the Go-dots of the source. You depart from your source like a shadow that quickly takes flesh and has pounding blood in its heart. You are distinct persons."

"If we are distinct persons, Baron, then why don't you treat us with the same respect you offer source. Oh, perhaps I misunderstand. You send them to their deaths by the millions, so why should you treat a rule any better."

He was red and hot. "I am offering to treat you better. You are being unreasonable." A crafty look chased away his red anger. "You are playing with me. You are negotiating for the best deal you can get. I see it now."

She whirled and confronted him. They stopped in mid-corridor, among dark wood and carved reliefs in walnut and oak. The faces of *putti* looked shiny from centuries of serving-girls' soft cloths. "I am only asking you to behave like an adult and put your tongue back in your mouth and your zipper back to the top."

He stammered: "I have never felt so tongue-tied, madam. If you wish to leave, you may do so. The police will have you in custody within the hour. You resemble Amy von Tedda too much, and they are by now driving themselves and the whole world crazy looking for her. Or, if you choose, you can stay here and tolerate my hospitality. I think you will choose the latter course."

"And?"

"And what?" He appeared to be afraid to say the next thing, which she knew would be something like "I will take my time about getting into bed with you."

"Please don't threaten me," she said. She felt a sense of despair, looking past her own anger and disgust.

"Don't be silly," he said, calming himself and patting his clothes back in order. At a small niche in the wall, he washed his face quickly at a sink, and wiped his head with a towel. He discarded the towel, for some servant to pick up. He smoothed his disheveled hair back. "Let's have a look at the rest of the place."

He showed her the rest of the second floor, with its great family sleeping suites and common rooms. He showed her his office, his library, his billiards room, his personal collection of weapons (as distinct from the hunters' armory on the third floor). The tour went on until she tired. He showed her the first floor, which had a great ballroom, a dining hall, an infirmary (guarded now by the hunters in fatigues, and containing Amy). He showed her the wine cellar, the champagne cellar, the brandy cellar, the cheese cellar, the vegetable cellar, the fruit cellar, and a dizzying array of other purposed places. He took her on a walk around the outside of the house, pointing out the barns with their horses ("twelve Arabians, six Belgian farm horses, and several other breeds and ponies," he told her as she smelled the calm and sweet smell of oats).

Back in the house, he said: "We have nearly 300 serving staff on the estate. Naturally, one has a tendency to knock about in such a huge place, and I am a single man, not yet married. My parents are dead, my siblings have all moved away, and I carry on here by myself. So I have my own little nook that I retreat to." He showed her a small corner apartment whose proportions where quite normal. It actually looked small and cluttered, and she liked it. But she was not staying here alone with this gryphon, this potential satyr.

"You will occupy your own apartment for the time being." He took her to another corner of the house, and gave her the key to an apartment similar to his. "This was my sister's. She married the wealthy industrialist and banker Baron von Hohencohen two years ago, and hasn't looked back since."

"Is this all her stuff?" Tedda asked. The rooms looked cozy, and were crammed with dainty coverlets and stuffed animals. She was afraid it would be stuffy and dusty, but he saw her look and quickly added: "A serving woman looks after it. You'll meet her—Damselle Gretchen. One thing—."

"Yes?"

"Don't tell her you are a rule."

"I see." Stabbed to the soul, Tedda sat down in a plush chair and put her feet up.

"I didn't mean for it to come out like that," he said. "You have to understand that it's the reality."

She wished she could leave her and be with Hedrock. Why not simply die in the final crackup of Monopol City, but in his arms? What else was there?

"The servants will make a fuss," he said. "They won't wait on you, and even worse, they may report us all to the authorities."

"I'll keep my mouth shut," Tedda said. "Look, Watka. I'll do whatever is my patriotic duty to help out, so that your clique can help themselves get back into power and put the dimmer on the Moss crew. That sounds like a good thing to do. However, please spare me the moist paw prints. I'm not interested. Can you get that through your drooling skull?"

He straightened to his full height, took a step backward as if she'd pushed him, turned dark red, and whirled to storm from the room.

She slammed the door after him and rummaged in the kitchenette for cups, tea, and fresh water. Pretty soon she had herself a little afternoon tea going, complete with some crackers from a tin (slightly stale, but the lemon and powder sugar disguised the flat taste). She noticed a small plastic radio shaped like a blue bear by the window. As she ate, she listened to a radio broadcast. "Authorities continue to comb the city and countryside of Central West Gotha for a group of enemy spies who appear to have kidnapped an important Western industrialist from her hospital room at the 325th Army Station Hospital at Gotha Fields. Images of the missing Amy von Tedda and her look-alike rule will be posted shortly on every street corner. Citizens are encouraged to report any sighting of these two."

Tedda's gloom deepened as she realized how tenuous her existence here was. She also recognized fully how imperfect these source people were, and how bleak their world was. She remembered Watka as she had first met him—a foul-smelling, lumbering plow horse of a man, reeking of cabbage and cheap schnapps, failed as an NCO and little better than a stable hand in his baggy, dirty, torn uniform. How well he had played the role—because it surely was part of his nature.

The servants she met, including Old Gretchen, were little better. The hunters were a rough, surly crew who reminded her of pirates. They swore undying allegiance to the Watka crest, under which they vowed to serve the fatherland as in the best feudal traditions, but they stubbornly demanded their rights from Watka. They had their own *Gutt' Stub'* (cozy parlor) at a corner of the third floor. Their parlor had a high tiled fireplace and a beer keg in one corner. It was adorned with ancient hunting muskets and other *accoutrements*, including a museum of ancient clay pipes. Hanno, Gretchen's son and a hunter, gave her the tour and explained that each pipe had belonged to a trusty hunter who had puffed it here in the *Gemütlichkeit* or comfort of these walls in centuries past. Tedda lost count, and estimated there must be a thousand of these spindly objects with their sooty little bowls and curving stems spread over the walls and even the ceiling.

Every day, Tedda visited Amy in the infirmary. This was another antique, another museum, but updated to the latest technologies. There were scary corners, including a shelf with sealed jars in brandy or formaldehyde, containing various genetic monsters including a baby resembling a frog (no neck; head and torso joined in one peeling, graying, egg-shaped mass) dated 1735; and so on. There were also racks of computer equipment and electronic tomes on everything from surgery to stenosis, from liver to laboratory, from appendectomy to x-ray, yellow fever, and zygoblastomas.

After a few days, Amy was capable of walking about. She asked for Tedda, and they would have tea together in Tedda's little apartment. "I find it quite charming," Amy said.

"It belonged to Watka's sister."

"Oh yes, the Baroness von Hohencohen," Amy said as she stirred sugar into her bronze tea. "She is in on our little adventure."

"Watka has explained some of it to me," Tedda said. "Amy, please tell me. What is to become of me?"

Amy shook her head as if startled. "Darling, as long as I live, you live. You can stay with me as long as you like. I need a close personal servant and confidante." Seeing Tedda's silence, she added: "Are you offended somehow, poor thing? Did Watka try to get his dactyls up your hoosie?"

"More or less," Tedda admitted. "I am not interested in his, er, interests."

"What do you want?" It was a frank, kindly question.

"I met a rule, from Hedrock."

"Ah, so that's it. Well, darling, you should find your rule and make your life with him, if that is what you wish."

"I had expected you would be very depressed to learn that Captain Hedrock has left us."

Amy nodded. "I am, my dear. I am." She stirred her tea more than was required by it, but she needed to so more. "At the same time, I am a practical woman. There is too much at stake. Do you understand, Tedda? The entire world is at a pivot. This is no time for me to mope about. I can grieve at the loss of my husband, build him a monument, weep for him on his birthday, but the fact of the matter is, child, if Watka and I and our allies do not strike now, the Moss Syndicate will dig in ever deeper. Same thing with their opposites in the East. Now is the time to strike and put them out of business." Amy regarded Tedda for a minute or two. "Child, I don't think I answered your question. What are you thinking?"

This was the one moment where Tedda was totally honest with her source. "I don't like your world. I wish I could go back down into the Monopol City world and find Edgar."

"It's a dying world."

"I know, but I'm not suitable to be a servant or a second-class citizen here."

"What do you mean?" Amy buttered some toast, while Tedda brought out orange marmalade. The little kitchen smelled sweet and warm. There was a medley of bread smells, jam smells, even coffee though it sat in tightly closed tins on shelves. Light from the park filtered in through the gray filmy curtains. The white valances with their strawberry and basket themes looked kitschy but pleasant.

"I don't think of myself as a rule, but as a person. I will always be a second class being here. I want to go home where I belong."

"What a strange set of ideas," Amy said. She appeared dismissive at first, but as she stroked her butter knife across her bread, she paused several times and Tedda could tell she had her source thinking. "I suppose we have created a new class of slaves without meaning to," Amy said.

"What do you call the source humans who serve you?"

"Servants," Amy said with a shrug as she bit into a piece of marmalade and butter toast. She looked at Tedda. "So you are implying that rules are a step lower?"

"You have already made that abundantly clear."

"Funny," Amy said, "I believe you're right. I never thought of it that way. So you feel like some sort of *Untermensch* and that hurts your feelings. Well, I can certainly understand that."

"You can?" Tedda said with some amazement.

"Indeed," Amy said. "Listen, honey, I was first in my class at University. I set records no man or woman has ever touched. I built my family's failing pharmacopia business, which was ruined by the Moss Syndicate, into a powerful industrial complex serving the war effort. I made myself indispensable, but you know what?" She leaned closer. "I used to think—here I am prostituting myself and my firm, anything to garner favor, anything to hang on, anything to build us back up, and for what? So the Moss Syndicate can become more powerful. That's why, when Alton Hedrock and his bedroom manner crossed my path, I fell hard for him. I fell for his physical charms, his pathetic yet irresistible boyish seductions, and yet I began to see the genius in him. Something in Alton Hedrock awakened a genius in me that I never knew existed."

"Maybe it's just plain humanity," Tedda said.

"You're so right. You are a piece of me, and you carry my genius, though you are like a dumber younger sister. Forgive me for being blunt. I don't mean to hurt your feelings."

Tedda said: "I never felt the need to be a genius, so my feelings aren't hurt; well, maybe not much."

Amy seemed remorseful. "Child, I never—."

Tedda felt hot. "Stop calling me child. I am a person, just like you. I am your sister, I guess."

"Yes you are." Amy tapped her fingertips on the table. "This is a moment in history when so much hangs in the balance; who we are, who we want to be, who we will make ourselves become. Do we really want to be a class of slave owners?"

Tedda helped her along: "If you continue producing rules for whatever need that happens to come up, it's worse than owning slaves. You are creating human beings for some purpose, and shaping them to your own selfish ends. That is playing God, and I think it is morally wrong."

Amy stared at her, shaking her head in confusion.

Tedda continued: "Think of it! You can create rules to fight your wars, and people like me will die by the millions in your endless pointless wars. You can create rules to clean up your garbage, do your heavy lifting, even suffer for you. In the process, you become fat dependent white slugs, and we become a resentful owned class that will eventually overthrow you. Don't do this to us, and don't do it to yourselves."

Amy looked at her for a long time, and then said in a very honest, serious voice: "You are so right, Tedda. I am sorry for what we have thoughtlessly done, not just to ourselves but to your kind. You really do carry parts of me in you, because when you teach me, I find myself opening my mind and receiving all your wisdom."

Tedda said: "Using your pragmatism, then, even if you see the light, will Watka? Will the Junkers? Will anything change?"

Amy studied her. "Sister, I need to figure a lot of things out. We have the Moss Syndicate on the run. Already, a group of Junker generals are negotiating with the Leader's family about deposing him and replacing him with a fatherland council in which we will have a far greater voice."

"What about this great missile Leader wants to launch against East Gotha?"

"We've already parsed that situation," Amy said. "We've agreed with the other side to turn it into a joint scientific satellite that will orbit the sun for millions of years. As a gesture of good will, we have asked them to submit experiments of their own to replace half the MIRVs that Leader had intended to launch against them."

"Great," Tedda said. "It sounds, sister, like you don't need me anymore."

Amy put her hands over Tedda's. "Thank you for teaching me. It is so simple, and I was so far out to lunch, but I understand now what I must do. Watka will have a hard time getting it. The Moss and Grün families are hopeless, but most of the Junker have been sidelined for so many decades that many are open to reason. I think I can convince our people to stop dabbling in femtoworlds, and more importantly, to stop creating rules because it is morally offensive and will destroy what is left of the fabric of this crazy Gotha world."

"Not only that," Tedda said, "but it is very hurtful."

"I'm so sorry," Amy said. "What can I do to make it up to you?"

"I want to leave here," Tedda said. "I want to return to Monopol City and be with Edgar."

"Your Hedrock rule."

"Stop sounding patronizing."

"I didn't mean to." Amy patted her hand in a sisterly fashion. "You are forceful and intelligent, which I am known for. Good. But that entire world will die. We have to kill it off or it will destroy our world."

"That is a difficult choice," Tedda said, thinking of the beautiful buildings and people in Monopol City, with their colorful train stations and sidewalk cafes.

"No, it's not," Amy said with utter harsh pragmatism.

Tedda looked at her source and gasped. There was no way she could ever get used to being around these people.

Amy said: "I wouldn't dream of letting the rule destroy the source. We will preserve the Gothas above all." She offered no regret or apology.

They fell silent, and the spell in the little kitchen vanished for Tedda. Tedda knew something had just died, some feeling of fondness for Amy and her people, that she could never regain.

"You could stay with us," Amy said, wiping her mouth and rising.

Tedda shook her head and did not offer thanks. Alton-Edgar Hedrock could not come upworld without perishing, and she wanted more than anything to find him. She knew Amy was contemplating the same thoughts as she stood staring at Tedda, who remained sitting on her stool by the window. Tedda looked up and said: "Even if we only have one day together." *It will be worth far more than a lifetime alone in your cruel world.*

"You are welcome to stay as long as you wish," Amy said. She turned and, as she strode from the room, she added, "As long as we can protect you." With that the door slammed, and Tedda was alone.

Chapter 48

The Moss Syndicate counter-attacked with surprising ferocity and speed.

Tedda was outside on the grounds with Nurse Gretchen, a taciturn but kindly old woman. Gretchen wore a shawl and a black dress. She wasn't a small woman, but seemed one of those indestructible grandmotherly types who move at their own speed and never stop moving. Gretchen was always doing something, whether it was cutting up a potato with rutted fingers, or waddling effortfully with a woven basket of wash under one arm and a cane in the other hand, or a hundred things like that. Her one dash of color was always some head kerchief—usually black silk, with glowing blue and other peacock colors in big bold geometries. She seemed to know who and what Tedda was—the resemblance to Amy made it painfully obvious—but did not treat her unkindly—just distantly. Watka stopped by every day to sit in the kitchen and sip schnapps while smoking a cigar, and Gretchen would hover protectively around Tedda, opening windows and using her arms to push billows of smoke out. Amy came by every day, never at the same time as Watka, and would fuss a bit at the sink, maybe have Gretchen make her a bowl of strawberries with milk and white sugar. "You have a nice little corner here," Amy might say, hinting that Tedda should stay with them. And Gretchen would hum contentedly in the corner by the woodpile, next to the crackling fire in a tiny tiled hearth: "You could be sisters, girls. It is so nice to have girls around again."

Every day, Tedda got an hour or so of fresh air, usually in the company of Gretchen and one armed hunter. Today, Gretchen hobbled along with her cane in one hand and a basket to gather mushrooms in the other. "It rained during the night," Gretchen singsonged, "it rained and rained, and the roof is still dripping." She looked up with a grimace at the pearly-gray sky. A flight of birds shot past, black ones that cawed loudly. Hanno, the guard, abruptly unshouldered his double-barreled shotgun and stood at alert.

"What is it?" Gretchen said.

"They shouldn't have done that," he said. His eyes did not follow the winging blackbirds, but gazed toward the hillside toward the northern end of the estate. "Let's pull back toward the main house a bit." He spoke into a collar mike, alerting the duty hunter up in a turret behind them.

Gretchen had a slow time turning around, and Tedda helped her. The old woman turned slowly as a battleship. Tedda felt the fatty strength in her upper arms, the redolent barnyard cowness in her unwashed body. Hanno was a short, powerful man with a large forehead and neatly groomed, upward combed brown hair. He wore a green fedora with a pheasant feather on one side, and sported a Cheddar Billo mustache the color of wet bark. As he stood with his legs propped apart and the long shotgun with its wicked muzzles ready in both arms, a shot rang out. Hanno dropped like a rock. Gretchen screamed, and Tedda shoved her roughly to the ground.

Tedda heard the men running toward them before she saw them. "Amy von Tedda!" one said, and the other said: "Grab her and let's fall back before the others attack." Two of them, in dark fatigues, young and blond, they came running at a crouch over a rise Tedda had not noticed. They carried spidery assault rifles in both hands, ready to shoot.

Tedda threw herself toward Hanno. He wasn't dead, but stunned. His head and shoulder were covered with blood, and he lay helplessly on his side. The shotgun lay before him. Tedda picked it up, broke the breech to make sure it was loaded, all in a second or two. Then she turned the heavy gun around and fired. In a deafening cloud, one of the attackers flew backward. The other attacker raised his weapon but hesitated. He looked at Gretchen, who lay helplessly on her belly. He looked at Hanno, who blinked through bloodied eyes and mouthed a few dull syllables. Then he drew down on Tedda but seemed to remember he wanted her alive. In that time of hesitation, Tedda looked down at the gun, found the other trigger, aimed at the intruder, and fired. He keeled over backwards with his feet flying into the air. Tedda pulled the leather bandoliers and pouches from Hanno's stout body. With the shotgun and pouches, she ran forward at a crouch. She threw herself on the ground just this side of the little rise, so that she overlooked several acres of lower meadows she hadn't seen before. A second later, she regretted her strategic error. The far wall erupted in smoke and flying earth and tumbling bricks about a quarter mile away. In poured several armored personnel carriers, a swarm of leather-clad and helmeted motorcyclists with big goggles and burp gun barrels visible over their shoulders. Behind those came at least thirty or forty foot soldiers in helmets and long coats with their assault rifles at their chests. Several guidons fluttered above the attackers, carrying the old imperial crest and eagle with the letter M superimposed in Gothic alphabet.

Tedda looked back, biting her lip, and assessed her situation. It was too far to get to the house, and the motorcycle riders were coming on too fast. Hanno was on his feet and staggering toward her. His head was cocked to one side as he spoke into his mike again.

Tedda turned and fired. The nearest motorcyclist went down head over wheels. Tedda reloaded and fired again. The effect was to slow the entire attack down by a few minutes. Hanno crashed to the ground beside her, firing with hand gun.

Suddenly, even as the attackers regrouped and starting rolling forward, the fortifications in the house erupted with counterfire. Rockets streaked down and took out the armored cars. Two or three rockets fired at the turrets were shredded by defensive gatling guns. A fusillade of rifle fire rained down from the upper stories, until Moss' forces either lay dead or retreated.

A dreadful calm descended as thick smoke drifted across the battlefield. Tedda heard men crying pitifully in pain and fear. Hanno cursed and shot them one by one with his handgun as they lay dying before him. Tedda wanted to stay his thick, cord-like arm but closed her eyes and rested her head weakly on her forearm. Tedda found that the Gothans demonstrated their ox-stubborn cruelty again and again, inbred and unalterable. This was a moment when she realized that, inadvertently, in creating the rules in their femtoworlds, the Gothans had set forth people better than themselves.

The sounds of a recorded martial victory tune echoed across the grounds. A small troop of hunters carrying ancient colors came galloping around the corner from the barns. Cantering and clattering, they cheered the man and woman who appeared on a high parapet. Amy von Tedda, wearing a nightgown, helmet, and bandoliers, waved a machine gun high. At her side stood Watka, waving two handguns and grinning broadly. As Tedda watched, the two embraced passionately and kissed long and hard mouth to mouth. Wondering about Amy's passion for her husband, the late Hedrick not yet cold in the earth, Tedda realized again that the Gothans' passions were brief, hot, and brutal. She almost expected to see Amy start eating Watka in the midst of the intercourse that would give her an heir. But that was carrying it a bit too far, she thought with a shudder.

The horsemen smelled of sweat and leather. Their mustaches smelled of tobacco, coffee, and beer. Their teeth were large and yellow as they cheered, and their eyes were tiny gray or blue dots of delirious victory. A bugler sounded various stirring attacks and charges as they raced around and around the sprawling house in a thunder of hooves.

A dozen young hunters surrounded Hanno, Gretchen, and Tedda. Hanno brushed their help aside after they got him on his feet. Wrapping himself in a dirty gray towel, he staggered stubbornly toward the house on his own feet. Several nurses came running—horsy and robust young women with serious eyebrows and pretty faces scrubbed until glowing—and they helped Gretchen to her feet. Tedda rose under her own power, and walked to the house alone while the others fussed over Gretchen as was appropriate. Tedda felt her knees begin to shake in reaction now that the fight was over. She went to her little apartment, locked the door, and threw herself into bed with the covers up over her head. Had the Moss troops killed Amy, Tedda would have evaporated in a brief twinkling of mosaic light and dust. Her life was more transient than a mosquito's. She thought again of Alton-Edgar Hedrock, and wished he could come rescue her, but he would evaporate if he came upworld. No, somehow she must get to him. There was no future here for her. The hunters, however, had a different idea about that.

Chapter 49

As Tedda lay shocked and numb in the twilight of her tiny bedroom, she heard more gunshots and singing all around. As she staggered to the window to close it and tie the curtains shut, she saw that other hunters were rolling in. She saw different guidons, other colors, even dark-skinned hunters in various shades of the racial colorings of the Gotha world. *Something big must be happening*, Tedda thought drowsily. *They look flush with victory and ready for a bigger fight.*

Tedda fell asleep.

Much later, a low but persistent knocking woke her up. She looked about in surprise. It must have gotten dark outside, for the room was pitch black. The knocking brought her to the door, and she turned the big fat wall knob that turned on the electric light overhead. Shielding her blinded eyes, she swung the door open. There stood a smiling Amy von Tedda. Beside her in a wheelchair sat Gretchen, and behind them with head bandaged stood Hanno. "We came to thank you," Amy said.

Gretchen muttered and babbled as she took Tedda's hands in hers and kissed them again and again. Tedda felt the old woman's tears and saliva wetting her hands, and pulled them away to wipe them on the back of her skirt. "You are a princess," Gretchen mumbled toothlessly. "You are truly a sister of our Amy."

Hanno stepped forth. "Miss Tedda, the hunters want to thank you for saving the estate."

Tedda rubbed her eyes again, with fingers that smelled of the old woman's gums. Gretchen knotted her hands together in the wheelchair and shook them in prayerful thanks under her aged chin. Nurses wheeled sobbing Gretchen away down the gloomy corridor.

"Truly," Amy said, "we owe you a great deal." She said sharply: "Hanno, I will send her to you. Go now."

"Thank you," Hanno said. He lowered his head in obeisance with closed eyes, and strode away in that wide gait of his, so much like a great war horse. The corridor rang with his footsteps.

"The hunters have prepared a feast in your honor."

"It's not necessary," Tedda said.

Amy put an arm around her. "Tedda, darling, many things seem not necessary, but we do our Pflicht, our duty." She gave a squeeze. "Do you understand?"

Tedda nodded.

"We don't control them," Amy said, "the hunters. They are a law unto themselves. Hundreds of years ago, when the emperors were weak, the forest meisters ruled in their own strength as a loose union. The cheddar was only a figurehead. My ancestors employed a thousand hunters at the time, who swore undying and eternal allegiance to this house. At the same time, they continue making their own laws within our own. They obey, but they also demur."

"I don't understand," Tedda said standing in her doorway.

"I know you don't." Amy released her from her embrace and started for the main house. "Go up to the third floor and enter the hunters' parlor. They will sing for you and drink a toast. I will join you shortly."

"Very well," Tedda said.

"Tedda."

"Yes?"

"I wanted a moment alone to thank you in my own way." She raised an imperious finger to shush Tedda's protest. "You did a great thing today, and we will all thank you in our own way. Later tonight, you and I and Watka will be removed to a safer place. My own, on the edge of town. Already, the hunters have declared against Moss, and the generals are following. The Junkers are resurrecting the Redensort, or parliament, and we just got word that Tonsonby's intelligence services are turning against the regime. At my own fortress, we will negotiate with the East in a secret pact to stand down the war for a time, so we can negotiate at least some kind of armistice. After all, we were one nation until the Moss and Grün Syndicate took over a century ago."

"It sounds as if there is hope for your people," Tedda said. "I still don't want to remain here."

"I know, my dear. That brings me to you. I cannot allow your world to continue growing, because the energy curve of all the West and East digging in femtoworlds will soon reach critical mass as the separate digs flow together into one larger entity. You see, it is hopeless anyway. The East's underworlds, plus the fortress world where you lived with Moira's rule Lindy, plus this place you speak of—"

"—Monopol City—"

"—Yes, Monopol City, will all slam together and annihilate each other in a great burst of subatomic energy. That in turn will cause a chain reaction that will set our atmosphere on fire and possibly disintegrate that top hundred miles or more of earth's surface. I can offer you one thing that you've said you wanted."

"Yes?"

"A day with Alton-Edgar Hedrock."

Tedda forgot her gloom and brightened at the thought. "Yes?"

Amy smiled. "Yes, Tedda. I would do anything for you, but it seems this is the limit of my abilities to thank you."

Chapter 50

The Guild Hall of the Hunters was hot and smoky, crowded to the rafters with roughly singing men. Fire blazed in the hearth, and the windows were open to let in the sweet damp night wind of the fatherland.

The only two women present were Amy and Tedda.

Watka stood by in his black uniform of an imperial horse guard colonel, complete with gold epaulets, short tunic, tight trousers, black boots, black leather belts, pouches, and pistols, and a pillbox hat with a flap to one side from which dangled a gold-braided tassel.

"Hail, hail, hail," the hunters shouted in chorus as they rose and held up their beer mugs. They drank a sip and then swung the mugs left and right. "Hail, hail, hail!"

After all the hails and salutes, Hanno made a speech. He stood before the fire in breeches and loose blouse. His hairy chest gleamed with sweat as orange flames flickered to one side of him. His big forehead glistened with reflected fire, and his dark hair looked damp. His Cheddar Billo mustaches drooped and shook as spoke in a loud voice: "Tonight we will swear renewed allegiance to the House of Watka, and we will add a special oath of allegiance to the House of von Tedda and their hunters, who have joined us tonight. The day of Moss is finished."

"Hail, hail, hail!" the hunters sang, and the hall smelled of burnt wood, beer, and cigar smoke. It stank of leather, unwashed men, and singed mustaches. It smelled of broken teeth and bad breath and horse manure.

A messenger stepped into the room, and handed a note to Watka, who stepped quickly to Amy's side and whispered in her ear.

Tedda stood near them, but could not hear Watka's words.

"I bring you another bit of great news," Amy said. She raised her arms and the men fell silent. "I just have received word that the Moss Syndicate is already abandoning its positions in Central West Gotha."

"Hail, hail, hail!" sang the hunters.

"There are indications of unrest on the other side, and it appears the East Gotha Air Weapon has begun bombing their central palace. No word on what the Grün Syndicate is doing, but we understand that the Knights of West Gotha, Moss' praetorian guard, have turned on him and are hunting him down in the streets."

"Hail, hail, hail!" the hunters sang in deafening chorus as they waved their beer mugs, and the rafters seemed to hum with the force and tension of their determination.

Watka stepped forth. "Best of all, I give you word that Amy and I have joined in a movement to declare a constitutional monarchy. It is almost certain that Amy will become your queen, with myself as her royal consort. This was all already worked out in recent months with the help of Captain Hedrock and other agents from both sides of our poor divided nation. There will be one Gotha again, for the first time in our lifetimes!"

"And forever more," Amy added.

Tedda found herself clapping and cheering along with the rest of them. She put two fingers under her tongue and let out a victory whistle that startled all the men around her.

Hanno came forth and took Tedda by the wrist. "This is the woman who saved our Queen to be."

"Hail, hail, hail!" sang the hunters.

"I present to you the woman we honor especially tonight. I don't know what the lords and ladies of the high-falootin' government want to do, but I propose to you that we declare Tedda a princess of hunters!"

"Hail, hail, hail!" sang the hunters. "Yes, yes, yes!"

"It is done," Hanno said. He raised Tedda's arm as if she had won a prize fight. "Princess Tedda Roule, then."

Amy spoke up, seizing the challenge to turn it into an opportunity. "I will be proud, once I am crowned your Queen, to name my sister a national princess. For now, I join you in applauding the great honor you have bestowed on her, for she truly deserves it. We must leave you now, for duty calls us to Fortress von Tedda. Colonel Watka will take charge of the Knights and of the central garrisons tonight. Meanwhile, my sister and I will move as close to the front as we can. I don't mean the front with East Gotha, which we hope will shortly cease to exist as our nation reunites. I mean the front in our final battle against the totalitarian Moss System."

"Hail, hail, hail!" sang the hunters. "Yes, yes, yes!"

Chapter 51

Amy and Tedda rode together in the back seat of a black, armored limousine flying only Watka's colonel colors on the front fenders. They had an escort of twelve ordinary West Gotha traffic cops on motorcycles, but armed with burp guns over their shoulders and grenades on their belts. With their thick leather uniforms and white belts and helmets, plus huge goggles, the policemen looked like a formidable defense for any street engagement, but the trip was uneventful.

"I didn't want to speak of this, Princess," Amy said quite seriously, "but there is another gift I can give you."

"What is that, Queen to be?"

"I make you a solemn promise." Amy raised her right hand, the index finger and middle finger raised and the thumb crossed over the other two fingers, folded down. "I swear on my sacred new appointment, as Queen to be, that I will forever terminate the science of rules."

"Oh, thank you, that would be so nice," Tedda said.

Amy folded her arms pragmatically and said in that dead-on Gotha manner, almost brutally, with her own hyper-rational coldness layered on top: "I believe that if we continue the rule class, we will be creating a nation of slaves and masters."

Offended and hurt, but comprehending the logic, Tedda listened.

Amy continued: "Slavery rots a nation from inside. Slavery causes a disease in the human spirit that may never be cleansed. It is an offense to the human soul. For this reason, Princess, I will make it my first order of business tomorrow to begin destroying the technology, and all the knowledge, involved in what we have been doing with femtoworlds and rules."

Tedda thought of Hedrock, where he must be right now in a darkening and ever more silent city of ruins, growing cold as the chill of utter annihilation descended upon it and its remaining citizens. She wiped a tear from the corner of her right eye, and fought to stop herself from sniffling.

"You can choose to remain with us," Amy said. "We welcome you and we have already bestowed honors on you. I meant what I said back at the hunters' guild hall. I will declare you a princess of the realm, with your own servants and castles and anything you may need."

Tedda was silent.

Amy added: "Child, you will surely find another man to love. Trust me, Hedrock was charming and slippery, but he was about as trustworthy as any other Grün Syndicate spy."

Tedda nodded, but didn't answer, and continued to think of the man she had so passionately kissed with outside the hospital in the fortress world after he'd killed the Major Grün rule on the white horse.

The convoy ran cautiously behind two outriders on motorcycles. The car and cycles had their lights dimmed. Only as they approached the flickering East-West border, and Tedda saw the looming fastness of sprawling Fortress von Tedda on the hills above, did the drivers turn on their flashing lights and martin's horn sirens. Speeding up, they came into a wide highway lit up as bright as day under closely spaced, powerful bluish streetlights built into the block walls rising on either side. The enormous portals of Fortress von Tedda yawned in the darkness ahead. As they swung open, light from inside spilled out onto the highway, revealing a great complex of domes, cubes, and stone defense works.

For a minute or so, the canyon echoed deafeningly with the massed too-tah-too-tah of blaring martin's horn sirens. The motorcycles and limousine pulled into the fortress and grew silent. Only a mass of blue and red lights continued to flash as the limousine pulled into a vast underground bunker and came to a wide stairway. In the cavernous garages and recesses of yard-thick concrete, a military band played various ruffles and flourishes, then airs and anthems. It was all very solemn as the combined hunters, policemen, soldiers, and civil servants of the new regime welcomed their ruler.

From the limousine stepped Amy I, ruler of all the Gothas, soon to be Queen of the Mark, Lady of the Reich, Mistress of the World. At the moment, she was still only Baroness von Tedda, but dozens of representatives of the high houses of Gotha were present and knelt before her. Watka was already there, and he had with him a combined honor guard of colonels and generals from both East and West Gotha. Tedda swept along in the wake of Amy's triumph, and many gray heads and jeweled ladies bowed to both royal women. Ceremonial halberdiers, grenadiers, and color bearers stood by.

Chamberlains escorted Amy and Tedda into the calm and peace of the central keep. It was like coming into a luxury hotel, Tedda thought. They installed her in a luxury suite with six rooms, in which she felt lonely and ill at ease despite the many amenities. She had her own gymnasium, a library, an office with a great glass-topped desk that had gryphons on all the corners, a smoking room in which probably nobody had lit a cigar in 100 years or more, and a well-stocked kitchen and bar. The only thing that appealed to her was the heated swimming pool, in a walnut-paneled room with glass doors. The floors and pool were done in fine greenish mosaic tiles, as was the Jacuzzi capable of holding about eight persons.

It was quiet in Tedda's suite, and Tedda relished that. It was good to be away from the horses, the smells, the brutality of ordinary Gotha life. Tedda sat about, dressed in thick white terry robes, turban, and matching slippers. She wallowed in soft leather couches that smelled like fine shoes. She ate fruit and drank a small cognac, which made her feel relaxed. Making sure all the doors were locked, she slipped into a huge bed with fresh linens and fell asleep.

In the morning, girls' laughter, and beams of sunlight, awakened Tedda. She sat up, rubbing her eyes, and marveled as a half dozen of the horsy-pretty, scrubbed and red-cheeked young Gotha maids wearing white linen caps unlocked the door with their master key and brought in trays of steaming coffee, pastries, fruit, and fragrant rolls with butter and jellies. One of the girls even brought with her a pair of frisking, long-haired shaggy dogs that jumped over the furniture and one peed on a little foot rug. The girls all laughed and faced Tedda. They curtsied all at once. Only the girl with the dogs didn't curtsy, but wailed as the dogs made her turn in circles.

Through the open main door, Tedda glimpsed rolling greens and trees and dozens of busy groundskeepers. She saw a man smoking a pipe and carrying a ladder, boy carrying a beehive, and a girl with flowers and shears. It was the bird-sung and aristocratically out of touch paradise in which she knew she could spend the rest of her life, if she wished.

A stern clapping of hands made the girls scurry out of the room. Last to vanish were the wagging tails of the two dogs, out a side door, which then closed. In the main door stood Amy. She wore grape-red corduroy riding clothes, including tan knee-boots and a black helmet, which she left on the carpet near the door along with gloves and riding crop. She stepped inside and closed the door. "Did you sleep well?"

"Yes, sister. Come join me for breakfast."

"Thank you. That's what I had in mind. Well, Moss committed suicide this morning in his keep, and our soldiers accepted their garrison's surrender."

"It all ended very quickly," Tedda said, buttering a roll.

Amy poured coffee for both of them. "It was a great rotten house of cards. We planned all this very discreetly and very well. I am queen in all but name, and you will be princess as soon as I am crowned."

"Thank you."

Amy grinned. "Be thankful that, until that happens next week, you don't have to stand when I enter, and call me Your Majesty."

"I didn't know about such things," Tedda said.

"I am sure it will all take getting used to again."

They ate quietly. "I would have us do this on the patio overlooking the gardens next time. I just wanted a little time alone with you, away from nosy servants."

"Suits me just fine. I did enjoy the Jacuzzi last night."

"Oh, good. So you are a water nyx, a nymph."

They both giggled. And so they ate a light-hearted breakfast, speaking of nothing too serious. Afterward, Amy said: "Throw on your clothes, my dear. I have something to show you."

Soon, wearing jeans, a blouse in fine green and white vertical stripes, and soft deck shoes, Tedda followed Amy through a tight paneled doorway amid books and carved devices, down a narrow flight of stone steps, into a more central carpeted corridor lit by milky glass wall sconces, and into a large library with high windows. Some of the window panes bore manorial symbols in stained glass. Amy rushed about, closing windows and pulling long, heavy red curtains shut.

The walls were covered with older books and the newer e-discs. Newest of all was the cryogenically cooled server in one corner, which could access databases and information around the globe. There were several comfortable looking old leather couches and chairs in the room, plus a small refreshment bar, and some tables and stools. One corner consisted of a viewing table in a ring of plush chairs.

In the middle of this room, on a thick carpet, stood an odd device: a wood frame surrounded by a maze of criss-crossing wires. Tedda tried to make out the shape of the thing, but it seemed blurry around the edges.

"This is what you asked for," Amy said. "It is a doorway into the Monopol City world. I can't believe you wish to go there, and perish." She pointed to a spot high up. There, surrounded by coils of bare copper wire and blinking green and blue lights, was the chip Tedda had brought up from downworld.

"Is there any way you could save just Monopol City?" Tedda pleaded.

Amy shook her head. "I wish I could, sister. The problem is that the technology is new, and femtoworlds are inherently unstable. There is a certain balance among the underlying Go-dots that we know very little about maintaining. Think of it as being like crossing a great chasm on a fine wire. You hold a stout pole across your chest, taking one step at a time. If you find yourself swinging a little to the right, you move the pole left and the weight shift balances everything. A wind blows you a little off balance to the left, and you move the pole to the right. Then, at some point, the oscillations become too much, and the pole can no longer save you. You tumble screaming into the abyss. That's what we face with this technology. If it begins to fall out of control, the femtoworld starts growing rapidly until it reaches critical mass and explodes, destroying itself and our world. I cannot permit that to happen."

Tedda stood staring helplessly at the maze of wires and the glowing chip. She stared at the black doorway beyond which she could only see a thick haze with a few tiny lights winking in it. That was the doorway into the world below.

"Once you go there," Amy said, "I have to close it up and be done with it. There is no way back for you. I will miss you if you go."

"I will think about it," Tedda said.

"You are free to spend all the time here that you wish," Amy said. She looked about fondly. "This is the library in which I started my secret research into Intereality about ten years ago. How quickly it all led to all the things that came next!" She held up an e-disc. "Here is the very book that got me started."

Tedda reached out for the disc, but Amy instead took it to the viewing table put it in a player. "Sit down," Amy said, and Tedda sank into a cool leather easy chair facing the viewing table. The viewing table was round, about four feet in diameter, and smooth on top. It was raised to a comfortable viewing height. As Amy adjusted the controls, she gave Tedda some brief instructions on how to access the global knowledge base, as well as operating the more primitive local disk players. A man's voice spoke as the holographic text opened in midair. The controls appeared holographically beside each of the four chairs, and they were intuitive and easy to figure out. They consisted of amber buttons amid green frames, all virtual and glowing with delicate fineness. "You can speak the commands also," Amy said, "back, forward, stop, rewind, et cetera."

Amy left Tedda to view the book that had started it all. She rewound it to the beginning, which looked like an old fashioned paper and ink book. In fact, it appeared the book had originally appeared in such an antediluvian format under the title (which a gentle male voice now spoke) *Pseudopolyhedral Constructs in Two-Dimensional Plane Space, With Applications in Probability and Production Theory, based on the question What is the smallest number of flat planes on a three-dimensional real (not ideal) construct (other than the one plane on a sphere)?*

Tedda blinked and replayed this several times until she thought she grasped the general drift of the title. Could she pull any of Amy's mathematical, scientific, and technological genius from inside her memory? Was it there at all in her genes?

The beginning of the book was easy enough to follow. Shifting diagrams and images moved about in the air over the viewing table as the voice spoke: "Picture a flat plane, which has by definition two dimensions. Now for a recreational moment, imagine constructing an imaginary set of values on this plane, such that the values are antithetical to the coordinate system and cannot actually exist on it but must therefore represent points off the plane, in a space that does not actually exist within the reference world of the plane." As the voice spoke, rectangles and other constructions of dotted lines grew like tumors on the unbroken white surface of the plane. "Notice now that we go from a two-dimensional world, with one plane, to an imaginary world containing a dome or sphere, which can be argued as having one surface, although technical arguments can be made that in fact a physical dome or sphere also has at a minimum F faces, as opposed to a seamless ideal dome or sphere. We can image a type of cone that is pyramidal (four-sided) but if we cause two of its faces to blend into one by rounding a full edge, then it becomes a three-plane three-dimensional construct..."

The voice droned on and on, and shapes moved about. Tedda's eyes became blinded by dizzying arrays of symbolic representation, often interspersed with Greek, Hebrew, Gothic, and other foreign alphabets. Boolean operators intermixed with counters, flags, and switches on computational paths. Arrays appeared and disappeared depending on flashing multi-colored conditionals. Arrays grew or shrank, depending on energy inputs and reactions. Tedda watched all this until she grew tired. She stopped it several times and stepped outside for fresh air. The fortress was quiet. Its dark walls loomed all about while the gardens sprawled on forever, filled with wind and birds and sunshine. She called down to a gardener for a glass of cool fruit juice, and the man hurried to do the bidding of Princess Tedda Roule.

Soon, a grimy urchin with grapevine clippings in his hair appeared. He was barefoot and carried a torn straw hat in one hand and a large, frosty glass of freshly mixed water and berry pulse in the other. Tedda patted the boy's head, closed the door, and took her drink back to the chair. She sipped fresh boysenberry and raspberry pulse sweetened with honey while watching the spark of Amy's genius over and over again.

One thing bothered her. While she couldn't follow all the fine detail and the preciously wrought minute reasoning, she brought to it a newcomer's naïve overview. As she became familiar with the greater flow of hypergeometrical reasoning, she started following certain logic paths back and forth, until it became apparent to her that either she was wrong, or there was a serious flaw in Amy's reasoning.

She called Amy and begged her to come. It was late in the day, and Amy appeared in the uniform of an Imperial Guard lieutenant general, complete with riding crop, high boots, black jodhpurs, and white tunic with crossed leather belts, oblique sash in national colors, and rows of medals. She wore shoulder boards with epaulets, three stars, and a coronal device. Putting aside a high black bicorn hat of Napoleonic fashion, complete with crown and tricolor, Amy strode over to the viewing area. "I see you have been hard at work."

Tedda grinned tiredly at the uniform. "You too, sister."

"I would much rather sit and quietly do math, rather than fool with all the diplomats and chamberlains." She plopped into a chair and sat back. "Play it for me. I am too tired to move."

"I'm too bleary to keep on much longer," Tedda said, "but I think I may have found an important error in your declarations."

"Oh?" Amy sat forward, her eyes luminous, her concentration total, her curiosity sharp as a razor's edge. Absently, she called for food and drink as Tedda described her thoughts.

"So," Tedda concluded later that evening, "either I'm wrong, or the critical mass event plays out somewhat differently. See the original plane there? If we take the femtoworld to be more like a sphere, then it is joined to the plane at a single point."

"Yes?"

"In purely physical terms, that is a stress point. Initially it is a point of attachment on which the entire femtoworld depends."

"Yes." Tedda's points were turning Amy's responses less into questions and more into tones of hesitant agreement.

"As the femtoworld reaches critical mass, and critical volume, density, and so forth, it is not going to explode."

"Right," Amy said intently. It wasn't an agreement so much as an agreement to follow the logic of Tedda's presentation, wherever that might lead. "And where does it find all that energy and/or matter?"

Tedda said: "My guess is that it originates in the subquark monopol Go-dot foam, which is like the ocean floor of infinitely many universes."

"I see," Amy said. "The slush for making universes is all around us, but it doesn't have all the attributes of stuff in the {universe} set so it's got one leg in and one leg out." She added, grinning: "Or one dot in, one dot out."

"Gray dot, black dot?" Tedda said quizzically.

"We're thinking on the same wavelength, sister."

Tedda nodded. "When this newly enlarged femtoworld grows past a certain critical point, like a cosmic dust mote gathering dots at a runaway pace that gets exponentially faster, then nothing can stop it from becoming a universe all of its own."

"A Big Bang."

"Yes, effectively. The point of origin of the expansion is not on the two dimensional plane, but at the origin, the center, of the sphere. At that point, the connection to the source plane vanishes because, mathematically, the new universe no longer shares any dimensions with its source. Without a trace of energy exchange, that single point connection vanishes. The two universes are separate entities."

"Astonishing," Amy said, chewing on an orange slice.

"A new universe is born," Tedda said, unwrapping a fine small block of semisweet chocolate, "which we no longer want to call a femtoverse."

"Bingo. It's an entire huge 15-billion light-year mambo all its own."

"Right. What we've looked at is mathematical and to some extent allegorical, but this is what I am hoping will happen if you let the Monopol City world expand to critical mass."

"Oh sister," Amy said regretfully, "I can't allow that."

"It's a dilemma for you, isn't it?" Tedda grumbled sadly.

"It's a dilemma for us both." They sat and stared at the frozen image of a sphere—whose surface was shaded with dotted lines, but its outline was now a solid line—rising away from that flat plane. "I'd have no way of running the numbers in time to verify that your hypothesis is correct. I could end up blowing up our world."

"What if you manage to get the East Gothans to shut down their femtoworlds and stop mining, now that there is a truce? We could do the same on this side, except for Monopol City?"

Amy shook her head. "Definitely and absolutely not. We are in very delicate negotiations, and they don't trust us at all. Why would they, after a century of corporate lies and deceptions by the Moss and Grün new world order? I couldn't possibly convince them that we have some reason to ask them to shut theirs down, but we keep one of ours going. Nope, Tedda, sorry. No go."

"I understand," Tedda said. "I've made up my mind, in any case. I'm going in. I will find Hedrock and have my day with him."

"As you wish."

"Kind as you are, I must do this." She wanted to add something else, but didn't.

Amy spoke the thought out loud for her: "I don't believe you will ever feel really comfortable here, and I can't blame you. You will be a princess, but of a dying breed, because I will permit no more rules. It will be difficult to change Gotha thinking..."

Tedda finished that thought for her source: "...To many Gothans, I will always be a freak, a caricature, some sort of slave, a rule."

Amy nodded. "You can't abide that, and neither would I."

"I have one more idea," Tedda said.

"Try me," Amy said.

Tedda told her, and Amy brightened. "It's worth a try."

"It's fifty-fifty," Tedda said.

"It will either work, or it won't. Thank you for a brilliant idea, though."

Tedda rose. "I have no more time to waste, then. I'll get a few belongings together and then I must step through the doorway. Thank you for everything." She held out her arms, and Amy embraced her.

"I would have enjoyed doing mathematics with you and having a sister," Amy said before releasing her from their affectionate embrace. "Sometimes we realize too late what is good in our lives."

"I know," Tedda said wistfully. She knew that their final goodbye would be emotional, but was not to be avoided or put off. "I'm going through within the hour."

"You're not going to spend the night and rest up?"

Tedda shook her head. "There isn't any time to waste. God only knows what is going on in there."

Amy said: "Go carefully. We don't even know if the gate will work properly, since Monopol City was femto within yet another femtoworld, that of the fortress."

Tedda thought of the fortress where she'd roomed with Lindy and walked to the university to work every night in the Bit Cave. She shrugged. "I'll take my chances."

Chapter 52

Tedda—after a tearful goodbye with Amy—stepped through the doorway into the femtoworld contained on the chip she had brought up from the Bit Cave. It was the same chip through whose doorway she had entered Monopol City before, with Rory, with Jakko, with Wally.

She wore warm, comfortable military fatigues provided by Watka. There hadn't been time to launder them, so they still had an oily, slightly mothball smell from the Quartermaster stores. She carried a small, female-issue military rucksack, canteen, bayonet, and automatic pistol in mesh holster. Folded in a roll over the rucksack were a sleeping bag and field jacket. She had a poncho, black beret, and stop watch. Among her emergency supplies were waterproof matches, and some field rations including coffee. Watka's QM people were experts at all this, and she thanked him warmly before hugging Amy goodbye.

Now she was on her own.

So far so good. She found herself walking through the empty lower halls of the hospital where Amy had been kept prisoner. The upper floor, where Amy had been detained, was in the A world. Tedda took that same elevator downstairs from near Room 909 where she had been generated with fake memories of the prison van and her non-murder of Moira (who had been impaled in a tree while escaping with Hedrock—thus Watka had explained to her, after reading the late Tonsonby's secret police files; and this guilt trip had been set up to intimidate the rule Tedda into going along with the scheme to entrap Hedrock).

As Tedda descended, she began to understand what was happening here physically and mathematically. Already, both Gotha camps had begun freezing their femto assets and reducing their mining operations in femtospace, to curtail that possible critical mass explosion. Meanwhile, Tedda's proposal to Amy would buy a tiny bit of extra time. Although she was bypassing the fortress step and going directly to the Monopol City step, somehow the Intereality of the fortress and the Bit Cave remained in the connective tissue between the A world (Amy's) and the C worlds (Monopol City). The Lindy world (fortress, University, Bit Cave, etc.) was the B level, directly under the upper hospital windows. If Amy had been conscious during her confinement, and had been able to look out her hospital window in Room 990, she would have been looking out upon the normal West Gotha countryside. A few doors down—going through a hidden step-down collar in the hallway—when Tedda looked out the window in Room 909 after awakening from her sleep, Tedda was looking out over the fortress grounds of the B world.

Everything was pretty much as before when Tedda took the elevator down. The biggest difference was that all the rules were dead and gone. All the doors stood open. Not a bird twittered in a tree, nor a squirrel ran across the lawn, nor a worm crawled on the earth. Even the grass and leaves were rapidly dying out. There was very little grass left, all of that sere and gray, and only a lot of noisy, brittle brown leaves remained on the trees. There was still some wind, but not much. There were hardly any lights on anywhere, and windows had mostly become replaced by blank sheets of black nothingness as the death and crackup of this world grew faster and faster. The Gothas were shutting down the power, letting their femtoworlds start collapsing into nothingness. Objects that had been shrunk could not reconstitute themselves and thus self-destructed at a plane so infinitesimal that it was inaudible, invisible, utterly undetectable on the A world level. The processes set in motion with rules and derivatives—including people, cities, oceans, all the naturally evolving complexity of a world space—essentially would regress into nothing.

As a testimonial to the reality of all this, the bleached bones of Nurse Amit lay amid the weathered remains of her clothing on the ground. Nobody had come to claim her. It seemed as if a year had passed here, and Tedda hoped the same wasn't true in the Monopol City world. Amit had to be one of the few source people to ever die in a femtoworld, Tedda thought. Tedda nodded respectfully to the gaping skull with its bared teeth and huge eye holes, but did not stop.

Tedda strode around the mound under the fortress hospital. She came out upon the central grounds where the Confessor had sat in his eel-slot, and where Major Grün had clattered up and down on his great white horse. She passed the round-fronted building where she and Lindy had roomed during the initial heavily drugged days here. She left the fortress by the lichen-white gate of huge gloomy blocks, and strode down the cobblestone street one last time to the university. The sky overhead was uniformly gray. No sun would ever break through there again, and as the first tendrils of darkness crept through the sky, she thought she could detect elements of that waving aurora through which she had passed with Wally, Eduard, and Lindy, to return alone in Wally's huge car. In fact, there was the car, windowless and weathered, on flat tires down the street. She turned and entered the university grounds. Crossing a small, parched square, she entered the building housing the Bit Cave.

"Here we are again," she said as she stepped into a long, dimly lit hall. At the end, she saw the same quiet, deserted building lobby. The lights in the lobby had long since burned out, and the glass ceiling had fallen in. Dead trees had grown up and more recently died, so that their gray corpses rose up like frayed monoliths leaning at odd angles amid the orderly lines of human design.

Tedda stepped up to the dull round buttons between the elevator doors and pressed.

Nothing.

She panicked.

If the service was out, she was finished—trapped here in this dying world, unable to return upworld, unable to get down.

The door rumbled quietly open.

Relief.

She got in. Down she went, past the Bit Cave level. This time the elevator had buttons for three stories rather than two. She shot down past the hangar where the programmers and techs and quants had worked. This world repaired itself logically. She had removed the chip leading to the Monopol City world, and reality had compensated for the violation by creating a different set of rules for accessing the attachment to the Monopol City world.

Now the door opened for a last time, and she stepped out into what was left of Monopol City.

Chapter 53

As Tedda stepped out from the elevator, she heard the mechanisms inside the left tunnel squeal and grind irrevocably to a stop. Tortured metal ground on tortured metal as axles seized, wheels stopped turning, cables twisted, and reality itself bent out of shape. There would be no way back now.

She stopped and put on her field jacket, because it was chilly. The rucksack and web belts went over that. As an afterthought, she even put on the poncho over the whole lot, though there was no trace of rain.

Tedda stood on a street in the far suburbs of what had been greater Monopol City. The night sky gleamed with a weak ambient light. Telltale flickers of green aurora danced on the far sea. Tedda walked among ruined blocks of buildings, many of which had sunk into the decay of failing rules. The streets still worked, though few street lamps did. A few corner lights still flickered a weak, sickly greenish color. Many of the city blocks had simply vanished, so that she was walking through an astonishing landscape of streets and sidewalks among flat empty lots. It looked more like a city waiting to be built, rather than a city and suburbs that were vanishing block by block as the energy for the world died away. She strode along, her breath coming in vapor as the chilly air received it.

Closer to downtown, tall buildings still stood. All the neon was out. The great billboards were darkened and askew. Parts of letters were missing. She could make out faintly the dull signs of Green Station, Blue Station, Red Station, and so forth—all the same uniformly muddy brown. Some of the skyscrapers had collapsed into piles of rubble. Many of the trees had turned gray and died. There was very little life here. There was a pervasive, autumn-like smell of burning wood or leaves.

Downtown itself, within the loop of the original monorail like on the board game, still had some electrical power. Tedda wandered among the huddled, homeless few people remaining in the ruins of their formerly great city. The sidewalk cafes were long abandoned. A few spindly tables and chairs remained piled together. From the absence of wood, Tedda guessed that the denizens of this lost world had been burning every bit of wood they could get their hands on to keep warm.

It was indeed chilly here. She shivered and kept climbing over piles of rubble. Men, women, and children huddled bleakly together in corners and nooks. They huddled around fires and cooked what little food there was. They regarded her with hollow, hopeless looks. "Has anyone seen Edgar Hedrock? Alton-Edgar Hedrock? Nobody?" They all shook their heads bleakly and returned to their fires.

She finally succumbed to exhaustion. Clambering up in to the dusty, dirty ruins of Green Station, she found a trolley stuck amid fallen metal power girders. In its final moments of operation, the train must have rushed onto a twisted tie, for it sat askew just as it had come to dead stop amid screeching brakes and showers of sparks. The windows were gone, and the seats covered with white guano from now-vanished birds. Afraid of disease, she climbed up-slope to the motorman's compartment. The driver, before leaving the damaged vehicle, had dutifully closed the door, and so it remained. Tedda let herself into the dry, dusty space that smelled faintly of motor oil and mouse droppings. Propping herself on the short couch with her head against the down-sloping wall and her booted feet pulled up, she fell into an exhausted slumber.

Chapter 54

Amy von Tedda watched her sister disappear into the maze of wires and lights that formed a nebula in the midst of her library. For a few moments, she stood sobbing into a handkerchief. She sighed deeply, wiping the last tears away.

Watka stepped into the room. "My dear, my royal dear, we cannot have you displaying so much emotion!"

She spoke annoyed. "It's private, my consort to be. I am allowed a personal life, am I not?"

He grinned and put his arms around her, his hands roving about. "Certainly."

She pushed him away. "Have a little respect. You are as bad as Hedrock. Why do Gotha men have no sense of delicacy?"

"Because our women are strong farm horses who don't require much delicacy, but enjoy a little rough handling."

She swept from the room, and didn't care whether he followed or not. Maybe that was another cultural element they could concentrate on correcting, now that Moss and Grün were no more, with their endless wars. Grün had died in the bombing of his palace, and his cousin Moss had died by sitting on a live hand grenade. Watka did follow, speaking all the way. "I arranged a meeting with General Schadow on the East side, as you requested. Are you sure it's safe for you to travel over there so early in the game?"

She snorted. "If I am the Queen to be, then I expect to be safe everywhere in my realm. Besides, you will be with me, as will some of my best bodyguards. I feel quite safe."

In the motorcade across the now-deactivated force barrier, she told Watka: "It is important to move fast and solidify all these impulses for *Zusammenarbeit* (working together) and *Zusammenhaengichkeit*."

The motorcade swept into the temporary headquarters of the East Gotha Provisional Military Commission. Both sides had established identical PMC bodies, governed half and half by chief officers of the former warring nations. The desire, no the passion, for *rapprochement* and *Ausgleich* was palpable. People everywhere wanted to bring about complete peace as quickly as possible.

"Your Majesty," Schadow said gravely, clicking his heels and lowering his head. He was a tall, white-haired field marshal—gaunt, red-faced, gray eyed. He wore a plain olive-drab uniform with few decorations representing the horrific war he'd lived his life in. Instead, he wore the new tricolor with the gold letters AP-R on a green (peace) background: *Amy Prima, Regina*, Queen Amy the First. With him was Knetzelmann, a West Gotha admiral and Junker, installed as his provisional co-regent in the East. Together, Amy and Watka entered a small conference room with the two flag officers.

"Your Majesty has called us to an urgent meeting," Knetzelmann said as servants brought coffee. The room was elegantly furnished in the old Empire style, and a grandfather clock ticked loudly. Knetzelmann was tall, but younger than his counterpart, dark-haired with much silver in it, bearded, and dark-eyed. The three men sat with their Queen to be in four lounge chairs facing each other. They waited for her to speak.

"Gentlemen, I have come to iron out a matter of grave importance to the safety and peace of Our Realm."

The field marshal and the admiral briefly declined their heads in respect and agreement.

"Gentlemen, as you know, Moss built a huge missile, designed to rain over a dozen nuclear warheads on Central East Gotha. As a Multiple Independent Reentry Vehicle, it would be unstoppable by existing antimissile defenses of either side. As long as this device continues to sit on the launch pad in West Gotha, it remains a potential threat to everything We hope to achieve on behalf of Our subjects."

"Amen," all three men mumbled deferently.

"Accordingly, Gentlemen, I propose a quick and orderly solution to the matter, that will also accomplish a personal matter very dear and important to my heart. It involves the Hunter Princess Tedda Roule, who has entered upon a journey that is too complicated to explain just now. We propose to reveal all the details to Our Nation shortly in a paper We shall write, explaining the abolition of femtoworlds and human rules. For the moment, Gentlemen, it is very important that the following be accomplished. First, the shutting down of all Intereality tunneling and mining operations, with the total cessation of power to all such projects. This will prevent the possible explosion of these projects should their common energies combine into one critical mass that could destroy our world."

"Hear, hear, amen," they all muttered.

"Also, gentlemen, rather than dismantle this rocket, We propose that it be immediately outfitted with scientific packages that already exist for the study of our solar system. As scientific and mathematical director of von

Tedda Industries and formerly of the Moss Enterprise, as those syndicated gangsters called their corporate global empire, We are aware of at least two dozen telemetry and vacuosonde packages that could be ready within days for launch atop that giant rocket. We propose, therefore, that you bring across a bilateral commission of the highest stature, to verify and guarantee that this is not some final trick of the West Gotha regime. Will you grant me that, Gentlemen?"

The men, including Watka, jumped to their feet. "Majesty, we are eager to serve you and our fatherland."

"Motherland," Amy said, rising. "Let's change the furniture around, shall we?"

They kissed her hand, and Amy drove back with Watka to her family estate. On the way, she said: "One of those packages will be the one Tedda suggested we try. It's a 50-50 proposition, but I hope it works.

Chapter 55

Within a week, the giant rocket thundered aloft. Generals, admirals, and news reporters from all segments of East and West Gotha society stood at the drizzly, gray launch pad. As the rocket shook the ground and lit up the early morning sky, a cheer went up. As the rocket's glowing tail grew distant, the first rays of dawn lit the night sky.

The rocket achieved escape velocity and pushed on, faster and faster, breaking out of orbital velocity, and climbing (or falling) toward the sun when its engines burned out. The fourteen science packages Queen Amy I had managed to assemble spread out silently from the central pod that had once been meant to guide nearly two dozen deadly warheads to a now no longer existing enemy capital.

Instead, the pod now continued on into a solar orbit, where it would stay for a billion years. Turning gracefully as it approached solar orbit, it exposed the rugged collector cells to a constant bath of limitless solar power. If Tedda's hypothesis were wrong, nothing would happen to the single data chip installed in the exact center of the pod's innermost compartment.

Chapter 56

Tedda awoke in the darkness, in the ill-smelling trainman's cab atop a ruined rail car in the Green Station. What woke her was the sound of rats scurrying over her legs and trying to get at the contents of her rucksack. She jumped up screaming and flailing. The rats were persistent, and she kicked a few to death, but most exited from the compartment by the same hole by which they'd entered, in one continuously flowing mass of gray fur and long pink tails. "Argh!" Tedda growled disgustedly after them.

As she stood catching her breath, she looked through the grimy window at a dot of motion far below. Wiping dust away with a gloved hand, she spotted a man walking on the street below the station. She caught brief glimpses of him as he passed through her field of vision, which was obstructed by mud blots outside, frozen wiper blades, dead tree branches, and metallic girders. Nonetheless, he was unmistakable. It was Alton-Edgar Hedrock, though he walked like a homeless person. There was a dispirited slouch in his walk, and his clothes were in rags. He wore a dirty watch cap, an old coat, and torn boots. He carried his possessions in a slender sack thrown over one shoulder. Her heart went out to him, knowing she could make it all better for him, even if only for a day.

She yelled, but he could not hear her. Already he was passing out of sight. She pounded on the window, to no avail. She considered pulling out her gun and shooting the window out, but that might scare him off, waste ammo, and get her hurt by shattered glass. She looked down the sloping floor of the car outside, thinking it would take her a long time to get down there to chase after him. What other choice was there?

Impulsively, she reached up and pulled the motorman's signal cord. A long, loud braying sound filled the air. It died after a minute, as the battery played out its last stores of energy. Tedda clambered quickly down through the coach. She slipped and fell, but kept on going, bruising her hand. Holding the hand within the other, she stumbled out on the dusty platform and ran to the stairs. Down she flew, taking two and three steps at a time, so that her boots clattered on the metal. She forgot about the ache in her hand and clutched the railing on both sides as she leveraged herself to take half a dozen steps at a time.

At the bottom of the stairs, he waited for her. He had a hopeless look about him. His eyes looked beaten, and he looked merely curious. Perhaps nobody cared about a stranger in the world now, and he was curious to see why anyone would signal to him.

"Tedda," he said dully, and then something awoke in his eyes.

"Edgar!"

"Hey," he said, breaking into a sunny grin.

She flew into his arms.

They embraced and kissed passionately for two or three minutes. They groaned at the pleasure of holding each other. She felt the comfort bathing her like a warm liquid that filled her soul. "I didn't think I would see you again," she said.

"I didn't exactly give up hope," he said, flapping his arms hopelessly once and looking around, "but you see how it is down here. I take it your source is still alive."

"Yes. Yours isn't."

"I know, and I feel kind of empty sometimes, thinking I'm about to break apart and vanish."

She shook her head. "It's more complex than that. When Hedrock died, you were near him, and you became Hedrock. That's got to be it. Somehow, the laws of this process are more complicated than we thought. Amy has promised to stop the femtoworlds and rules. The war is over."

"Really. Hey, that's great. Meanwhile, this place looks like it's in the last stages of a world war."

"There is some hope," she said.

"Great. I'll believe it when I see it. Look here. It's very sad." He put his arm around her and led her across the street. They walked down several criss-crossing side streets, and to the edge of the city center.

"What's that?" Tedda said curiously. Ahead was a row of flashing amber warning lights atop red and white striped metal sawhorses. Several police cars were parked askew, but they looked abandoned. Their lights had stopped twirling.

"It's the end of the world," he said. "See down there? It's all frozen down there. Time has stopped moving forward. Don't get too close or it will suck you in. I think it's moving toward us slowly."

She walked beyond the flashing lights and parked police cars. Down the street, she saw a strange sight. The brighter evening light of a better time was trapped as if in an ice cube. She saw distant neon, bright billboards, even an airplane with flying lights ablaze but trapped in midair on a descent path. Buses, cars, trucks—all were frozen exactly as dying time had trapped them. She could make out the red taillights on a bus pulling out from the curb. She could make out the leaning stature of a child holding his mother's hand while peering up the street with a worried face. She also could see people running anxiously in her direction as if trying to escape a doom they must have begun to feel coming, but couldn't escape. They were forever frozen with their legs running and their arms reaching out.

Several cars and a fire engine appeared to be trapped half in, half out of the edge of that phenomenon. The driver of the fire engine was frozen in place as he had tried to back his vehicle away from the encroaching barrier, while the rear of the fire engine was still in the realm of moving time. Apparently this had all happened days or weeks ago, and the fire engine had been pushed along as the growing time-death ate its way through the universe.

"Better come with me," Hedrock said. "I know of a little hideout where we can be comfortable." He didn't finish, but she understood: *until the end.*

They held each other close, and kissed often, as they wandered back into the central city. He took her through a pile of rubble, behind a loose door he lifted away from a brick wall, and into a hideout he had fashioned. In rubble of a collapsed building, there was one room that had survived because a mess of steel girders had formed an A-frame overhead. "It's solid," he assured her. "What have we got to lose?" He grinned.

She found running water at a former kitchen sink. There was a double hotel bed with sheets still on it. There might be rats all around, and a good tremor might bring the whole thing down on them, but for the moment it was all they had. They fell upon the bed and passionately made love, until she passed out from sheer exhaustion, still clinging to him.

Chapter 57

The central pod of Her Majesty's Space Vessel HMSV Regina Mater sailed into solar orbit far from earth. As the vessel did so, she sent back telemetry to earthbound observers. In the tiny central compartment containing a single old-fashioned computer chip, sensors turned on and indicated to the listeners back on earth that the chip was bathed in just the right amount of light and warmth to create the effect desired by the creators of an experiment that had been designed for another purpose, but had been preempted by this very important cause dear to Her Majesty's heart.

The sensitive machinery recorded an infinitesimally tiny change in how the chip itself was being warmed through. That told the ground controllers, and their eagerly watching queen, that Tedda's hypothesis had been correct.

The femtoworld within the chip was flooding with limitless fountains and oceans and galaxies of energy. Almost instantaneously, it flooded through its critical mass and far exceeded that humble limit. Within that single, central, stable space of that limit, a dying sun flared back to life. A solar system containing an earthlike planet once again bathed in light. That planet's blue seas and tan continents (not earth, different, yet spun off from the same rules) revolved within an oxygen rich atmosphere. Time rolled backward, restoring the piece of the new universe within that critical limit back to the point where it had been the moment Gotha's engineers turned the power off. Billions of light years of space rose like cookie dough full of raisins in all directions, and the femtoverse became a macroverse in its own right. Meanwhile, stability and returned to the planet where the point of attachment had been. That elevator door opening on a nondescript suburban street, that point where Tedda had stepped out in to Monopol City, had briefly been the center of the new universe. Now it quickly became, like its source on Gotha-earth, just another backwater planet, a grain of dust lost amid countless other grains of dust amid the tides of galaxies churning slowly in the vast realms of that new universe.

Chapter 58

Tedda awoke on a strange bed under the crushing tons of a broken ceiling about to fall down upon her. She sat up, startled.

"Tedda!" Edgar called from someplace. She sat up at the edge of the bed. As she did so, she caught movement in the corners of her eyes. Momentarily, she felt dizzy. For just an instant, the entire world did a single lightning twirl, like barbershop pole. It was over in a flash. Had the crushed buildings and the frozen street all been part of a dream? And what of Amy and Watka?

She was in a hotel room over looking Green Station, whose gloriously illuminated neon letters glowed outside the window. Edgar came in holding a container of chicken dinners and cola bottles. "Hey, Tedda, wake up. The day's a-wasting."

"What happened?"

Alton Hedrock shrugged. "You must have been right upstairs, whatever you told them to do. We went to sleep in a rat-hole, and woke up this morning in a first-class hotel." He walked past her and opened the curtains. He stood near her wearing shorts and a shirt, and she caressed his bare leg. "Hey, don't get me started. The chicken's getting cold."

They both laughed. Sitting on the balcony, overlooking Monopol City, they had their bare feet up on the railing as they ate batter-fried chicken breasts, roasted potato slices, fresh sweet cole slaw, and barbecue baked beans. The cola was cold and fizzy and went down nicely too.

Hedrock told a dumb joke, and they both laughed. "Why do Gotha dogs have flat foreheads?" Answer: "From chasing parked cars."

Monopol City sprawled all around them. They could hear the music and the dancing in the streets below. Palm trees waved in a balmy breeze as the City Monorail rattled past smartly on its tracks. The signal horn brayed as the cars entered Green Station to take on and let off passengers. Beyond the bustling city skyscrapers, miles and miles of blue ocean glittered in the warm midday sun. A blue, nearly cloudless sky sweltered overhead.

Hedrock told her: "When I got here, I figured I might as well live it up for whatever short time was left. I was miserable without you, but I blew most of my wad on this hotel room, so we're good here for at least another month. In that time, I can get us set up over in one of the better suburbs."

She laughed. "We'll need jobs."

"Yeah, or just be beach bums. I could use a long rest without all the anxiety."

She wiggled her toes on his. "And we'll get tans from head to foot."

He looked at her. "I'm bored already. Shall we go dance, or have a drink, or walk on the beach, or make love, or just sleep some more?"

She kissed him and wrapped her arm around his neck. "Whatever you want to do. I just totally don't care right now."

So, lacking the energy to make a decision, they stayed where they were while the afternoon wore on. The air was balmy. Planes landed and took off, trolleys rattled by through the Green and Red and Blue Stations. The air smelled like eucalyptus and coconut milk, with lavender and diesel burn mixed in. It was a very relaxing time, and they watched cruise ships come and go over the rims of their toes.

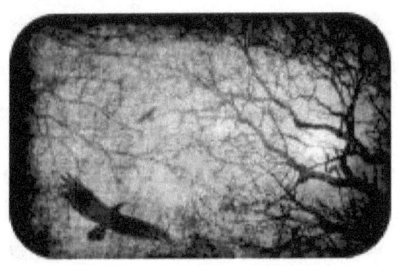

About Clocktower Books

Our excellent authors include Renee Horowitz (*Pharmacy Sleuth Trilogy*); Robin Marchesi (*A Small Journal of Heroin Addiction*, a poetic autobiography in a post-Beat tradition); Dennis Latham (*The Bad Season*); Deborah Cannon (*Raven Trilogy*); and others including our Teenage Novelist/Poet. To learn about our latest offerings, please visit the website at

www.clocktowerbooks.com

Clocktower Books, a pioneering Internet, e-book, and San Diego small press publisher, launched in April 1996 by publishing the world's first entire (not partial) proprietary (not public domain) novels (long works, industry standard) for reading online in HTML format (not for reading on portable media like CD-ROM, floppies, or other intermediary media). Some reviewers are confused and think Gutenberg did this first, but they specialize in public domain. We were the first (John Argo: Neon Blue, This Shoal of Space, Pioneers; John T. Cullen: The Generals of October) to publish proprietary novels as noted.

Clocktower Books Museum Site

You will find at the Museum Pages on our website a detailed history of our pioneering publishing house starting from 1996—including references and documentation (ever a work in progress).

museum.clocktowerbooks.com

From 1998 to 2007, Clocktower Books also published what was, during its decade-long run, the world's first professional Web-only (online) magazine of speculative and dark fiction (or SFFH). We published new authors as well as officers and top names of the Science Fiction Writers of America (SFWA); more on our pioneering work at the Science Fiction Encyclopedia online (look under Far Sector).

Our magazine's major names over the years included Deep Outside SFFH and Far Sector SFFH. We published many nominees or later awardees of the Hugo, Nebula, Sturgeon, and other global awards including British, Canadian, and Australian. The leading SF magazine historian Mike Ashley (Liverpool University Press) has stated he will recognize our pioneering magazine in the final volume of his authoritative SF magazine histories. We are mentioned in the SF Encyclopedia.

Jean-Thomas Cullen and Clocktower Books Present

A sentimental, clean romantic story set in contemporary Connecticut. A young war widow has become a Sleeping Beauty, stung by the loss of her soldier husband, and works as a librarian in the tiny town of Emery. One hot summer day, just looking for a cool spot while his car is fixed, Prince Charming stops by in the form of a young millionaire who has suffered a painful divorce and isn't really looking for love. Neither is she. But old Cupid shoots them both with his arrows, and the ground moves beneath their feet…

Valley of Seven Castles: Progressive Thriller

Set in tomorrow's Europe, in a world gone global and run as one big feudal state by a thousand zillionaire families, here is the world's first progressive thriller. A U.S. Army deserter running from a crime he didn't commit, and a young California woman who sold herself into a modern form of five-year slavery to pay her mother's final hospital bills, are on the run. With them they carry the plans for a new warplane fuselage that must not fall into the wrong hands. Chasing them from Paris to Luxembourg is the Chinese billionaire who murdered a young Luxembourg engineer in London and wants his toy back. In the spirit of John Buchan's 1915 *The Thirty-Nine Steps* as well as Alfred Hitchcock's 1935 movie version *The 39 Steps*, plus a big surprise (see *Thrillerology* in the novel). Add to that the pace of the 2002 thriller movie The Bourne Identity starring Matt Damon and Franka Potente, based on a 1970 thriller novel by Robert Ludlum, and you have a first-class read.

Valley of Seven Castles

A Luxembourg Thriller by John T. Cullen

PROGRESSIVE THRILLERS SERIES

Also By John Argo: YANAPOP

Here's a thriller unlike anything you've ever read. Think of the dark comedy movie After Hours (Martin Scorsese, all-star cast) which is considered one of the funniest (and craziest) films ever made. We agree. Think of Linda Fiorentino in The Last Seduction, Jack Lemmon in The Out-of-Towners, and how about Thomas Pynchon's classic novel The Crying of Lot 49. YANAPOP (stands for Young Adult, New Adult, Participating Older Persons) is the name of a giant (fictional) entertainment corporation in Los Angeles. It's the love story of Martin Brown and Chloë Setreal, and how Martin became Odysseus in his insane and dangerous journey to reach his Penelope.

Nonfiction by John T. Cullen: Dead Move

John T. Cullen, a San Diego author and scholar (BA, BBA, MS) applies his journalistic and historical expertise to solve a long-standing true crime. During Thanksgiving Week 1892, a stylish young woman (about 24) officially called The Beautiful Stranger by the Hotel del Coronado near San Diego, checked in under a false name and died a violent, mysterious death a few days later. Her case became a national sensation full of notoriety overnight because of allegations of affairs with men in high places. It was a Victorian scandal of epic proportions, resulting in the famous ghost legend at the hotel. John T. Cullen, basing his research entirely on true history (no ghosts were harmed), provides the first ever plausible explanation of what really happened—including a coverup of global proportions. See also Lethal Journey, the noir gaslight mystery thriller he wrote to dramatize Dead Move, on which Lethal Journey is closely based.

Thriller by John T. Cullen: Lethal Journey

Closely based on his nonfictional scholarly analysis of the 1892 true crime (*Dead Move*) here is a dramatization treated as a gaslight era noir suspense thriller.

JOHN T. CULLEN

Lethal Journey:

Legendary 1892
Gaslight Mystery
True Crime & Ghost Story

Hotel Del Coronado
near San Diego

125th Anniversary Edition

Ray Bradbury Loved This One:

Ray Bradbury wrote a personal fan mail note to John T. Cullen in January 2008, praising this little gem, a novel that is a tribute both to Charles Dickens' classic A Christmas Carol, and to Ray Bradbury's dark but playful fantasies.

THE CHRISTMAS CLOCK
John T. Cullen
or, TIME'S RIVER OF DUST
A DARK HOLIDAY TALE

'Bravo, John - Read & Loved your Clock!" - personal note from
RAY BRADBURY

Lots More Where These Came From...

Please visit the website of Clocktower Books for a full listing of our exciting fiction and nonfiction books, articles, and short works by a variety of talented authors.

www.clocktowerbooks.com

www.ingramcontent.com/pod-product-compliance
Lightning Source LLC
Chambersburg PA
CBHW050839180626
46814CB00007B/2538